# American Reset

## Book Three of The Economic Collapse Chronicles

Mark Goodwin

ISBN: 1495236641
ISBN-13: 978-1495236648

# ACKNOWLEDGMENTS

"I am the vine; you are the branches. If a man remains in me and I in him, he will bear much fruit; apart from me you can do nothing."

-John 15:5

I would like to thank Jesus Christ for making me the person I am today.

Thanks to Jeff and Dutch for sharing their military knowledge and for helping the book to be more technically accurate in the area of weapons and tactics.

Thanks to my wife and family for their prayers and support in the good times and the bad.

Thanks to John Aman and Catherine Goodwin for editing.

# Foreword

*American Reset* is a work of fiction, but the threats that materialize in the book are real. Many of the numbers stated in the book are forward projections made by the author and based on real numbers.

*American Reset* looks at the current political and financial problems our country is facing and simply does the math. Plan accordingly.

Technical information in the book is included for educational purposes and to convey realism. The author shall not have liability nor responsibility to any person or entity with respect to any loss or damage caused, or allegedly caused, directly or indirectly by the information contained in this book.

For more information on preparing for a financial meltdown or other natural or man-made disasters, visit the author's website at www.PrepperRecon.com.

Except for a few people and one cat whose real names were used with permission, all of the characters, places and incidents are products of the author's imagination or are used fictitiously. Any resemblance to actual people, places or events are entirely coincidental.

# PROLOGUE

"See how the faithful city has become a harlot! She once was full of justice; righteousness used to dwell in her—but now murderers! Your silver has become dross, your choice wine is diluted with water. Your rulers are rebels, companions of thieves; they all love bribes and chase after gifts. They do not defend the cause of the fatherless; the widow's case does not come before them. Therefore the Lord, the LORD Almighty, the Mighty One of Israel, declares: 'Ah, I will get relief from my foes and avenge myself on my enemies. I will turn my hand against you; I will thoroughly purge away your dross and remove all your impurities. I will restore your judges as in days of old, your counselors as at the beginning. Afterward you will be called the City of Righteousness, the Faithful City.' Zion will be redeemed with justice, her penitent ones with righteousness. But rebels and sinners will both be broken, and those who forsake the LORD will perish."

-Isaiah 1:21-28

Over the past six months, the political and economic landscape of the United States changed dramatically. Decades of deficit spending caught up with the American economy and the bill finally came due. Monetary creation by the Federal Reserve reached its limit when confidence in the US dollar hit a wall. High inflation threatened to jump to hyperinflation if the American central bank raised the rate of increase for the money supply just one more time.

Rising interest rates demanded that a growing percentage of the federal budget be allocated to servicing the national debt. As lenders became aware of the domino effect that rising rates were having on America's ability to pay her debts, the rates on US debt went parabolic and new lenders became scarce. The International Monetary Fund stepped in to stem the crisis in hopes of delaying a global economic meltdown.

The first crack in the veneer appeared just weeks prior to the last election. Despite the best efforts from Washington and the IMF, a severe fiscal shortfall left Electronic Benefit Transfer cards underfunded. The EBT card system facilitated access to SNAP benefits for millions of Americans each month. Many Americans were totally dependent on the benefits for food. When the cards were funded at fifty percent of their normal payments, massive rioting overtook large cities throughout the country.

Paul Randall ran as an independent candidate in the last election. His platform was to get America back on a sustainable path by drastically reducing welfare and warfare spending and adhering to the founding principles in the Constitution. Randall won the popular vote and polled the most electoral votes, but none of the three candidates received the required 270 electoral votes to win via the Electoral College. Rather than honor the will of the people, Congress elected Democratic presidential candidate Anthony Howe who swore to ban all semi-automatic firearms through executive order.

Matt and Karen Bair were preppers prior to the riots, but they were not prepared for the level of chaos spreading around the US. They made a hard decision to sell their home for what they could get and move to the mountains of Kentucky to be near Matt's cousin, Adam. They settled on a small farm just across the woods from Adam's homestead near London, Kentucky.

Days after Anthony Howe's inauguration, skyrocketing interest rates triggered a crisis in the $700 trillion dollar, interest-rate-derivatives market. Thanks to the 2005 bankruptcy reform, holders of derivatives were assigned super priority over bank depositors who were considered unsecured creditors. The bank accounts of millions of Americans were wiped clean by the crisis. An unprecedented amount of new money was created so the FDIC could reimburse depositors for their losses. Before the money could be credited to the depositor's accounts, the IMF demanded a ninety percent bail-in of all deposits over $5,000 in order to make loans to keep the Federal government afloat

Soon, the dollar became utterly worthless. People who listened to the warnings of Paul Randall during his campaign diversified their wealth into tangible assets that could be exchanged in barter networks. Gold, silver, ammunition, hygiene products and even coffee became the currencies of choice.

A new wave of riots broke out after the collapse of the currency which dwarfed the EBT riots. Municipal governments in large cities were bankrupt and unable to compensate their police forces. Law-abiding officers who had no underhanded means of supplementing their incomes left police forces en masse. President Howe was quick to use the opportunity to enact martial law. He used the new Federal Ration Notes as currency to keep and recruit Federal troops for his totalitarian police state.

Many state governors rallied behind Paul Randall to resist martial law and President Anthony Howe's gun and resource confiscation objectives. Those states banded together to form the American Coalition States. The Coalition consisted of several states and territories in the northwest, south and Texas. The Dakotas, Montana, Wyoming, Idaho, Eastern Washington, Eastern Oregon and Northern Colorado made up the Northwest Coalition. Kentucky, Tennessee and the Carolinas made up the Southern Coalition. At first, the conflict over the division was rhetorical. But the Coalition eventually used military force to evict all Federal agencies from inside their borders.

The president initiated the first act of violence against the Coalition by attacking the compound of Pastor John Robinson who had been very outspoken against Howe during the campaign. Howe underestimated the organization and readiness of the compound at Robinson's Young Field and the Federal forces suffered a humiliating defeat.

Howe ramped up his campaign of aggression by sending DHS enforcers to all neutral states. West Virginia was one of the first neutral states to be locked down. West-Virginian patriots fled from the oppression and poured into Eastern Kentucky as refugees. Matt and Karen took in a young couple from West Virginia, Justin Clemens and his wife, Rene.

Once the neutral states were well occupied, President Howe turned his attention towards Kentucky. Matt Bair and his cousin, Adam Bair, were part of the Eastern Kentucky Liberty Militia. Their mission was to perform raids on federal convoys moving supplies into Kentucky. In one such raid, just outside of Pikeville, Kentucky, the militia was counter-ambushed by a barrage of federal forces. Wesley Bair, Adam's brother, was killed in the failed raid along with several other members of the militia. Matt Bair was captured and imprisoned in a DHS work camp. Adam escaped capture by moving through the woods and away from the federal soldiers. Justin Clemens and Gary Brewer also evaded the enemy in the raid. They were cut off from Adam and the other survivors and had to make their way back to the London area.

# CHAPTER 1

"Keep me as the apple of your eye; hide me in the shadow of your wings from the wicked who assail me, from my mortal enemies who surround me. They close up their callous hearts, and their mouths speak with arrogance. They have tracked me down, they now surround me, with eyes alert, to throw me to the ground. They are like a lion hungry for prey, like a great lion crouching in cover. Rise up, O LORD, confront them, bring them down; rescue me from the wicked by your sword. O LORD, by your hand save me from such men, from men of this world whose reward is in this life."

-Psalm 17:8-14

Matt lay in his cell on the cold steel floor of the shipping container. As tired as he was, he couldn't sleep. He tried to discern his location by listening to the sounds from outside the container. He could hear indiscernible voices. "I wish I could tell what they're saying."

Matt sniffed the water in the bucket. "It smells like sulfur. It's probably well water. I'll be dead if I don't drink it."

Matt cupped his hands and drank the water. His stomach was growling. He hadn't eaten since before the ambush, the day before.

"There is no way to know what time it is." Matt spoke out loud just to break the silence.

He could tell the light coming through the cracks of the container door was natural light. The light moved quite a bit since he had been watching. It must be well after noon. He felt like he'd been in there for more than a day.

The door swung open and daylight flooded in. Matt turned away and hid his eyes. He had been in complete darkness except for the light coming through the cracks. His eyes were adjusted to the pitch-black interior of the shipping container.

A voice came from someone Matt couldn't see because of the blinding light. "Breakfast, lunch and dinner."

"Where am I?" Matt asked the voice.

"Hell." The voice laughed. The door to the container was shut again and the blackness returned.

Matt groped around to find his bearings. The moment of bright light had blinded him to the darkness again. A few minutes later, Matt's eyes adjusted well enough to see the bowl the man brought in. Matt sniffed the bowl. "Oatmeal."

There were no utensils so Matt turned the bowl up to sip out the cold porridge. No sugar or salt. Hunger is the best seasoning of all. Matt finished the bowl and licked it clean.

Matt thought about his wife. Karen must be worried sick.

He thought about the rest of the team. He wondered who made it and who didn't. The only person he knew for sure that survived was himself. The gruel had quelled his hunger pains for the time being and sleep overtook him.

# CHAPTER 2

"Trust in the LORD with all your heart and lean not on your own understanding; in all your ways acknowledge him, and he will make your paths straight."

-Proverbs 3:5-6

Adam Bair started out on his long journey home. This trek would have been hard enough, but he had the grief of his brother's death that weighed on him like a battleship anchor. He would have to mourn Wesley's demise later. For now, he needed to get home to his wife and daughters. The reverse ambush scattered the entire team. Adam was lost in the woods. He didn't know where he was and he knew even less about the location of his cousin, Matt, and the rest of the team.

He crossed a small creek. He had no means of purifying the water, so he dug a gypsy well about two feet away from the stream (A gypsy well was simply a hole dug near a stream or river. The water would push through the earth between the hole and the stream. This layer of earth would filter out most pathogens.)

He whispered to himself, "This water looks clean, but who knows what could have died in it, two miles upstream." The hole slowly filled with water. Adam cupped his hands and drank as much as he

3

could. He then continued along the edge of the tree line.

About a mile up the path, he found a blackberry bush. He looked at the small undeveloped berries. "Too green." The bitter taste was one thing, but getting stomach cramps or diarrhea was something Adam couldn't afford.

Several miles along his hike towards the Kentucky-Virginia border, Adam ran into Fishtrap Lake and followed the shore east. Eventually, the lake tailed out into Levisa Fork which was a river that ran south. The recent rains swelled the river to nearly fifty feet across with rapid currents.

"I'll just have to walk until I find a bridge or better place to cross. This ain't happenin' here." Adam followed the bridge around for several miles. He finally came upon Levisa Road which had a bridge and took him over the river. *The road should lead to a checkpoint if I follow it south*, he thought.

Levisa Road followed the twisting and turning course of the river. Adam stayed on the western side of the road so he could flee to the tree line if he spotted an enemy vehicle. If he needed to find cover on the river side of the road, he could be forced into the sweeping current of the river. He heard a vehicle coming in his direction. Adam quickly jumped into the veil of the brush. He drew his pistol and laid still as the pickup truck drove past him. The truck had several armed men in the bed.

"Militia," he whispered to himself. He could have yelled out for a ride to the checkpoint, but it didn't seem wise. A startled fellow militia member might shoot first and ask questions later. Adam listened for more vehicles that may have been traveling with the first truck before exiting the concealment of the roadside brush. It was certainly a positive sign. The men must have been traveling to the checkpoint. *That means we're still in control of it*, he thought.

Adam finally arrived at the militia camp. There was no sentry posted at the rear of the camp. "That's not good," he muttered. The last thing he wanted to do was enter the camp on foot and unannounced. He spotted two militia men walking toward their tent, still several hundred feet away. He yelled and waved his hands in the air. Adam wanted to make sure they had plenty of time to identify that he was not a threat before approaching.

"Hey fellas!" Adam yelled out.

One of the men said something on his radio and the other thumbed off the safety of his AR-15. Adam kept his hands in the air as he drew near.

"How you doin', bud?" one of the militia men asked.

"I'm good, I need to speak with whoever is in charge," Adam stated politely.

"Alright, are you armed?" the man quizzed.

"I have my pistol in my back waist," Adam confessed.

"Would you mind if we hold on to that until we can verify who you are?" the man inquired.

"I'm fine with that." Adam slowly passed the weapon to the man he was speaking with.

"What brings you here on this fine day?" the man asked curiously.

"I'm with the Eastern Kentucky Liberty Militia. We had an operation near Pikeville yesterday. I think it was a trap. We were overrun by Federal troops," Adam explained.

"We heard about that. How did you end up here?" the man asked.

"I walked," Adam replied.

"Long walk." The man picked up the radio and said, "Stan, we got a fella here, says he was in the fireworks yesterday, over by Raccoon Road."

"What's his name and what's he look like?" the radio came back.

"Lieutenant Adam Bair," Adam said when the man looked at him.

The man relayed Adam's reply and gave a short physical description of Adam.

Stan radioed back, "Hang tight for a minute. I'll call that in and see if he checks out."

"I'm Charlie, by the way, and this here is Pete," the man said.

Pete nodded, but didn't say anything. Adam could tell he was still keeping his guard up. *That's fine. He probably should*, Adam thought.

Minutes later, Stan called back. "That's him. Get him something to eat and bring him on up to the checkpoint."

Charlie handed the pistol back to Adam. "Thanks," Adam exhaled as he tucked the pistol back where it had been.

They stopped by the chow tent and grabbed Adam a bottle of water and an MRE, then continued toward the checkpoint.

"You all by yourself out here?" Charlie asked.

"We split up when we got hit," Adam said. "My brother and another guy died in the operation. I don't know who else may have survived. It was a real mess."

"I'm sorry to hear that," Charlie said. "About your brother, I mean."

"Thank you," Adam said as he tore into the MRE. He opened the M&Ms and began pouring them into his mouth as they walked. Adam was famished.

When they arrived at the checkpoint, Stan introduced himself and said, "It's an honor to have you here. Please sit and eat your meal. I'll talk while you eat."

Adam nodded and sat down at the picnic table just off the road.

Stan continued, "We weren't an organized militia before the crash. We all know each other through work, church, relatives and such. Most of us are from Pikeville and didn't get involved until after it was occupied. We all know people who are still in Pikeville. We got out as soon as DHS started rolling in there. They have the roads blocked now. There ain't no gettin' out for those who are still there."

"Who are you taking orders from?" Adam continued working on the MRE menu number twenty, spaghetti with meat sauce, while they chatted.

"The Kentucky National Guard," Stan responded. "Can we give you a lift somewhere?"

"I'd love a ride home. My wife is probably worried sick." Adam dropped his head as he thought about having to tell his brother's widow, Shelly, the bad news.

"Sure thing, brother," Stan arranged for Charlie and Pete to drive Adam home. "You guys take it slow. If you see any trouble, come on back and we'll figure something out," Stan said as they entered the truck.

# CHAPTER 3

"Let us consider, brethren, we are struggling for our best birthrights and inheritance, which being infringed, renders all our blessings precarious in their enjoyments, and, consequently trifling in their value. Let us disappoint the Men who are raising themselves on the ruin of this Country. Let us convince every invader of our freedom, that we will be as free as the constitution our fathers recognized, will justify."

-Samuel Adams

Unlike Adam, Justin Clemens and Gary Brewer kept their battle rifles and full militia gear for their return home. They were more than 100 miles from London, Kentucky.

"What's your call?" Justin deferred to the older and wiser man.

"We're not far from Prestonsburg, we could walk there and try to get a ride or get a message through, but I don't trust anyone right now," Gary replied.

"It'll be a long walk without any provisions," Justin commented.

"I have a sister in Hazard. That's about fifty miles from here. We can forage for acorns and wild garlic for two days. There's fresh water all along the way. But this is a group decision," Gary said.

Justin approved Gary's plan. "I think that sounds like a plan. I agree. I don't know who to trust. I wouldn't want to just walk up to anyone. I've got no identification or anything to use as currency besides my gun."

Gary shook his head. "Same here. Let's start heading west. That should run us straight into State Road 80. We can follow the tree line most of the way to Hazard."

They stopped by the small stream at the bottom of the hill to fill their canteens. They hadn't planned on being gone more than twelve hours, so they had no means of purification. "I'd rather take the small risk of getting something from the water than the greater risk of getting dehydrated," Gary said.

Justin replied, "I guess the moral of this story is to at least have some water-purification tablets when you go out on a mission. They weigh practically nothing and don't take up much room."

Gary said, "I just had a thought. What if we used the Betadine swabs from our IFAKs?"

The militia all carried an Individual First Aid Kit for all combat missions. The kits held an Israeli Battle Dressing or IBD, an ACS chest seal, Quickclot and an assortment of other first aid supplies. Among the supplies were Betadine swabs for disinfecting wounds.

"I don't know," Justin said. "It's iodine. It's the same ingredient as water-purification tablets. I just don't know what else might be added in there."

"If it was poisonous, I don't suppose you could clean an open wound with it," Gary said.

"That sounds logical," Justin replied. "You try it first, and if you die, I'll tell everyone not to use Betadine to purify water."

Gary punched Justin in the arm. "Smart aleck."

They both laughed, filled their canteens and put two of the swabs in each of their canteens. The two men walked several miles through the woods.

Gary broke the silence. "We should've ran into the road by now."

"I wish I had my phone for GPS," Justin replied.

Gary said, "DHS would probably have us by now if you had your phone. If it's pinging a GPS satellite then they can find you."

"That's true," Justin declared. He put his hand up for Gary to stop. He pointed in front of them and whispered, "Deer."

Gary shook his head. "That's a big buck."

Justin looked at Gary as if he were asking for permission.

Gary said, "I'm hungry too, but we can't take the chance of being heard when we take the shot. We don't know how far we are from Pikeville. We could be around the corner from a DHS outpost."

Justin shook his head in agreement and continued the march toward home. Soon, they arrived at a paved road that ran north and south.

"Should we follow this road?" Justin asked.

"I'd say we should," Gary answered. "Question is, do we go north or south. Home is south, but so is Pikeville. And it's infested with DHS grunts."

Justin recommended, "Why don't we stay back off the road and follow it south, at least 'til we see signs of trouble. If we spot any DHS vehicles, we'll turn around."

Gary patted Justin on the back. "I'll second that motion, soldier."

Justin smiled and they followed the road south from the cover of the brush. Not long after, they came to a crossroad.

Gary looked at the signs. "US 23 south runs straight into Pikeville. I'm pretty sure it'll hit State Road 80 if we take it north."

"North it is," Justin replied.

A few hundred feet down the road, they hit a bridge that crossed the Levisa Fork River. "I think we should run across this bridge one at a time," Gary said. "There's no cover on the bridge and no other way across the river. If a patrol rolls up while one of us is crossing, whoever is still in cover can give the person crossing some suppressive fire."

"Sounds like a plan," Justin agreed.

Gary continued, "Keep in mind, this road is probably a regular thoroughfare for DHS. So, if it's more than one patrol vehicle, don't engage. If we're drastically outnumbered, we'll have a better chance of surviving if we just run for it."

Justin nodded his approval and the two men approached the bridge.

"You cross first," Gary scanned both directions and said, "Go!"

Justin shot across the bridge at breakneck speed.

Gary shook his head and muttered to himself, "Oh, to be that young again." Once Justin was safely in the cover of the roadside brush, Gary made his crossing. He ran as fast as his knees would carry him. Gary caught his breath and the two men resumed their trek.

They hit their desired course, State Road 80 southbound, in only thirty minutes. The two men soon discovered a meadow on the side of the road.

"There's a pond over there in that meadow. Let's go check for cattails." Gary was hopeful.

"Okay," Justin concurred.

"Did you ever eat cattail?" Gary asked.

"No," Justin answered.

Gary explained, "Most of the plant is edible. The roots have a lot of starch which can give us some energy to get us home. You just chew the starch out of the root and spit out the fiber. It's a little too rough to digest. I doubt they will have any of the big flower spikes this early in the season. If they did, they could be roasted and eaten like corn on the cob. We can still peel them and eat the tops as well. It's a little like cucumber."

The two walked to the pond. "Sure enough, those are cattails," Gary proclaimed. The duo collected as many cattails as they could. They peeled the tops and ate them raw. They bound the roots into bunches and stuffed them into their pockets to eat later.

As the sun began to get low, they scouted out a remote campsite. "We should be sure to make camp far enough from the road to have a small fire. These cattail roots will be much tastier if we roast them." Gary said.

"I think we'd be safe on the other side of that hill." Justin pointed to a knoll in the direction they were traveling. They continued on to the proposed area and built a lean-to shelter out of branches and debris from the forest floor.

They roasted the roots for their dinner. "We have about twenty miles to go, 'til we hit Hazard," Gary said.

"We'll make it." Justin chewed the root he had just toasted. They took turns sleeping and keeping watch.

# CHAPTER 4

"Wait for the LORD; be strong and take heart and wait for the LORD."

-Psalm 27:14

Karen Bair and the rest of the girls sat somberly at Adam and Janice Bair's home. Adam's two daughters, Mandy and Carissa, sat close to their mother. They seemed to fear losing the whereabouts of yet another parent. Shelly, the young bride of Wesley Bair, said, "I know we can't call, but couldn't two of us drive over to Lt. Joe's and see if he knows anything?"

"I agree with Shelly," said Rene, Justin Clemens's wife. "I'll ride over there with her. Joe knows me. Justin and I stayed at his house for a couple days after we left West Virginia."

"Adam was very specific," Janice protested. "He said we shoul leave until they return."

"What if they don't return?" Shelly asked. "How long s sit here? We can't just sit here forever. I need to know v happened to my husband."

"If something went wrong, we need to know," there's trouble, we might need to bug out. DHS

Karen's heart sank to her stomach. This was worse than before. Only moments ago, she was sure she would be reunited with her life-long beau. Then, Matt wasn't in the truck. Now, she was back to not knowing if he was alive or dead. The excitement and disappointment left her drained. She sat on the couch and the tears began to flow.

Adam fought back the tears as he took Shelly's hand. "Wesley loved you with every ounce of his being. I want you to know that you'll always, always have a home here with us. You're my sister, and we're your family."

Shelly kept crying, but hugged Adam. She had no living family. The last time Shelly saw her parents was at her and Wesley's wedding. She never heard from her parents again after that. Most folks assumed they were murdered on their way home to Louisville. After the collapse, police were all but non-existent and the cities were war zones.

Adam regained his composure and gave everyone the best details he could. Karen listened, but each word left her feeling like she knew less than before it was spoken.

Karen said, "I have to go home. It's getting dark and I haven't been home to feed the cat all day. Miss Mae is probably starving."

Janice said, "Why don't you bring her back over here. You can stay here tonight."

"I'll be alright," Karen said. She almost resented Janice because Adam was alive. She knew she shouldn't, but she just couldn't help it. An hour ago, they were all sisters bound by circumstance. Now, Janice's husband was alive and safe. Even Shelly had a definite answer, not that Karen was in a hurry to be in her shoes.

"I'll go home with you," Rene said. Karen and Matt were letting Rene and Justin stay with them. They had fled the occupation of West Virginia by DHS.

"Alright, let's go. Goodnight all," Karen said.

Everyone wished them goodnight and they headed home. On the way back, neither Karen nor Rene spoke.

Once they arrived home, Karen said, "We have to stay positive. We have to hope for the best."

Rene nodded her head in agreement as she petted the cat. "Do you want to play Rummy? Justin and I used to play it a lot. It might keep our minds off of things."

"Okay, but you'll have to refresh my memory on how to play," Karen agreed. "I don't think I can go to sleep for a while."

Rene went to get her deck of playing cards. It was one of the few possessions she still owned. When they left West Virginia, she and Justin came with two backpacks and the clothes on their backs. Karen considered how much more trying it must have been for Rene. Although, Karen's worldly possessions were not comforting her much in the time being. The card game did lighten their mood and took their minds off the situation enough to eventually get sleepy.

When Karen put her head on the pillow, the anxiety gave way to sorrow and the tears began to flow. "God, please watch over my husband, wherever he is. Please let him be alive and please bring him home to me." She continued to pray and cry until she slipped into an unconscious rest.

# CHAPTER 5

"The harder the conflict, the more glorious the triumph. What we obtain too cheap, we esteem too lightly; it is dearness only that gives everything its value. I love the man that can smile in trouble, that can gather strength from distress and grow."

-Thomas Paine

Matt watched the light appear again through the cracks of the door at the end of the container. *It must be morning. It feels like I've been here a week already, I can't believe this is only day two,* he thought. Matt had no way of knowing how many more days his captivity would last. *It's Sunday, we should be going to church and going over to Adam's for lunch afterwards.* Of course, Matt didn't even know if Adam was alive. His stomach growled. He heard the lock being removed from the outside of the door. "Breakfast?" he muttered. The oatmeal he received the day before was bland, but Matt just wanted something to stop the pangs of hunger. Matt was ready for the light this time. He squinted one eye and shut the other completely. The light flooded the shipping container and with it entered a fellow prisoner and a guard. They walked to Matt's cell.

"Hand him your filth bucket," the guard said to Matt.

Matt did as he was instructed. The other prisoner handed Matt a new bucket with fresh water.

"I'd like to call my attorney," Matt knew it was a shot in the dark, but it didn't cost anything to ask.

The guard laughed. "That's funny, but still, no talking. I'll crack your skull if you open your mouth again."

The guard and the other prisoner left and the darkness returned. Matt opened the eye he kept shut while the door was opened. It was still adjusted to the darkness. *I guess yesterday's fresh water bucket is today's toilet. I hope they're sanitizing those well between cycles. If not hepatitis, E. coli or a myriad of other diseases will kill us all. Maybe that's the plan,* he thought.

Matt had no way of passing the time other than praying and reciting Bible verses. He had already done that and felt there was nothing left to say.

Matt spoke aloud to himself, "I need to start some kind of regiment. I'll lose my mind if I don't." Matt did a few sets of pushups, crunches and squat thrusts. He worked out some of the nervous energy which made him feel a little better.

*I wonder why they haven't interrogated me yet. Maybe they're waiting for my mental state to deteriorate so I'll resist less. Maybe they already know everything they want to know.* Matt thought through the events of two days ago. He considered the attack and how Adam had said it was a trap. *I don't think there ever was a supply convoy.* Matt remembered where they had received the information on the supposed convoy they were to ambush.

"Michael got all that information from his brother-in-law. Then, on the day of the operation, he conveniently came down with the flu. That guy is a rat!" Matt muttered.

There was nothing Matt could do about it now. He undressed and used yesterday's fresh water bucket to bath himself and rinse out the prison clothes he was wearing. He wrung out the shirt and pants and hung them in the chain-link fence that sectioned off his cell.

"I have to get out of here." Matt said it again to strengthen his resolve, "I have to get out of here!"

His mind raced. What had Adam taught them about escape and evasion? "Get out fast. The longer you are in captivity, the lower your odds of escape are. You are usually processed into deeper levels of security and you lose your strength and will to escape over time."

"With the amount of food they're feeding me, I'll be losing my strength. As for levels of security, I may already be in the belly of the beast," Matt whispered softly to himself. He had to break the silence, even if it were only with whispers. "Then what? Study my opponent and surroundings and formulate a plan. Sleep and drink lots of water. The water I can do, but sleeping is harder. Tools, I have nothing." Matt looked at the metal handle of the bucket. "What good could that possibly do? I'm not Slick Gyver. I can't pick a lock with a bucket handle. That's alright. I'm thinking. Adam always said your mind is your greatest weapon and your best survival tool."

Matt continued to recount the instructions Adam had taught his team on escape. Several hours later, Matt heard the lock being removed again. "I really hope this is food."

The door swung open and Matt saw several new prisoners being brought in. He made a conscious effort to start analyzing the gear worn by the guards. They wore a hybrid of military and civilian police attire. It was a grey uniform with a red KBR logo. They had Tasers, batons, handcuffs, radios and holstered side arms. Matt thought it was curious that there were KBR guards working in a government prison camp. He heard Halliburton was issued several contracts for constructing and maintaining the camps. He also knew KBR was once a subsidiary of Halliburton. But from what he knew, they were no longer affiliated after the criminal charges and bad behavior of KBR in Iraq and Afghanistan. *Of all the private security firms*, he thought, *these guys are probably the nastiest of the military industrial complex.*

Soon, Matt's lonely container was filled with new hostages.

"There will be absolute silence in here," one of the guards yelled. "If you violate that, you don't eat. Trust me, as bad as the food is, you'll want it by the time it's served." The new prisoners were placed in their respective cages and the door was shut.

*Still no food*, Matt thought. He was in the end cage, so there was only one new prisoner next to him. Matt could see him, but could tell the man could not see him in return. The man's eyes had not yet adjusted to the dimness.

*I'll let him get settled before I try to communicate with him.* Matt had been talking to himself all day, and no guard had said anything to him other than the one he asked to bring him a lawyer. *I'll whisper really low to be safe. They may want to keep us from communicating so we don't coordinate a riot*, Matt thought.

Two hours later, Matt could see the light through the cracks getting low. He heard the lock being taken off of the door again. "Finally!" Matt whispered softly. He could smell the oatmeal. Breakfast, lunch and dinner were served.

With his belly somewhat full, Matt found a good position and went to sleep.

# CHAPTER 6

"Woe to those who rise early in the morning to run after their drinks, who stay up late at night till they are inflamed with wine. They have harps and lyres at their banquets, tambourines and flutes and wine, but they have no regard for the deeds of the LORD, no respect for the work of his hands. Therefore my people will go into exile for lack of understanding; their men of rank will die of hunger and their masses will be parched with thirst. Therefore the grave enlarges its appetite and opens its mouth without limit; into it will descend their nobles and masses with all their brawlers and revelers. So man will be brought low and mankind humbled, the eyes of the arrogant humbled."

-Isaiah 5:11-15

Anthony Howe prepared his notes for the staff briefing. It was his first day back in the White House. He actually enjoyed his time in the subterranean bunker at Mount Weather during the riots, but it was time to put things right in Washington. It was a symbol of power. Howe knew he needed to display a strong hand in the streets of D.C. if he expected the rest of the country to see him as their ruler. DHS adopted a zero-tolerance policy for protests in D.C. and violators were quickly hauled away to various work camps around the country.

President Howe's staff was still unaccustomed to having a regular briefing on Sunday. It's not that any of them were missing church, but they were missing out on barbecues, tennis, golf and other pastimes that they were afforded at their private clubs. While the rest of the country and even D.C. had fallen into a state of utter chaos, the politicians and elites in the nation's capital found a way to maintain a higher standard of living. Lobbyists, senators and congressmen redirected resources to keep their favorite country clubs afloat. One would secure a reliable flow of electricity, another would make sure the choice cuts of meat and the best produce were brought in, others would ensure there was a steady flow of wine and spirits. While there was no fully functioning currency in America, power proved to be a readily accepted form of tender. Defense contractors offered complementary security services as well as armed escorts to and from their private sanctuaries.

The few Republican lawmakers remaining in the city were completely on board with the new program. The dissenters in the Coalition States left D.C. to assist in governing their respective states. Those who stayed in Washington and voiced their opposition to the regime were carted off to CIA black-site prisons and held under the 2012 NDAA indefinite detention clause. The complete lack of any true conservatives allowed the private country clubs to indulge every whim of their clients. Drugs and prostitution became less hush-hush and the debauchery at the private clubs rivalled ancient Rome.

Howe began the cabinet meeting. "People, the First Lady has made me hyper-aware of the pig roast being held at Belle Haven today, so I'll try to get you out of here at an acceptable time. I know those of you who have been cooped up with me at Mount Weather are particularly ready for a little recreation."

Howe laughed in such a way to let everyone know he really didn't care if they made it to the pig roast or not. He held no contempt for the absolute hypocrisy of the feast being held while there were reports of starvation and cannibalism pouring in from the major cities due to a lack of food. He simply didn't care about anyone but himself.

"I suppose the first order of business should be resource

allocation. I'll let Secretary Brown brief us on the current situation," Howe said.

Department of Health and Human Services Secretary Gerald Brown was a holdover from the prior administration. The previous president, Mustafa Al Mohammad, asked Howe to keep Brown on as a personal favor. Howe always granted Al Mohammad's requests. Al Mohammad had asserted himself as President Howe's handler for those who ruled from the shadows. All of Al Mohammad's requests were thinly-veiled orders.

"Thank you Mr. President," Brown said. "With the help of the military and DHS acting under the authority of the National Defense Resources Preparedness executive order 13606, we have been able to acquire vast amounts of food resources from farms around the Federal States. We're also steadily acquiring fuel and transport vehicles to move food into the cities and stem starvation. You're all aware that we've had to write off Detroit and Chicago as a loss. They are unsalvageable. Several other large cities such as New York, Philadelphia, Indianapolis and Atlanta are probably beyond the point of saving. It is the recommendation of HHS to focus our efforts on the cities that can be rescued rather than spreading our resources too thinly and potentially having an even higher die-off. We have put together a triage schedule that uses a health analysis of each city within the Federal States to prioritize our assets and labor. We will dedicate our energy to the areas with the highest likelihood of survival."

The president was deep in thought. "Gerald, is there any way we can preserve New York City? It is the icon of America to the world."

Brown responded, "If we did, Mr. President, it would be at the expense of many other cities. New York City's most prominent are already out of Manhattan. Most have homes upstate. The buildings and basic infrastructure are not going anywhere. My recommendation would be to let nature take her course in the city. Afterwards, we can clean it up, fix the things that are broken, give it a fresh coat of paint and repopulate it. I hate to sound cold, but the residents who are still alive in New York are expendable."

The president let Brown know that his comments were valid. "No, Gerald, it's not cold. It's the simple truth. I think I can stomach that plan. Perhaps we could even make New York a place of privilege. It could be the phoenix that rises from the ashes. It could be the visionary prototype for our new utopian society. Once completed, we can relocate new residents into the city as a reward for their faithfulness to our agenda. We'll make it a symbol of hope for other cities to look to. Thank you for your report, Mr. Secretary."

Brown replied, "It was my pleasure, Mr. President."

Howe continued, "Next, I'd like to hear what you have for us, Melinda."

Treasury Secretary Melinda Chang observed the economic collapse from a front-row seat over the past six months. Her position allowed her to see into the gut of the cancer-ridden financial system of America. "Yes, Mr. President. Our recommendation is to switch the Federal Ration Notes over to a single unit currency. While having each type of note backed by a specific class of commodity did instill confidence in the new money, it has created complications. One of the most significant problems has been the need to print different types of notes. The Federal Reserve can't keep up with the demand on their presses. A single unit currency would still derive its value from a basket of commodities, but would be interchangeable for any class of commodity. We would continue to use the notes already printed. The five-unit fuel notes and the twenty-five-unit food notes would simply be used as a five or twenty-five-unit general note. They will also be less confusing for consumers. The transactions will be more familiar, they will seem much like dollars. In time, we will also be able to regulate the supply of the new Federal Ration Notes to stimulate the new economy."

Howe nodded his approval. "I think it's an ingenious plan. Did you work with Jane Bleecher from the Fed on this?"

"Yes, sir," Chang replied.

"And have you consulted with the IMF about it?" Howe inquired.

Chang answered, "We did run the general idea by IMF Director Stanley Klauser. His only concern was that we needed to regulate the amount of new notes that are produced. He suggested a cap of five percent annually after the initial period of monetary supply. Five percent is very restrictive to the type of growth we would be able to stimulate under our previous Keynesian models, but without the support from the International Monetary Fund, we won't be able to sustain any value in a new paper currency."

Chief of Staff Alec Renzi made a comment. "Have we considered developing a fractionally gold-backed currency?"

Howe snapped, "And admit Paul Randall was right about fiat currencies? Are you out of your mind? We are in the middle of a war with Randall and his Coalition States. As in every war, the main battlefield of this war is in the arena of popular opinion. Admitting he was right about gold and silver is tantamount to admitting we caused the collapse. Use your head, man!"

"You're right, Mr. President. I'm sorry," Renzi confessed.

"Let's move on," Howe puffed. "I think you all know I've appointed California Congressman Juan Marcos as our liaison to China in the West Coast relief effort. You all know he is a Republican, but he's on our side. It's important to show the American people that were are willing to work together. Paul Randall has created enough division. Marcos has a working relationship with the Chinese company, Hangyun, which is offering relief to the major port cities on the West Coast. The assistance will be in exchange for special privileges and control over the ports. Secretary Vance, how are things coming along with Congressman Marcos?"

Secretary of State Cordell Vance was assigned to provide oversight to Marcos and the Chinese. It was a given that China's role in the ports was a threat to national sovereignty, but the West Coast was beyond the efforts of D.C. to save. At least the Chinese would be more cooperative than the Coalition States. Granting control to the West Coast ports to China would keep them out of the hands of the Coalition.

Secretary Vance said, "Things are progressing nicely on the West Coast. Hangyun has agreed to offer relief assistance to Western Oregon and Western Washington. They are providing Chinese MREs to residents on the West Coast. Los Angeles was already a war zone by the time the Chinese arrived, but many other cities have greatly improved their odds of survival with the help of our friends from the East.

"With the aid of the Chinese military, Hangyun will help to secure the ports from terrorist attacks initiated by the Coalition States. We'll also be safeguarded from attacks from our traditional enemies around the world who may take advantage of us while we're down. Secretary of Defense Hale, I believe you're working with China on an agreement to provide security for the eastern borders of Western Oregon and Western Washington?"

The Department of Defense Secretary Scott Hale answered, "Yes, thank you, Cordell. I know what many of you must be thinking. We understand the risks of allowing Chinese boots in Oregon and Washington, but we've already lost the eastern halves of those two states to the Coalition. That puts the western territories of those states at risk of invasion by the Coalition as well. We would rather deal with the risks associated with the Chinese occupation than to have the rest of those resource rich states fall to our enemies in the Coalition. Our current military is stretched too thin to effectively defend the West Coast. The massive desertions made by soldiers who responded to Paul Randall's invitation to join the Coalition has left us very understaffed in all branches. The massive amount of new DHS recruits can't replace the battlefield experience we lost."

President Howe said, "Thank you, Scott. Rosa, can you brief us on the development of DHS's joint effort with FEMA to convert the relief camps and prison camps into labor pools?"

Department of Homeland Security Secretary Rosa Ortiz answered, "Yes, Mr. President. As you mentioned, we'll be bringing more of those camps online over the next few weeks. The prison camps will be used for more hazardous work and utilized in remote areas that dissuade escape. The FEMA relief camps will institute a mandatory work program for all residents as well, but the residents will be paid a stipend of ten Federal Ration Notes per week, in addition to food and housing. They will be allowed to spend their notes at commissaries within the camp. We hope this will help them to be more content at the camps. FEMA-relief-camp residents will not be allowed to leave voluntarily until order has been restored in the nation. Their only option to leave the camp voluntarily will be to join DHS in our battle against the Coalition. We believe this will greatly add to the number of new recruits. FEMA-relief-camp residents who do not comply with the work programs or attempt to leave without permission will be transferred to the prison camps. We simply cannot allow huge swaths of displaced persons to wander about the country during a civil war."

Howe stated, "Rosa, I received a call from Brian Casik, the CEO of Halliburton. He's concerned that religious meetings inside the camps could become breeding grounds for malcontents. Do you feel that's a valid concern? We need to keep Halliburton on our team, DHS isn't in the position to take on security, logistics and management of the camps."

The DHS Secretary concurred. "Not only do I feel religious meetings have the potential to become problematic, I think all forms of religious expression do nothing but pit people against each other. This entire conflict stems from Paul Randall's Christian worldview."

"And what could I do to help this situation, Madam Secretary?" Howe offered.

"I think banning religious materials like Bibles from the camps would be a good start. These are state-sponsored camps. To have religious materials inside the fences violates the principle of separation of church and state. And I think it would ease the concerns of Mr. Casik"

"Consider it done. It sounds like you've got things under control, Rosa. Good work," Howe complimented.

"Thank you, Mr. President," Ortiz replied.

"Scott, can you let the cabinet in on Operation Black Out?" Howe requested.

"It's top secret, Mr. President," The Defense Secretary answered.

"Everyone in this room knows we are at war, Scott," the president scolded. "They've all seen how this administration handles insubordination. No one here is in a hurry to end up in a CIA black-site prison. Besides that, they all have the DARPA chip implanted in their hands. Regardless of whether you think they can be trusted, do you think I appoint fools to these positions?"

Anthony Howe had an uncanny talent for switching from cordial to a seething, hate-filled maniac in nanoseconds. He could go from compliments to insults and threats in the same breath.

Scott Hale quickly complied. "Yes, Mr. President. Operation Black Out will be a strategic attack against the Coalition utilizing electromagnetic pulse technology. The EMPs will be generated via high-altitude detonations of nuclear devices over specific geographic targets within the Coalition. This will cripple their electrical grid and disable most of their vehicles and all computing equipment. We will allow for a three-month period after the attacks for the citizens of the Coalition to expend their resources and become weak. Afterwards, we should be able to walk through and reclaim the territories with minimal effort."

Howe gleamed as he listened to Hale lay out their dastardly plan. If anyone disagreed, they dared not voice their opposition.

# CHAPTER 7

"Be joyful in hope, patient in affliction, faithful in prayer."

-Romans 12:12

The morning sky was just starting to reveal the first hint of daybreak. Justin had slept a few hours before his watch, but it was very hard to stay alert. The long walk the day before and the intensity of the attack two days ago had taken all of his energy. He needed to sleep for a couple of days to get caught up on his rest.

He woke Gary and said, "The sooner we get started, the sooner we can both get some real rest."

Gary stretched the stiffness out and got up to begin the final leg of the long hike. "Let's do it, then."

The two set out toward Hazard. They found a creek to refill their canteens and added two more of the Betadine swabs to each one. They gave the iodine a few minutes to react with any potential pathogens, then drank those canteens and refilled them, adding one more swab to each.

When they hit an oak grove several miles along their journey, they stopped to fill their pockets with acorns. The small bit of mush inside of each was a lot of work to get out, but it provided enough energy to get them to their destination.

Once they arrived on the outskirts of Hazard, they kept to the roadsides so they wouldn't stick out. Before long, they were at Gary's sister's house. He went to the back door to knock. Gary's sibling, Laurie, wasn't expecting him and let out a loud scream when she saw him at the back door. Gary put his finger to his mouth and took off his boonie hat so she could see it was him.

Laurie let the two men in and Gary gave her a detailed account of the engagement. "You two must be starving. Let me make you some toast, bacon, eggs and coffee before I drive you back to London." She was up and had things out of the refrigerator before they could answer. Both men were anxious to get home to their families, but they were also starving.

The men ate and Laurie drove them back to London. In little more than an hour, they reached the city and Laurie dropped Justin off first.

Karen and Rene ran outside when they heard Laurie's car pull in the drive. They were both observably optimistic. Rene's optimism was soon replaced by elation when she saw Justin step out of the vehicle. Karen's face went white with despair when she saw Matt was not with them.

Gary and Laurie drove away and Karen quizzed Justin for details.

He told her all he knew. "We were crossing the road to get away when DHS vehicles drove up on us. Matt couldn't cross so he went back into the woods. Gary and I kept going."

"Why did you leave him?" Karen asked.

"We had no choice. It was Matt's call to split up," Justin answered.

Karen was hesitant. "Do you think he's alive?"

"Karen," Justin answered, "there is absolutely no way of knowing that. All I can say for sure is that I did not hear any gun fire in Matt's general vicinity after we split up. I honestly think that I would have heard a shot if he was killed. I was specifically listening for gunfire from his location to know if he was taking fire."

"Okay, that's something. Thank you," Karen replied.

Rene hugged Karen and Miss Mae rubbed Karen's leg. Karen reached down to pick up the little cat. She held the animal close as she scratched her behind the ear. Miss Mae always had a way of knowing when someone was in need of a little affection.

# CHAPTER 8

> "The purpose of government is to enable the people of a nation to live in safety and happiness. Government exists for the interests of the governed, not for the governors."
>
> -Thomas Jefferson

Paul Randall finished getting his notes together for the meeting Monday afternoon at his Kerrville, Texas ranch. The doorbell rang.

"I'll get it, sir," Sonny Foster called out from the other room. Sonny was Paul's right-hand man. He served as Paul's campaign manager during the previous presidential campaign. Randall had intended to make Sonny his chief of staff had the decision awarded him the office, but that didn't pan out. Sonny still proved to be invaluable to Paul Randall and to the Coalition movement.

Sonny escorted the guest to Randall's office.

"General Jefferson, welcome," Paul said.

"Hi, Paul," the General replied.

Sonny said, "Governor Jacobs should be here shortly. I have individual laptops set up over here so we can teleconference with the governors of the other Coalition states via our secure VOIP network."

Paul's wife, Kimberly, walked into the office and gave the General a hug. "It's so good to see you, Allen. I'm putting together a tray of cookies and a coffee service tray for your meeting. Do you have any special requests?"

"I would appreciate a pitcher of water if it wouldn't be too much trouble," Jefferson replied.

"No trouble at all." Kimberly disappeared into the kitchen to prepare the refreshments.

The doorbell rang again and Paul said, "That must be Larry. I'll go let him in."

The security on Randall's property rivalled that of the White House. Anyone who made it to the front door was obviously a friendly, the doorbell was simply a courtesy to announce one's arrival.

Paul opened the door. "Larry, it's good to see you. Come on in."

The men found their seats and Kimberly brought in the coffee, water and cookies. "Don't you boys make a bigger mess out of the country than what you've already made," she joked. The men all laughed as Kimberly excused herself.

The men started their meeting and Paul Randall laid out his agenda for the material he wanted to cover. "Gentlemen, thank you all for making the effort to be here either in person or via teleconference. It's not my intention to recreate the Constitutional Convention here today. Rather, I would like everyone to start a brainstorming campaign over the next few days. I do not believe that we need to rewrite the Constitution. We are not the entity in this civil war that has broken away from our heritage. I don't think anyone present today would disagree that it is the Federal States who have broken away and are in rebellion. I would also say that they have already invested much time and energy into rewriting the Constitution over the past several decades.

"With that being said, I also believe that there is great danger in deifying the founders or attempting to canonize the founding documents as being the divinely inspired words of God. We should remember that even in 1787, there were compromises made between those who wanted a smaller government and those, like Alexander Hamilton, who wanted a federal government with a strong hand. Hamilton believed in a central bank, a standing army and many other principles that, despite Aaron Burr's best efforts, bore fruit and corrupted what could have been a great government."

The men chuckled at the Aaron Burr comment.

Randall continued, "Gentlemen, today we do not have Alexander Hamilton or his ilk to dissuade us from what is possible. I believe we have an opportunity to correct the blemishes that found their way into our founding documents. I think we have been given the chance to make clarifications on gross injustices such as abortion that our founding fathers could never have anticipated. I think we have the opportunity to put up safeguards that will restrict a federal government from growing into the behemoth that we presently find ourselves having to fight against.

"In all of this, I think it is important to remember that we are but mortals. I pray that we will look for divine counsel in seeking a better path. Our forefathers had many advisors from the Church. The Black Robe Regiment was a group of pastors who were instrumental in the battles as well as the politics of the American Revolution. I believe it is important to seek input from men of God in clarifying and defining our Constitution. One such man who has proven to be both a patriot and a man of God is Pastor John Robinson of Liberty Chapel in Idaho. He has been spreading the message of freedom from the pulpit for several years. I would love for all of you to think about who else might be a good fit for what I would like to call our Black Robe advisory board. Psalm 33 tells us 'Blessed is the nation whose God is the Lord.' Personally, I'm tired of living in a country that is cursed because our god is not the Lord. To turn this around, we must put up safeguards to protect our children from the falsehoods which have been taught through the public schools. They need to know that they were created by God who has a plan for their lives. So much evil has come from teaching our children to believe the myth that they evolved from an ameba.

"I really believe this war is a gift, a second chance to safeguard our blessings of liberty. Let us not squander it by bowing again to the federalists and liberals."

The sounds of claps could be heard coming from the men watching via teleconference. The men continued their meetings. General Jefferson gave a brief update on the state of the military campaign and each governor of the individual Coalition States gave a report on the condition of their respective state.

Paul Randall closed the meeting with prayer then said, "Gentlemen, talk to your state-level and federal-level representatives about the issues they would like to address. We'll get back together via teleconference on May first and use those notes to come up with some proposals for the individual state legislatures to vote on. I realize that our representatives as well as all of us were elected prior to the meltdown and that things have changed. We may have to discuss a vote of confidence from our constituents to ensure that we still represent the people. God bless you all and stay safe. I'll talk to you next week."

# CHAPTER 9

"We must, indeed, all hang together or, most assuredly, we shall all hang separately."

-Benjamin Franklin

Matt awoke. He couldn't detect any light coming through the cracks of the door. It was maddeningly black. Matt tried to go back to sleep, but couldn't. He began praying quietly to God and reciting Bible verses as they came to mind. His stomach was starting to growl again, but if the schedule remained as it had been over the past two days, the small serving of porridge wouldn't arrive for another fourteen hours or so. Matt felt his way to the fresh water bucket. He placed the fresh-water bucket on the farthest corner of the cell and the sewage bucket nearest to the cell gate. This made it easy to discern them in absolute darkness. Matt cupped his hands and drank to quell the rumblings in his stomach.

Matt heard a very faint "Psst." It was coming from the cell next to his. He felt his way through the darkness to the chain-link fencing separating his cage from the one next to him.

"Hello?" the voice whispered ever so faintly.

"Hi," Matt replied in a volume just above silence.

"I'm Theodore Morris. I'm a doctor, folks where I'm from call me Doc," the voice whispered.

"I'm Matt," he whispered back.

"How long you been in here?" Doc asked.

"Two days, this will make three. Seems a lot longer though," Matt replied.

"Any idea what happens to us next?" Doc inquired.

"Not at all," Matt said. "Did you see any details about where we're being held?"

"I was blindfolded when they brought me in," Doc said.

"Me too," Matt whispered. "Where are you from?"

"Huntington," Doc answered. "I was suspected of giving aid to wounded militia and brought in for questioning. I was held all day yesterday with wrist restraints and a blindfold, but no one ever questioned me. I guess questioning means you've already been found guilty. I never thought I'd see this in America. I heard folks warn of it, but never paid them any mind. I labeled them as kooks. Well, I guess I was the kook for not believing them. I suppose I had a comfortable life and didn't want to believe anything could change that. Even when it started happening, I tried to stay neutral. I didn't want to get involved. I guess my side has been chosen for me now.

"When I treated those boys, I didn't even know they were militia. I suspected something, but didn't ask any questions. I didn't realize it was a crime, 'til now. Someone must have sold me out."

"Sounds like a popular pastime," Matt said softly.

"What's that?" Doc quizzed.

"Selling people out," Matt answered. He gave his new friend the abbreviated version of what happened to him.

"I picked sides a long time ago, but I'm in the same boat you're in," Matt said.

The men sat silently for a while, then Matt noticed a faint glimmer of light through the crack of the door. "Day break," he whispered.

"Oh yeah," Doc acknowledged.

Two hours later, they heard the lock being pulled from the door. Matt closed one eye so it would not adjust to the light. He recommended the same for Doc.

"Smart thinking," Doc said.

The light flooded in and a guard yelled, "Everybody up. Hi ho, hi ho, it's off to work you go. I'm going to kick wrist irons and leg irons under your cell doors. The last prisoner to get his on is getting his face kicked in." The guard walked down the corridor of the container, kicking two sets of handcuffs under each door. Matt's cell was the last cell, he had an unfair disadvantage to get his restraints on. His heart started to pound thinking of the cruel punishment for being last. As soon as the cuffs appeared under the cage door, Matt grabbed them and put them on. He was still last to get them on.

The guard could see the despair in Matt's eyes. "Just kidding," he laughed. "Everybody get up. We're going to get you boys suited up so you can go mine coal."

One of the prisoners near the front door protested, "That's slavery!"

The KBR guard drew his weapon and Matt could see the man at the other end of the container cover his face with his hands. POP, POP, POP. The guard fired three shots very deliberately and in quick succession. He did not hesitate and appeared to have no remorse for his action when the man fell to the ground. These were some bad people.

The guard holstered his weapon. "President Howe wants me to remind you that the work program is absolutely voluntary. You are free to opt out at any time. Do I have anyone else who wishes to opt out this morning?"

The only sound was the ringing inside of Matt's ears from the gun being fired in a metal shipping container. The men were chained to a single chain that was about thirty feet long. One guard led them to a prefabricated building where they were unhooked and given jumpsuits, boots and hard hats, one at a time. While he waited for his turn, Matt took the opportunity to survey the surroundings. The camp was filled with shipping containers similar to the one Matt was housed in. Outside of the fences were several mobile homes. "Those must be the living spaces for the guards," he whispered to Doc. Matt looked around for signs of civilization. It was all trees and he could hear no noises outside of the camp other than the sounds of the forest. The fence was twelve-feet high and had razor wire strung across the top. Security lights faced both directions from each of the four corners. A guard came to Matt, disconnected him from the central chain and led him inside to be equipped.

A man at a desk asked Matt, "Shoe size?"

"Eight," Matt said.

"Tens." The man handed Matt a pair of oversized work boots.

Matt was uncuffed long enough to put on the work boots and jumpsuit and hastily taken back to the central chain outside. As he waited for the others to be outfitted, he drank in the beauty of the surrounding forest and the light. He had been suffocated by darkness for nearly three days now and forgot how beautiful it was to see light and color. Another guard walked up the line handing out some type of food ration bar. Matt knew not to expect much from the taste, but he was so hungry, he didn't care. When his bar arrived, he opened it and began eating. It had the texture of dry cardboard and the taste of wallpaper paste. But it was filling the gaping space in his stomach and he was grateful for that.

Everyone was herded to a school bus while still attached to their single common chain. Matt looked out the window as they drove to the mine to look for any distinguishing landmarks. There were power lines running into the prison camp, it had to be within a reasonable distance of a town. One guard stood watch over them, so he and Doc dared not even whisper to each other while on the bus.

Twenty minutes later, they arrived at the mine which was inside of a fenced-in area similar to their prison camp.

The men were herded off the bus, uncuffed, and sent down the mine shaft elevator, six at a time. Matt made a mental note of the number of guards. There were four guards on the bus plus four more inside of a guard house at the entrance of the fence, all armed with M-4 rifles and side arms. Down inside of the mine, there were four guards, also armed with M-4 rifles and side arms.

Two fellow prisoners acted as foremen and trained the new prisoners on the different tools inside of the mine. They worked for ten hours, were given two more nutrition bars during the day, and returned to the prison camp.

Once they returned to the shipping container, they were fed porridge again and fresh water was brought around by a fellow prisoner. Matt gave himself a cat bath with the fresh water from the day before. The light in the crack of the door faded which meant the day was over. He and Doc whispered about the events of the day and Matt asked him what he thought of the possibility to escape.

"I'm willing to die trying," Doc said. "This is no way to live."

Matt agreed and repeated everything Adam had taught him about escape and evasion. "I think we should study these guys for a couple days, watch the schedule, and devise a plan. This seems to be the only safe time to talk. The rest of the day we're being watched like a hawk."

Doc agreed. The work in the mine released all of Matt's nervous energy and he slept much more soundly that night.

The next day, the same schedule was repeated.

# CHAPTER 10

"That the people have a Right to mass and to bear arms; that a well-regulated militia composed of the Body of the people, trained to arms, is the proper natural and safe defense of a free State...."

-George Mason- Father of the Bill of Rights

Early Tuesday morning, Adam pulled into Matt and Karen's drive and parked his truck. Justin was in the garden with Rene. Adam walked over, "Hey guys."

"Hey," Justin said.

Rene was bent down putting some of the seedlings in the dirt. She shielded her eyes from the morning sun as she looked up at Adam. "Hi."

"Still no word from Matt?" Adam asked.

"No," Justin replied.

"Where's Karen?" Adam inquired.

"Still in bed," Rene answered.

"She doin' alright?" Adam quizzed.

"Nope," Justin responded. "She was only out of bed for about two hours yesterday. She hardly ate and never got out of her robe."

"We're doing everything we know to do," Rene commented. "I tried to get her to eat, but I don't want to push her. I don't really know what to do."

"You guys are a big help, just taking care of the animals and the garden and such," Adam complimented. "I'll go in and see if I can get her to come around."

Adam let himself in the house and put on a pot of coffee. Once it brewed, he made a cup for himself and one for Karen. He also made two pieces of toast and put butter and jelly on it. He carried it to Karen's room and knocked on the door. "Karen, can I come in?"

"Yeah," she said weakly.

He sat the toast and coffee on the night stand. He walked over to the window and opened the curtains. Adam sat in the rocking chair near the bed and picked up his coffee. "This is good coffee, you should have some."

Karen sat up and took the cup. She sipped it slowly.

"This is a tough time for everybody," Adam said. "Shelly is really having a hard time, too. So am I. And so are the girls. We really need to stick together. If you isolate, it is going to be even harder on the rest of us. Shelly and the girls really need you to be there. We're going to have a little memorial service tomorrow morning for Wesley, I think you should come."

"Okay," Karen said.

"Eat your toast," Adam said.

"It's just so hard to eat," she said. "If I only knew that he was alive or dead, it would be so much easier."

"Justin said he didn't hear any gunshots after they were separated," Adam affirmed.

"That doesn't mean anything. They could have captured him and executed him at the camp," Karen argued.

"That's not consistent with military strategy," Adam explained. "If you're going to take the risk of detaining a prisoner, you're not going to take them back to camp and kill them. There is much less risk if you kill them when you find them."

"I just wish I knew. If I only knew he was alive." Karen picked up the toast and took a bite.

"I know." Adam patted her hand.

"I'm so sorry about Wesley," Karen said. "I'll come by later today to see Shelly. How is she?"

Adam replied, "She's in about the same shape you're in. You may not be able to make each other feel better, but you can comfort one another through the sorrow."

Adam patted Karen on the hand again, offered a smile, and left her alone to get dressed. He returned to the garden. "Justin, did you get some rest yesterday?"

"He didn't get out of bed at all yesterday," Rene commented.

"Good, we need to run over to Gary's real quick." Adam stated.

Rene lost her chipper tone. "No, please don't leave." The tears began to well up in her eyes.

Adam cut her off before she could get herself worked up. "Rene, I promise I'll have him back before sundown. I need you to be strong. I need you to look after Karen. If she sees you falling apart, she is going to get more depressed. You have to get her up and moving around. Walk her over to my place to see the girls and Shelly."

Rene wiped her tears and shook her head. "Alright, I will."

Adam knew it was a lot to ask after she had waited for three days for her husband to return. And of the four wives, only two husbands had returned. Not wanting to alarm her further, he said to Justin, "Grab your rifle so we can give it a good cleaning when we get to Gary's."

Justin washed up and grabbed his rifle. The two men jumped in the truck and drove off.

"Are we really going to Gary's?" Justin asked.

"Yep," Adam said.

"But not to clean rifles," Justin guessed.

"Nope," Adam declared.

Seconds later, Adam began to fill Justin in on the mission at hand. "I think the ambush at Pikeville was a trap. The person who gave us the information conveniently had the flu on the day of the operation. I thought we'd stop by Michael's and see if he's feeling any better. You and Gary can go to the front door to check on him. I think he'll be surprised that any of us survived the counter ambush. If he's guilty, he'll make a run for it. If he rabbits, I'll be in the woods behind his house with the .308."

"Sounds like a plan," Justin said.

Adam continued, "His wife's brother works for DHS. He was a total dependent of the welfare state before the meltdown. Like most of the new DHS recruits, he only took the job because Howe cut off all of his benefits. The brother was the one that supposedly sold the information on the convoy. It's my guess that there was some serious monetary gain on Michael's part for furnishing the information on our locations. DHS knew exactly where everyone of us were. I also believe Michael's wife is complicit in their operation. That makes her a traitor. She may draw down on you. Can you shoot a woman if you have to?"

Justin's eyes opened widely and he blew out a big puff of air. "I can shoot anyone who threatens me or my team members."

Adam wanted to be sure. "You have to know that before you walk into this situation. We already have one widow, possibly two."

"I'm sure," Justin said.

"I'm going to have to interrogate them. We need to get some

information from them before we administer their punishment for treason. Can you handle that?" Adam asked.

"I'll do whatever you need me to do. This is war, I never expected it to be pretty," Justin replied.

"Good," Adam said. "That's what I wanted to hear." Adam was impressed with the answer. Justin spoke and carried himself like a much older man. He was very mature for his age. Or, this conflict had forced him to grow up fast. Adam heard a lot of young men talk a big game in Iraq and Afghanistan, but after the bullets started flying, it was a different story. It was refreshing to see a young man Justin's age speak about battle with sobriety and respect.

When the two arrived at Gary's, Adam filled him in on the mission. He agreed that it sounded like a solid plan.

"Is it just us?" Gary asked.

"Just us," Adam replied.

Adam put on his ghillie suit and camo face paint before they left Gary's. "I'll lay in the back and bail out right before you reach Michael's drive. Don't even stop, just slow down to about ten miles an hour."

Justin and Gary acknowledged that they understood. Gary drove his truck so Adam's truck wouldn't set off any alarms.

Gary slowed the truck down, right before Michael's drive. Adam bailed out and ran for the tree line. He found a quick sniper nest, deployed his tripod and removed the covers from his scope. He thumbed off the safety of the AR-10 and laid perfectly motionless. Adam watched as Gary and Justin walked to the door to knock. Less than a minute later, Michael was coming out the back door with a bug out bag on his back. He ran directly for the very tree line Adam was sitting in.

"Oh, this is too easy," Adam said to himself. He waited for Michael to get about halfway to his position, then took the shot.

POP! The .308 hollow point round hit in the center of Michael's knee and his leg almost folded in half, backwards. Michael screamed in agony as he grabbed his leg which was gushing blood.

Adam stood up from his cover and walked down to Michael's location. He kept the sight trained on Michael. "Roll over!" Adam commanded.

"I can't," Michael cried in pain.

POP! Adam put another round in Michael's shoulder. "I said, roll over."

As much pain as he was in, Michael complied. Adam quickly put zip-tie restraints on Michael's hands and removed all of the contents of his pockets. Adam grabbed him by the back of his bug out bag and started dragging him back to the house. "I should have dropped you at the door. I would have saved myself some work."

When they arrived at the house, Justin helped Adam get Michael inside while Gary held Michael's wife, Susan, at gun point. Adam quickly put restraints on her hands and feet as well. Next, he opened his first-aid kit and took out two Quickclot sponges and two Israeli Battle Dressings. He stuck a Quickclot sponge in each of Michael's wounds and secured them with a bandage.

Next he opened Michael's bug out bag to inspect the contents. He soon found several rolls of silver coins and a small pouch with five ounces of gold. "Is this the ransom you got for my brother's life?" Adam quizzed.

"There is more in the bedroom dresser," Susan cried out. "Just take it and leave us alone."

"Shut up!" Michael yelled.

Adam looked at Susan. "Do you think we're here to rob you?"

He grabbed Susan by the arm and dragged her into the bedroom. "Let's keep them split up for now." He closed the door and zip tied her feet to her hands so she was completely immobilized. "Which drawer is the rest of the bounty in?"

"Are you going to let us go?" she pleaded.

Adam drew his side arm, bent down and pressed it to her ankle. "Which drawer?"

"Top left," she muttered.

Adam opened the drawer and found five more tubes of one-ounce silver eagle coins and five more one-ounce gold coins. "Where's your brother?" he asked as he counted the loot.

"Somewhere in West Virginia, I don't know," Susan replied.

"Do you have his number? Can you call him?" Adam asked.

"No, he calls me if he needs to talk to me," Susan said.

"Even if your life depended on it, you couldn't get hold of him?" Adam asked.

"No," Susan began to cry.

Adam grabbed the woman by the face and squeezed. "Is Michael going to give me the same answer when I ask him that question? Because if you lie to me, I can promise you will die a very painful death."

"I can call him," she relented.

Adam dropped her face. "Good. Let's get you straightened up and make that call."

"Can I have a drink?" she asked.

"Sure, what do you want, water?" Adam offered.

"Whiskey," she pleaded.

Adam thought for a moment and said, "Okay, one drink. Where is it?"

"In the kitchen, over the sink," she said.

Adam walked out of the bedroom and closed the door behind

him. He went to the kitchen and found the whiskey. Justin and Gary looked at him as he walked back through the living room with the whiskey in his hand.

"What are you doing to my wife?" Michael asked.

"I'll be back with you in a minute." Adam winked at Michael and gave him a nod to let him know he wouldn't forget about him.

Adam walked back into the bedroom and shut the door. He opened the bottle and put it to the woman's lips. She tried to chug the liquor, but Adam pulled it away after a small drink. "We can't have you slurring when you call your brother. I'll be right back." He placed the bottle on the dresser where Susan could look at it. The carrot-and-stick approach was going to be very effective with this one.

Adam returned to the living room and sat down in the chair near Michael.

Michael said, "The Quickclot is starting to burn. Can you take it out? I'm sure the bleeding has stopped."

Adam looked at him and ignored the request. "Whose idea was it to take the payment to set us up?"

Michael pleaded, "DHS already knew about us. It was only a matter of time until they caught up with us anyway. Susan's brother told us they would be coming for the militia."

Adam continued the interrogation. "How did Susan's brother know you were in the militia?"

"She may have mentioned it in casual conversation," Michael replied. "Are you going to let us go? If not, I'm not telling you anything else."

Adam said, "Justin, go look in the kitchen and tell me what cleaning supplies you can find." Adam unhooked the bandage on Michael's knee. He unwrapped it and removed the Quickclot sponge.

Justin called out from the kitchen, "Bleach, Pine-Sol, Comet, dishwashing detergent.…."

"Bring me the Pine-Sol," Adam replied.

"Okay, wait! What do you want to know?" Michael pleaded.

Adam disregarded Michael's request. He opened his knife, stuck it in the wound channel of the knee and pulled it to the side to open it up even further.

Michael screamed like a banshee as Adam poured the cleaner into the gaping wound.

Justin and Gary looked on in horror.

"You guys can walk around outside and make sure no one is coming by to see what all of the commotion is about." Adam could see his methods of interrogation were getting to them.

When Michael finally stropped screaming Adam said, "I don't have a lot of time to negotiate with you. I have to get Justin home to his wife before sundown. I promised I would because she was distraught by the thought of him being out of her sight again. He was wandering around in the woods for two days and she had no idea where he was. You know why? Because you set him up. Does that make sense?"

Michael nodded in fear.

Adam said, "Now I'm going to ask you, Susan, and your brother-in-law how all of this was set up. If the stories don't line up perfectly, it's going to get very painful for everybody."

Adam wiped the blood and bone fragments off of his knife on Michael's cheek. "Well, not me, of course, but for you guys."

Michael stuttered in fear and pain as he explained the details of the set-up. "Susan's brother, Milton, said they were on to us, and that I should distance myself from the militia."

"They were on to us because she told him about the militia after he took the job at DHS?" Adam wanted clarification.

"More or less," Michael said.

Adam said, "I understand that you don't want to get your wife in trouble, but from now on, let's use "yes" and "no." If I hear 'more or less' again, I'm going to get angry. Is that fair?"

Adam pulled out another Quickclot sponge from his IFAK. Michael's knee was bleeding profusely. "And how did you get to the point of accepting money to sell us out?"

Michael winced as Adam stuck the sponge in the wound. "Milton told Susan that DHS would pay a lot of money for information."

Adam finished for him. "And you said okay."

Michael pleaded, "Adam, you've got to believe me. They were on to us. The militia was going to get hit whether I took the money or not. Please, Adam."

"What other action is being taken against the militia in this area?" Adam asked.

"There is something planned for Lt. Joe's," Michael said.

"A raid?" Adam inquired.

"Yes, a raid," Michael said.

"When?" Adam quizzed.

"Friday," Michael answered.

"What's done is done. You've been cooperative, I'll see what I can do." Adam got up to return to the bedroom.

He walked into the room where Susan lay hog-tied on the floor and shut the door. "You ready to call your brother?"

Susan asked, "Are you going to let us go?"

Adam didn't answer. He drew his knife and grabbed Susan's big toe.

"Alright!" she screamed. "I'll call him! What do you want me to say?"

Adam gave her the directions, "Tell him that two of the militiamen escaped the raid and you have information about where they'll be and when, but you need to be paid for the information. Tell him the guy with the information wants five ounces of gold and tell him you want two ounces for yourself. Tell him he has to come by himself."

"Can I have another drink?" Susan begged.

Adam cut her hands loose and left her feet restrained. He handed her the bottle and took her phone off the night stand. "That's enough." He took the bottle and handed her the phone.

She dialed the number. "Milton."

Susan did exactly as she had been told. "But five ounces won't leave anything for me. Make it six total and you've got a deal."

Adam shook his head. She was a good liar. Even her own brother didn't suspect a thing.

"He'll be here tomorrow night around nine o'clock," she said.

"Good job," Adam said.

He put new restraints on her hands and went outside to get Justin and Gary. "Let's throw these two in the bed of the truck. I'll keep them in the barn for now. Her brother is coming back here tomorrow night. We'll need her here for that operation. I want to grab him and see what else he knows."

Justin and Gary put the two turncoats in the bed of the truck and tossed a blanket over them so no one would see two prisoners being carted around. Adam went through Michael's things looking for items of value. He cleaned out his gun cabinet and all of his ammo.

They jumped in the cab of the truck and headed back to Gary's to retrieve Adam's truck. "My recommendation is to start a widow's fund with this gold and silver we took off these crooks. I was thinking we should give a quarter of it of it to Shelly now. We'll take a quarter to the other widows who lost husbands in the attack. I'll keep the other quarter to the side, if Matt doesn't make it home, we'll give it to Karen."

The men agreed that it was a good plan. Adam retrieved his truck from Gary's, then took the prisoners to his barn. He was still able to get Justin home just before dark, as promised.

# CHAPTER 11

"A free people ought not only to be armed, but disciplined; to which end a uniform and well-digested plan is requisite."

-George Washington

Justin shut the door of Adam's truck and yelled, "See you in the morning," as Adam drove away. When he walked in the house, no one was home. "Adam rushed me home and no one is even here," he commented to himself.

Miss Mae came in the room to greet Justin. "Hey, cat." He crouched down to pet the small animal rubbing on his leg.

"Meow," Miss Mac was hungry.

"I could use a snack myself," Justin replied. He took a chunk of the venison roast from the fridge and some beans and rice. He pulled a few small pieces of venison to give to Miss Mae and stuck his in the microwave to warm up. "You better eat that before Karen comes home. I don't want to get in trouble." Justin had seen Matt catch it on more than one occasion for overfeeding the slightly overweight pet.

Justin sat down at the table to eat his meal. Miss Mae was still asking for more. Just as he tore off another small piece for the cat, he heard the key hit the door. "Rats," he said.

"You're home!" Rene said as she and Karen walked in the door.

"Yeah, I didn't know where you guys were, so I helped myself to dinner," Justin said.

"That's fine, we ate a late lunch at Janice's," Karen said. "Did you feed Miss Mae?"

"No, well, yes, I mean, she was begging, so I gave her a really small bite of my venison," Justin said.

Karen rolled her eyes and said, "That's fine."

Justin asked, "Did you guys see Adam before you left Janice's?"

"No, we must've left right before he got home," Karen said. "Why?"

"Just wondering," Justin kept eating. He was really fishing to see if they had seen any curious activities such as Adam loading two human-sized packages into the barn.

Justin inquired, "Rene, did you finish with the garden this morning?"

She answered, "No, two guys came by today who were offering handyman services. I told them we were fine, then one of them asked where my husband was. I said you were around back. Then he asked if I could go get you. I said you were too busy. He looked around, then he kind of looked me up and down. I told him that we handled everything ourselves and didn't require their services. I had the garden hoe in my hand. I turned the blade side up, in case I had to swing it at him, ya know. I guess he got the hint. They finally got back in their van and drove away. It gave me the creeps. When Karen went over to Janice's, I went with her. I didn't want to stay here by myself."

"That was smart." Justin was concerned. "Why didn't you take the

AR-15 when you went to Janice's?"

"I had the pistol," Rene replied.

Justin said, "If you ever have to defend yourself, the rifle is going to be so much more effective, Rene. A pistol is a great thing to have when you don't expect trouble. We're in the middle of a societal collapse and a civil war. It's safe to say you should expect trouble in times like these. Karen, I'm a guest in your house, so I would never tell you what to do, but I'm sure Matt would want me to encourage you to carry a rifle as well."

"Thanks, Justin," Karen said. "You're right. I've not been thinking straight since Matt went missing. Speaking of rifles, did you get yours cleaned up?"

"What do you mean?" Justin asked curiously.

Karen said, "Didn't you and Adam go to Gary's to clean your rifles?"

Justin slipped up. "Oh, yeah. We did, but something came up," he covered.

"I bet," Karen said. "What came up?"

Trapped like a fox in a snare, Justin said, "I'm not supposed to discuss it."

Rene jumped into the inquisition. "What happened, Justin?"

There was no way out. Justin decided his best course of action was to negotiate for impunity. "You have to promise you won't say anything to anybody; especially Adam."

"We promise," Karen said.

Justin added, "And Janice, you can't say anything to her. It'll get back to Adam that I said something."

Rene said, "Our lips are sealed. What happened?"

Justin proceeded to give them a sterilized version of the events at Michael's house. He left out Adam's interrogation methods and the fact that Michael and Susan were being held hostage in Adam's barn.

The two girls listened intently. Karen asked, "Could this guy, Milton, know where Matt is?"

Justin regretted saying anything already. "Karen, there is no way of knowing what the guy knows until Adam gets him alone."

"Make sure he asks him about Matt," she demanded.

"Of course," Justin replied. "You know we'll do everything we can."

Justin saw the glimmer of hope the news gave Karen. He had no idea if it was a false hope or possibly a real lead to finding Matt, so he didn't know how he felt about spilling the beans.

# CHAPTER 12

"The uniform, constant, and uninterrupted effort of every man
to better his condition . . . is frequently powerful enough to
maintain the natural progress of things toward improvement, in
spite of the extravagance of government, and of the greatest errors
of administration."

-Adam Smith

Young Field was a 500-acre farm north of Boise, Idaho. Pastor
John Robinson had set up a large scale community retreat at Young
Field at the first signs of the collapse. Most of the people from the
Liberty Chapel congregation who followed Pastor John to Young
Field lived in campers, fifth wheels or RVs. The folks there survived
the winter months by communal living. They continued to share the
burdens and blessings to get the community established. Pastor John
gave a short speech at a barn dance about two weeks ago. He
encouraged the congregants to use their spare time to peruse their
own individual talents and industry.

After lunch, Pastor John walked through the make-shift bazar set
up outside of the barn that was used for church services, meetings
and barn dances. He approached a table constructed of two
sawhorses and an old door. "Howdy fellas, what wares or service
might you be offering today?"

Oliver Stillwell and Harry Wilder had a disassembled AK-47 laying on the table and a couple of other guns leaning up against the wall of the barn behind them. Harry said, "We're cleaning and repairing firearms, sir."

Oliver added, "You gave us the idea at the dance."

Pastor John said, "That's a great trade. How much do you charge?"

Harry replied, "We're not charging anything, sir. Since we defected from the Federal States, the people of Liberty Chapel have made sure we've had everything we needed. This is only a small gesture of our appreciation for the hospitality we've received."

Oliver winked and said, "But we do accept tips."

Pastor John laughed and said, "You two are a welcome addition. We're so glad to have you."

Harry said, "I think making Wednesday a half day was a great idea."

Pastor John replied, "Most of the planting is done, so the work load is lower than in the past few weeks. No sense wearing ourselves out when there's nothing to do. We still have too many daily chores for everyone to be off both Saturday and Sunday. If we took the weekends off, several tasks would be piled up come Monday morning. It made more sense to break up the downtime. Everyone gets the whole day off on Sunday and a half day on Wednesday, they seem to like that."

Oliver said, "That gives us Wednesday afternoon for the bazar. I think it's perfect."

Pastor John's wife walked up behind him. "Hi, John."

The pastor hugged his wife. "What bring you to the bazar, my dear?"

"Well," she answered, "one of the ladies has set up a clothing swap table. Some of us are trading clothes that don't fit any longer or for the sake of having something different to wear. There won't be any Macy's sales or Walmarts for buying new clothes for a while. Cindy set up a table right next to the exchange. She's making alterations. That's handy. A lot of us have lost weight since the meltdown. Most of us had a little to lose anyway. Well, I'm off to make a few deals."

Oliver and Harry both wished her good day as she trotted off with her clothes for swapping.

Pastor John asked, "Now, about those tips. What types of tips have you boys received."

Oliver raised up a five-inch-long, unevenly-cut bar of a waxy looking substance. "We cleaned a couple of rifles for Gus and he gave us this."

"Alright," the pastor said. "And what is it?"

Harry answered, "Soap. He has a table down at the end of this row. He's selling it."

"Ain't that something," Robinson replied. "He made it?"

Oliver replied, "From scratch. He has a process to make lye. He burns hardwood and keeps the ash. He soaks it in water and somehow gets lye from that. He heats it up and mixes it with hot lard from the hogs and makes this soap."

Pastor John said, "God has certainly blessed us to have a great selection of skills. These are hard times, but I'm convinced I'm going through them with the best people on Earth. Fellas, I can see you have a few weapons to work on, so I'll let you get back to work. Besides, I see that Isaac doesn't have any one waiting and I need to get a quick haircut."

Oliver said, "Thanks for stopping by, Pastor."

Pastor John walked to Isaac's spot at the bazar where he cut hair. There was no other sign of it being a barbershop. There was only a small table, one that might have been a night stand in another life, and a chair with a sheet draped over it. The small table held an assortment of scissors, combs and razors. "Good afternoon, Pastor," Isaac greeted.

"Hello, Isaac," John replied. "Nice and short in the back and sides."

Isaac pinned the sheet around the pastor. "Absolutely."

The two men talked about the weather and the general state of affairs at Young Field. Now that they were dependent on the success of the crops, weather was the most important topic of the day. It was no longer the icebreaker, small talk of the world gone by.

Two Idaho National Guardsmen in dress uniforms walked up to Pastor John as Isaac finished his haircut.

"Are you Pastor John Robinson?" the first man asked.

"Yes, how can I help you?" the pastor responded.

The man answered, "Governor Goldwater is requesting your presence at the governor's home next Monday. Coalition Commander-in-Chief Paul Randall would like to have your input in ironing out some safeguards to ensure the Constitution is never violated to the degree it has been in recent years. He wants to protect it from the left so future generations won't have to endure another civil war. At least not in the Coalition States anyway."

Pastor John asked, "Paul Randall will be in Idaho?"

The guardsmen replied, "We're not at liberty to get into many details at the time, sir, but I do believe the meetings are via teleconference. They utilize an encrypted VOIP."

"I'd be honored," Robinson said.

"We'll pick you up at eight o'clock in the morning, sir," the man replied.

Pastor John said, "It's less than an hour to the governor's house in Boise. I can get there on my own."

The man said, "Governor Goldwater insists that you have an

armed escort, sir."

Pastor John said, "In that case, I'll see you at eight o'clock Monday morning."

The men said farewell and Isaac finished the pastor's haircut.

"What do I owe you, Isaac?" the pastor asked.

"Nothing," Isaac responded.

"Nonsense. First Timothy five says a worker is worth his wages." Pastor John pulled out three rounds of .223 ammunition and laid them on Isaac's small table.

"Thank you very much, pastor," Isaac said.

Ammunition was the currency of choice in Young Field. Three rounds of .223 was the equivalent of around fifteen dollars in pre-collapse currency. Other flea markets around the country didn't trade in ammunition anymore. Reports had circulated about folks who had been robbed and killed with the very bullets they used to barter with. That wouldn't be a problem among the community here at Young Field. Ammunition made a perfect currency for trade among one's own mutual assistance group.

"You have a blessed day, Isaac," Pastor John said. He had a lot of prayer and preparation to complete over the next few days. This opportunity to provide spiritual guidance to the Coalition deserved his full attention and all diligence.

# CHAPTER 13

"Listen, I tell you a mystery: We will not all sleep, but we will all be changed—in a flash, in the twinkling of an eye, at the last trumpet. For the trumpet will sound, the dead will be raised imperishable, and we will be changed. For the perishable must clothe itself with the imperishable, and the mortal with immortality. When the perishable has been clothed with the imperishable, and the mortal with immortality, then the saying that is written will come true: 'Death has been swallowed up in victory.' 'Where, O death, is your victory? Where, O death, is your sting?'"

-1 Corinthians 15:51-55

The morning sun peaked through the curtains and Karen opened her eyes. She knew better than to look over to see if Matt was in the bed. She had looked the past four mornings and he wasn't there. Each time, it solidified the fact that it was not all just a bad dream. She rolled over and looked anyway. The same sinking feeling she felt the previous mornings returned. Miss Mae was on Matt's pillow. The cat looked at Karen as if to tell her that she shared her pain.

There was a knock at the bedroom door. Rene poked her head in. "Karen, we have to get ready for the memorial service."

Karen said, "Okay, I'm awake."

Rene closed the door and Karen forced herself to get up. She put her clothes on and went to the kitchen to make a pot of coffee.

Justin came in carrying several eggs. "Good morning, Karen."

Karen strained to smile, "Good morning, Justin."

Justin asked, "Can I make you an omelet? I've got some of Mr. Miller's homemade goat cheese. There's still a couple pieces of the bread Rene made. You can have some toast with your omelet."

Despite the depression, Karen's stomach was complaining. "That would be very nice, Justin. Thank you."

Rene, Justin and Karen ate breakfast and headed over to Adam's for the memorial service. Justin grabbed his full-auto Colt M4 captured in the raid at State Road 421 back in February. He handed his old AR-15 to Rene. "Are you going to bring your rifle, Karen?"

Karen knew what Matt would say. She went back in the bedroom, opened the safe and took out Matt's AR-15 and followed Justin and Rene out the door.

Rene asked, "Adam is going to speak at the Memorial?"

Karen answered, "Yes, he officiated Wesley's wedding." The memorial was a nagging reminder that Matt could be dead, but Karen knew this was going to be a tough day for everybody.

When they arrived at Adam's, the mood was very somber. Adam had a shoe box on the table. It held a tattered teddy bear, a plastic toy revolver and the neck-tie Wesley had worn in his and Shelly's wedding. There was a candle burning next to the box and a bouquet of purple and yellow wild flowers lay on each side of a photo of Wesley in a silver frame.

Karen walked into the living room and sat next to Shelly. She put her arm around her and suddenly felt guilty for feeling so bad. At least Karen still had hope. For Shelly, there was none. "How are you holding up?"

"I'll make it," Shelly said. "But I'm angry. They stole my husband. We didn't even have a chance to really get to know each other as a married couple. Four months wasn't even enough time to have our first fight."

Adam walked in, "Shelly, whenever you're ready, we'll get started."

"I'm as ready as I'll ever be," she answered.

Adam closed the box with the tie, the bear and the toy gun. He tucked it under his arm and led everyone out to the backyard and past the garden. They walked to the beginning of the woods where a large oak sat with massive protruding roots.

Adam said, "Wesley used to come sit under this tree and read his history books. Because of his understanding of history, he probably saw this battle on the horizon before any of us. This box contains the tie he wore when he got married. It has his bear that he was never without as a child and his toy pistol that he played cowboy with."

Adam broke down, he began sobbing violently and was unable to continue.

Justin walked over and patted him on the shoulder. Justin said, "I didn't know Wes as long as the rest of you, but the short amount of time I spent with him was inspiring. We were both involved in the DHS ambush on State Road 421. After you share an experience like that with someone, you feel like you've known them a lot longer than you have. We were all together at the Pikeville raid that went so terribly wrong. Wesley was a brave man. He was very good to me. You have all been very good to me and my wife. We came here with nothing, and all of you haven't stopped giving ever since we arrived."

Adam regained his composure but was unable to say anything else.

Justin kept going. "I'm not really the Bible scholar that Adam is, but I know Jesus is the Messiah. I also know that Wesley believed that and we will see him again. I think it was Paul who said something in First Thessalonians to the effect that we shouldn't grieve like those who have no hope, because we know we will see our fellow believers again. Of course we miss them. And of course it hurts. But this is not the end."

Janice hugged Justin and said, "That was beautiful."

Adam picked up the shovel and dug a hole near a wide root of the oak that rose so high above the ground that it almost made a bench to sit on. He placed the box in the ground and covered it up. Janice started singing Amazing Grace and soon everyone joined her. Shelly placed the bouquet of wild flowers on the mound of dirt. The tears streamed down her cheek as she said, "Good-bye, my love."

Karen, Rene and Justin knelt down near Shelly to comfort her. Mandy held Carissa as she cried. Janice stood by her husband as he kneeled near the memorial site and wept.

Janice was the first to walk back to the house. Mandy and Carissa followed her. Next, Karen, Justin and Rene walked back. They each had a cup of hot tea while they waited for Shelly and Adam to grieve.

Janice put together some things to eat. This allowed those who wanted to eat to go ahead. Those who weren't hungry could eat later if they wanted. They spent the day talking and crying and remembering Wesley.

# CHAPTER 14

"Among the natural rights of the colonists are these: first, a right to life; secondly, to liberty; thirdly to property; together with the right to support and defend them in the best manner they can."

-Samuel Adams

Karen and Rene hung out at Janice's until late after the memorial. Adam and Justin geared up for their "secret" mission. Karen knew what they were doing, and she suspected Janice did as well. She kept her promise to Justin and didn't say anything about it.

Rene hugged and kissed Justin as he walked out the door. "Be safe," she implored.

"I will," he stroked her hair as he walked out the door.

Adam assured his two girls, "Daddy will be home tonight to tuck you in."

They both seemed to have full confidence in his statement, at least more so than Janice, who said, "Be careful."

Karen noticed the way Janice held her eyes as Adam closed the door. *She knows something,* she thought. *Probably knows exactly what we know.*

The four women conspicuously avoided the subject of where Adam and Justin were heading. They all had a cup of tea and Shelly finally made herself a small plate of the finger foods that were still laid out in the kitchen, buffet style. They chatted for an hour or so after the men left.

"So, how is your garden doing, Janice?" Karen asked.

"Good." Janice took a sip of her tea. "Mandy and Carissa have been a great help. We've planted most everything. The green beans are already sprouting, and we put the tomatoes and pepper seedlings in the ground also."

Shelly said, "I haven't been much help."

Janice said, "Shelly, you're being human. No one faults you for that."

"I know," she replied, "but I am going to start getting on with life tomorrow. I really needed this memorial; you know, to sort of help me process things."

Rene moved over to sit next to Shelly and put her arm around her and gave her a hug. "You'll be fine. I know you will."

Shelly said, "Thanks."

Mandy asked, "Did you leave lots of food out for Miss Mae this morning?" Like many twelve-year-old girls, she was especially considerate of animals and always wanted to be sure they were well cared for.

Karen responded, "Oh my goodness! I forgot all about that! We better get going. The toilette paper will be completely off the roll and it will probably be shredded all over the floor by now. Serves me right."

Rene added, "It will probably be completely dark by the time we get home."

The two girls said their good-byes and headed home.

The woods were pitch black by the time they started out. Shelly flicked on the tactical light attached to her AR-15 to illuminate her path. Karen unscrewed the knob that secured the tactical light to her weapon. She removed it and used it as a regular flashlight.

"I'm glad to see Shelly is doing better," Rene said.

"Me too," Karen agreed.

"What about you?" Rene asked.

"What about me?" Karen said.

Rene clarified, "I mean, how are you holding up? You know, what's going through your head?"

Karen sighed heavily, "I don't know, Rene. I feel guilty if I start having a pity party. I think about Shelly who has no hope of seeing Wes in this lifetime, but then I think at least she has closure. I sort of got my hopes up when Justin said they were going to get this guy who might know something, but I'm afraid he won't know anything and I'll be right back where I started. I just don't know how long I can take not knowing. Does that make sense?"

Rene didn't answer. Instead, she asked, "Did you leave a light on in your bedroom?"

They reached the point where they could barely see the house through the woods.

"No," Karen said. "It was light when we left and I thought we'd be back before dark, so I didn't leave any lights on at all."

Rene said, "I thought I saw a light in the window. It could have been a reflection, but let's turn off the flashlights to be sure."

"Okay," Karen pressed the button on the rear of her flashlight.

"There it is again!" Rene said in a panicked whisper.

"Someone is in the house!" Karen's adrenaline kicked in and her heart pounded.

Rene looked at Karen. "What do you want to do? Should we go back to Janice's?"

Karen said, "I don't know. I'm worried about Miss Mae. She's in there. If they're crazy enough to break in, they might be crazy enough to hurt my cat. Besides, they could clean us out. Before the collapse, stuff was just stuff. If it was stolen, you could go to work, earn more money and replace it. Now, if they steal our stuff, we might not survive. Given enough time, they can cut the safe out of the floor and steal the whole safe. They could worry about getting it open later. If that happens, that would deplete most of our resources. We're going to need our stuff to survive this depression."

Rene asked, "So what do you want to do?"

Karen said, "Kill 'em."

Rene nodded. "Do you have a plan?"

"Not really," she whispered.

Rene inquired, "Mind if I make some suggestions?"

Karen replied, "Go right ahead."

Rene started brainstorming. "Justin and I played paintball with the militia once in a while. One of the games we played was called capture the fort. When our team was the one trying to capture the fort, we would try to draw the other team to the windows and doors of the plywood shoot house. Then, another team member would try to pick them off."

Rene bent down and started scratching in the dirt as she continued putting together a plan. She cleared an area on the ground of leaves and rubbish. She placed a stick in the middle of the area and drew a box around it. "We'll stay on one of these three sides, so we'll always have the cover and concealment of the forest. When we shoot, we'll make sure we have a tree for cover. Every time we shoot, the muzzle flash will give away our position. See these three lines that represent the three wooded sides of the house? We'll always make sure we're both on the same line, so we don't get confused and shoot each other."

Karen's heart was pounding, but she still managed to crack a joke. "Yeah, that would be bad."

Rene asked, "How many rounds do you have?"

"I don't know?" Karen said. "How many bullets goes in this magazine?"

"Thirty," Rene said. "But Justin never fills his all the way to the top. I have twenty-eight rounds in the magazine plus one in the pipe. Is your gun chambered?"

Karen shrugged. Rene took the weapon, removed the magazine and checked the chamber. A shell flew out and she forced it back in to the magazine. "It's really tight with this round. I'm guessing you had twenty-nine rounds in the magazine before." She racked the weapon for Karen and handed it back to her. "We're going to have to shoot and move. One of us is going to have to draw fire and the other is going to try to snipe off the shooter when they come to the window to return fire."

Karen said softly, "Alright, which job should I do?"

Rene asked, "How tight are your groups with that rifle?"

Karen said, "What do you mean?"

Rene said, "I should probably be the sniper and you should probably try to draw fire. Your sweater is brown and your jacket is red. You should take off your jacket now and leave it behind this tree. Move up to the edge of the tree line and see if you can make out a target. Plan your retreat before you take the shot. Look for a path that will allow you to move without hitting a lot of tree limbs or branches to make noise and create peripheral motion in the brush. If you see a form through the curtains, take a shot, then move back diagonally into the woods. I'll wait to see if they poke their heads out. I'll take my shot then move back to where you are."

Karen replied, "Okay, now?"

Rene said, "Now."

Karen moved slowly into position. She found a thick tree trunk for cover. She eyed out a good path of egress and found the bedroom window through the reflex sight. She had no magnification optics on the weapon, but she was pretty close. She waited for a light but saw none. She was far enough around the corner to see the edge of the driveway. Karen saw the bumper of a vehicle. As she looked closely, she could see that it was a van. "Those are the guys that were here bugging Rene yesterday! What creeps!" she said to herself. Karen saw light through the window, but couldn't make out a form. Confident that Miss Mae would be well hidden, she took a shot. She followed Rene's plan and retreated back into the woods. She found a safe spot behind a fallen tree and took aim towards the house again.

Within seconds, the curtains were pulled to the side and a dark figure was peering out into the night. Karen saw the muzzle flash from the direction of Rene's rifle and heard the loud crack of the shot. Seconds later, gunfire was ringing out from the window towards the woods. Karen dropped down behind the shelter of the large tree. When the gunfire slowed, Rene worked her way over to Karen's position.

"Are they still in the house?" Karen asked.

"Yes," Rene whispered. "I think I got one."

"How many are there?" Karen asked.

"I don't know." Rene sat low with her head concealed behind the fallen tree.

"I saw a van in the driveway," Karen said. "Is it the same guys that were here yesterday?"

Rene crawled around to the side of the log and peered towards the drive. "Same van. Maybe the rest of them will just leave."

Karen replied, "That would be great, but we don't know what they've already loaded into the van. Should we try to shoot out the tires?"

Rene said, "If we do, they're trapped and have no option but to fight. Then we're committed to killing them or being killed. I don't think that is a good idea. We have no idea of how strong a force they are."

"I see your point," Karen said, "but resources are tight already. We can't afford to let them steal anything."

Rene sat quiet for a moment, then said, "Let's try this. You circle back around towards the side we approached from. Lay down about ten shots to the bedroom window. Hopefully that will make them think the driveway isn't covered. I'll be set up to take out anyone who approaches the van. If I miss, they can still get away and we won't force them into a fight to the death. Does that work for you?"

Karen replied, "Yeah, but don't miss."

Rene said, "Give me thirty seconds to get over there, then pick about three or four trees to move back and forth from to make you appear to be more than one shooter. Don't shoot more than fifteen rounds. Save a few rounds in case you are attacked. If we do run out of ammo, what's the plan? Should we try to get back to Adam's?"

Karen said, "No, I don't want to bring trouble over there. Especially not with Mandy and Carissa there. I say run and hide in the woods until they're gone."

Rene said, "I don't like that plan, either. I suppose you're right, though. If it comes to that, keep moving as fast and as far as you can. Don't worry about getting lost. We'll get back home eventually, but we have to survive tonight first."

Rene moved into position and so did Karen. She counted the seconds and started taking pot shots at the windows of her bedroom. She lost track of time and lost track of how many rounds she fired. Soon, she heard two shots in close succession from Rene's rifle. She sat quietly for a moment then began to work herself around to Rene's position. As she approached, she could make out a dark form on the ground near the passenger side of the van.

"You shot him," Karen said.

"Yeah," Rene replied with a shaky voice.

"Did you see any more of them?" Karen inquired.

"No," Rene's voice was still shaking "Someone else must still be inside."

"Why," Karen asked.

Rene answered, "He was trying to get in the passenger side. The driver must still be in there."

Karen said, "Unless he was trying to get in the passenger side because it was his closest form of cover."

Rene said, "Could be, but how do we know?"

Karen said, "If he's the driver, he'll have the keys."

"No way," Rene said. "I'm not checking his pockets."

Karen said, "If you're sure he's dead, I'll check them."

Rene was confident. "I hit him right in the head. He dropped straight to the ground. I shot him again to be safe. He's dead, I'm sure."

"Cover me." Karen started crawling towards the corpse. She took the shotgun out of his hand and began rifling through his pockets. His front pockets were warm and wet. He must have urinated when he died. Karen felt her stomach turn sour and she fought to keep from getting sick. She was ready to abandon the mission when she heard keys rattling. She reached one last time to retrieve the keys and headed back to the tree line. Sure enough, there was a Ford key that likely matched the Ford van. Karen showed it to Rene.

Rene said, "I hope you're right. Still, we need to clear the house, room by room. Do you know how to clear a house?"

Karen shook her head, "Matt used to make me practice clearing the house when we lived in Florida. I guess it really will come in handy."

"Okay," Rene said, "I'll take point and you stack up behind me. I'll turn toward the inside of each room and you cover straight ahead of each doorway. We'll stack back up for each room."

Karen said, "I'll give you a squeeze on the shoulder when I'm ready and you'll signal with a nod when you're ready?"

"Yes," Rene said. "And don't shoot me."

"I won't shoot you!" Karen insisted.

Rene asked, "Did the dead guy's gun have a sling?"

"No," Karen answered.

Rene said, "Too bad, we could have taken it in as backup. Let's prop it up behind the van. If we run out of bullets and have to retreat, it'll be here. In fact, I should see how many rounds are still in it. I heard a few shotgun blasts, but most of the gunfire was from a pistol."

Karen said, "Then that means there is at least one more shooter."

Rene worked the pump of the shotgun to eject the remaining shells. "Or it means he switched guns. Only two shells left." She reloaded the shells and propped the shotgun against the van.

The girls approached the front door cautiously. Rene entered the room first and Karen followed smoothly behind her. Next, they went to the kitchen. When it was cleared, the girls stacked back up and reentered the living room. They cleared the bathroom and the bedrooms checking under the beds and the corners of each closet. Another corpse lay bleeding all over Karen's floor. A semi-automatic pistol sat on the floor near his head.

Karen said, "I guess this pistol belonged to pee pee pants' out there and he took the shotgun from Charlie here."

Rene asked, "Do you always give nicknames to your victims?"

"So far," Karen said sarcastically.

Karen turned on the lights and could see the greying skin of the body on her bedroom floor. "We've gotta get him out of here before he starts to stink." She bent down to look under the bed. There was

Miss Mae hiding behind the suitcase. "It's alright, you can come out whenever you're ready." Karen knew the cat would likely stay hidden until at least tomorrow morning.

They started to drag the body but noticed they were creating a trail of blood through the house. Rene suggested, "Let's wrap him in the shower curtain and drag him out of the house."

Karen agreed, reluctantly. It was a cheap plastic shower curtain, but there were no more Dollar Stores and it would be hard to replace.

They wrapped the corpse in the shower curtain and dragged him to the back door. Once outside, Karen insisted that they unwrap him and try to salvage the shower curtain. The two girls went to the shed and found a shovel. Karen scouted out an open area in the tree line far from the creek so their water source wouldn't be fouled. The two girls took turns digging with the shovel and eyeballing the size of the grave. Once they hit a depth of about three feet, they hit a series of large tree roots.

"That has to be deep enough," Karen said. "What do you think?"

"I don't know," Rene stepped down into the grave. "This seems like it should do the trick."

They went back to drag the man to the grave. He was heavy and the two women were tired.

"One down, one to go," Karen said as they kicked him into the hole in the ground.

"Let's get this over with," Rene wiped the sweat from her face.

Twenty minutes later, they were patting down the dirt on the shallow grave. "Should we say something over the grave?" Rene asked.

"Yeah, good luck," Karen said as she walked away. She was angry that the criminals had pushed her to such a place as having to kill another human being. There would probably be other emotions later, but for now, she was just mad.

The two girls got cleaned up and ready for bed, but neither of them were going to sleep anytime soon.

# CHAPTER 15

"Though the flame of liberty may sometimes cease to shine, the coal can never expire."

-Thomas Paine

Matt woke to the sound of the steel door being opened on his container. The hard work in the coal mine was at least making him sleep better. He felt the agonizing stiffness in his joints and back from both sleeping on the hard metal floor of the container without a mattress and from the tough work in the mine. The guard opened the door and yelled, "Five minutes!"

"God give me strength, just for today," he whispered as he stretched his aching body. Matt cupped his hands and drank as much water as he could from the bucket in his cell. The guards in the mine weren't very big on giving breaks. Matt needed to hydrate as much as possible right now.

Doc whispered from the next cell over, "You ready for another day?"

"Do I have a choice?" Matt replied.

Another prisoner came through with the tasteless nutrition bars that they were fed each morning for breakfast.

Matt said, "Thank you."

The man just smiled and nodded at Matt. As soon as Matt finished his ration bar, the guard began making his way through the container with the restraints. Everyone put their hand and ankle cuffs on quickly since these guards had shown they held no reservations about killing anyone they deemed to be uncooperative.

Matt placed the shackles on his feet, then his wrists. He looked over at Doc and whispered, "Hi ho, hi ho."

Doc forced a smile and whispered, "Off to work we go."

Matt followed the routine of going through the line, getting his jumpsuit and work boots and loading onto the bus. He was very careful to observe the actions and attitudes of the guards on the bus. This was only the third day of the work commute, and he could see the guards becoming noticeably more complacent. The absolute silence rule was already replaced by an occasional "Shut up!" when the whispering became loud enough to aggravate the guards. That was good, because if Matt was going to make a move, it would have to be soon. The ration bars were not enough for Matt to maintain his weight. He had been about twenty pounds overweight prior to the collapse. Less availability of the sweet treats Matt was so fond of contributed to a loss of about ten pounds since the meltdown. He had probably lost another three or four pounds since he was locked up only five days prior. At that rate, he would be too frail to escape in a month.

Matt whispered to Doc, "What happened to that guy, Wendell, who came in with you Sunday night? They took him to the infirmary after our shift Monday. Haven't seen him since."

Doc replied softly, "Don't know. I'm starting to suspect that 'infirmary' is a euphemism for 'shallow grave.'"

They arrived at the mine, unloaded and were herded into the elevator. Through the day, Matt thought about the different tools in the mine that could be used to effect his escape. *The pick would be a great weapon, but there was no getting it out of the mine; same thing with the shovel.* Matt made a conscious inventory of all the small pieces, belts and pulleys on the massive drilling machine and the loading machines. Surely, the machines wouldn't work if any of those pieces were missing. At the end of the day, Matt grabbed the wire brush broom and started sweeping his area. Matt noticed one of the wire bristles fall out. He thought nothing of it at first, but then went back to pick it up. When it was time to return to the surface, Matt stuck it in his mouth.

On the ride home, Matt pulled out the wire and began toying with it inside the keyhole of his handcuffs. Just before they reached the prison compound, Matt popped the cuffs. The bus came to a halt, Matt relocked the handcuffs and stuck the wire back in his mouth.

In the shipping container that night, Matt washed up and called Doc over to the chain-link fencing that separated their cells. "I figured out how to open the handcuffs with a piece of wire. I tried to feel around for the locking mechanism inside the cuffs, but couldn't really figure out how to manipulate it. I finally tried sticking the wire inside the area where the cuffs come together. I wedged it between the teeth of the lock, tightened them just a bit and then opened the cuffs. They popped right open. Why don't you take the wire and try it on the way to the mine tomorrow. I'll try to get another couple of pieces of wire from the broom."

Doc said, "Alright, but then what?"

"I don't know yet," Matt replied. "But let's just focus on that for now. Once we're proficient with popping the cuffs, we'll think of the next step. I'm sure everybody wants out of here. We have the least amount of guards when we're on the bus. If we're going to make a move, that's the time to do it."

"Should I tell Carl over here in the cell next to me?" Doc asked.

Matt said, "I think it'll take all of us. I can't imagine anyone being a snitch. Of course I never thought someone in my unit would sell me out, either. Still, I think we have to take that chance."

Doc said, "Our time here is limited anyway. I think the plan is to use us up until we can't work anymore. After that, it's a one-way ticket to the infirmary."

# CHAPTER 16

"War—An act of violence whose object is to constrain the enemy, to accomplish our will."

-George Washington

After Wesley's memorial, Adam and Justin loaded their gear into the cab of the truck. They stopped by the barn and fed their two hostages. Adam grabbed a pump sprayer and a two-gallon gas can. He placed them in the tool box of his truck.

"Stand up," Adam said to Michael. Michael stood and Adam led him to the truck bed where Adam quickly restrained him. Adam hogtied Susan and threw the canvas tarp over them so no one would see them while driving down the road.

Adam and Justin picked up Gary who was waiting outside when they arrived. Adam laid out the plan. "Gary, I want you up on the hill near Michael's house as a lookout. Don't break radio silence unless there's a threat. If Milton comes to the door alone as planned, depress the talk button on the walkie three times. The static created by the talk button will be our cue that all is well.

"Justin, you sit back in the bedroom until Milton arrives. If he tries anything or gets the drop on me, come out shooting."

Justin said, "It's going to be a tight fit back there with all three of them tied up on the way home."

Adam said, "Michael and Susan aren't coming back."

Justin and Gary didn't ask for any further clarification on that comment. When they arrived at Michael's, they unloaded the hostages into the house and Gary drove the truck up the hill and parked it inside the tree line so it wouldn't be spotted.

Adam sat Michael and Susan on the couch. "Can I have a shot of whiskey?" Susan pleaded.

"I'm going to need you to stay sober for a little while," Adam replied.

Just before nine o'clock, Adam's ear piece made the three distinct sounds of static to let him know his guest had arrived and was indeed alone. Seconds later, there was a rap at the door. Adam nodded, took cover in the kitchen and Susan called out, "Come on in."

Milton walked through the door. "What time is this joker supposed to get here?" As soon as he shut the door, Adam walked into the living room with his M4 level at Milton's face.

"Hands on your head," Adam said calmly. "Justin, come on in here and search him."

Justin placed the zip tie restraints on Milton's wrists. He removed the Smith and Wesson M&P .40 pistol from Milton's service holster and cleared his pockets of a wallet, six one-ounce gold pieces, a pocket knife and keys.

"Why don't you have a seat next to your sister?" Adam said.

Milton asked, "What's all this about?"

"I need to know if DHS took any prisoners at the ambush you helped to set up," Adam asked politely.

Milton said, "Why would I tell you? You're going to kill me anyway."

Adam said, "Justin, bring me a rag from the bathroom and see if you can find any tape around here."

Justin went to the bathroom and came back with a washrag. He went to the kitchen and scratched around in the drawers. He walked back in the room holding a roll of masking tape. "No duct tape. Will this work?"

"I guess it'll have to," Adam answered.

He stuffed the rag in Susan's mouth and wrapped several layers of the tape around the woman's head to secure the cloth.

"What are you doing, man?" Milton asked frantically.

Adam replied, "If you're going to be a wise guy, it'll cost your sister." He picked up a pillow from the couch, held it over Susan's shoulder, drew his .45 1911 pistol and shot her in the shoulder.

Her screams could still be heard through the wash cloth. Tears streamed down Susan's face and blood gushed from her shoulder.

"Ready to talk?" Adam quizzed.

Susan looked longingly at her brother as she sobbed and gasped for air through her nose.

Milton said, "Only one guy survived the attack. That was the report I heard. I promise, I don't know anything else."

Adam asked, "Where did they take him?"

Milton bargained, "If I tell you, will you let us go?"

Adam pulled Michael off the couch and said, "Get on your knees."

Michael cried out, "Milton, just tell him. Come on, man. Tell him, please!"

Milton said, "Okay! I'll tell you! Can you just give my sister something to stop the bleeding?"

85

Adam grabbed Michael by the shirt and dragged him into the bedroom.

Michael begged, "You said that you would see what you could do. You said we were cooperative and that you would let us go!"

Adam said, "I said I would see what I could do. I'm putting a bullet in your head to be merciful. This is not about vengeance for my brother's death. This isn't even about justice. My orders from Franklin were to burn you and Susan alive in the house. Do you know how painful that would be? And that's nothing compared to what I had in mind for you. Trust me, I'm a creative person. I've thought about some pretty bad ways for you to die. But I want to prove to myself that I'm a better man than you. I'm going to give you two minutes to get right with your Creator. Use that time wisely."

Michael cried and pleaded with Adam to spare him, but two minutes later, Adam put the pistol to Michael's head and pulled the trigger. A spattering of brain and blood was broadcast all over the floor.

Adam dragged Michael's lifeless body back into the living room to make his point to Milton. He could see the tears welling up in Justin's eyes. "Justin, why don't you go check on Gary. Make sure he's alright."

Justin shook his head and walked out the door.

Milton pleaded, "Please man, don't kill me. I'll tell you everything you need to know. The guy they caught, they took him to a work camp over in West Virginia. They use the prisoners to mine coal. I'll tell you anything you want to know. The camp is right on the other side of the river, just north of Williamson, West Virginia."

Adam asked, "What do you know about an operation to take out a militia communications hub near Wood Creek Lake?"

Milton said, "It's Sunday, predawn. Probably around five in the morning."

Adam asked, "Who is doing it? Is it military or private contractors?"

"DHS," Milton answered.

"Sit tight," Adam walked outside.

"Justin, you okay, buddy?" Adam put his hand on his shoulder.

"Yeah." Justin was still visually choked up.

"I have to try to get my cousin back, bud. I hope you understand," Adam said.

"I know, I thought I was ready for all of this." Justin wiped his cheek with his hand.

"Nobody was ready for all of this. It ain't normal. Nothing about war is normal or good or fun," Adam explained. "We do what we have to do and hope we can still live with ourselves after the fact. Let's go find Gary. We need to figure out where we go from here."

Justin nodded and the two walked up the hill to find Gary.

"I think I know where Matt might be," Adam said. "The problem is, if this guy doesn't come back to base tonight, his commanding officer is going to wonder what happened to him. If we keep his sister and try to send him back in as a mole, we risk him ratting us out anyway. She turned on him in a second. My guess is that this ain't the tightest family."

Gary said, "Maybe his commanding officer will just assume he ran off with the gold coins. Didn't this guy use to be a junkie?"

"Yeah, maybe," Adam said. "There are no good options here. Susan isn't going to last long anyway unless we get her patched up. Franklin's orders were to kill Michael and Susan and interrogate Milton. I think we've got all we're going to get out of him, so we should just get rid of him, too. Gary, can you fill up that bug spray container with gas and come inside and start dousing everything down? I figured the sprayer would let us use the least amount of fuel to burn the house down. Make sure you get Michael's keys to his truck. It's an old beater, but it might come in handy for parts. Milton's old Camaro is a stick. Think you can drive that back if Gary drives Michael's truck back, Justin?"

"Yeah, I can drive a stick," Justin said.

"Okay, let's finish up and get home," Adam walked back down to the house; Justin and Gary followed him. Gary retrieved the gas and the sprayer from the bed of the truck. Justin walked back in the house, picked up Milton's pistol, keys, coins and other belongings and went outside to wait.

When Adam walked in, Milton said, "Susan is unconscious. She needs blood."

"She'll be fine," Adam said. "Get down on your knees and face the wall. Do you want to take a second to get right with God?"

Milton pleaded, "Come on man, I helped you out."

"And I appreciate it," Adam replied. "I'm not going to torture you or burn you alive, but the reality is that my unit was completely wiped out in the raid you helped to facilitate. I have to take care of my brother's widow and resources are tight. We simply don't have the man power or the resources to keep prisoners. Thanks to you, that is. You have no one to blame but yourself. Take a minute to pray. I'll be right back."

Adam walked into the kitchen. He looked at the bottle of whiskey sitting where he left it the day before. When he came home from Iraq and Afghanistan a few years back, he turned to drugs and alcohol to cover up the guilt, pain and memories of the things he saw and did during his tour. All of those old feelings were coming back. He was using all of those old skills to extract information and fight yet another war. While he knew this was a just war because this one was truly in the defense of his country, the Constitution and even the safety of his own family, the bottle reminded him how quickly it could erase all of this unpleasantness. By the time he was back to the truck, he could be feeling just right. Adam picked up the bottle, opened the top and took a deep sniff. The fumes put the taste of the alcoholic spirit in his mouth. Adam thought past the initial feeling of relief that was promised by the bottle in his hand. He remembered how it had also allowed his pain and anger to erupt. How much pain and agony it had brought to his home. He recalled the fear in his children's eyes. He considered the feeling he felt when Janice packed a bag for her and the girls and left him. Adam counted the cost of having his present discomfort erased against the absolute horror that it would heap upon his loving family.

Adam poured the bottle all over the kitchen cabinets, curtains and wooden door frames. He lit a match and tossed it into the puddle of spilt whiskey.

He walked back into the living room and felt Susan's pulse. She was already gone. "Okay, Milt."

"No, please!" Milton said.

Adam put the gun to his head and squeezed the trigger. Milton's body fell limp onto the floor. Adam took another match and lit one of the curtains that Gary had sprayed with gasoline. The room was engulfed with flames by the time he closed the door.

The three men drove the vehicles back to Gary's. When they arrived, Michael's truck and Milton's beat up Camaro were parked inside of Gary's old barn.

Adam asked Justin, "Do you have those coins?"

Justin handed the 6 one-ounce gold coins to Adam.

Adam handed one back to Justin, one to Gary and dropped the others in his pocket. "I'm going to hang on to one of these, and the others can go to the widow's fund if that's all right with you boys."

Gary said, "They can all go to the fund, that'd be fine by me."

Adam said, "Stick it in a coffee can and bury it. Make sure you tell your wife where it is. This war ain't over, yet. It still might be a widow's fund. You do the same, Justin."

Justin nodded that he understood what Adam was saying. They had all seen enough killing and dying in the past weeks to come to terms with their own mortality.

Justin and Adam jumped in Adam's truck and headed home.

During the drive, Adam said, "Make sure you don't say anything to Karen about the work camp. For one thing, we don't even know if he'll be there. The other issue is we only have three days to prepare for the hit on Joe's place. We have to get through that before we can even start looking for Matt."

Justin said, "What if I went across the river and scouted out the camp? At least if I could locate it, we'd be that much closer to knowing where it is and what we're up against."

Adam said, "You can't do it by yourself, and there is no way I can go with you. Franklin is going to be counting on me to help plan the counter-attack at Lt. Joe's."

Justin said, "I know that area. Rene and I used to deer hunt by Cabwaylingo State Forest."

"How far is that from Williamson?" Adam asked.

"Ten or fifteen miles," Justin answered.

Adam thought for a second. "You just can't. There are too many variables, and you can't cross over into enemy territory on your own. You need at least two pairs of eyes for a recon mission like that."

"Then I'll take Rene," Justin said.

Adam shook his head in disagreement.

Justin stated his case, "Rene and I had nowhere to go and Matt took us in. We owe it to him to do what we can if there is even a chance that we can get him back. Rene is a good shot. She knows how to move silently through the woods and she is better trained than a lot of the guys in London Company. We used to play paintball with the other militia guys and their wives in Huntington."

Adam knew he was right. Matt was his cousin, he felt it was his responsibility to go get him, but he also had a responsibility to London Company and planning the defense for the communications hub at Lt. Joe's. "I guess I have no choice but to delegate this. I don't feel right about Rene going, but I don't know who else I'd send with you. I'll need Gary for planning the operation at Joe's. You're authorized for recon only. Find the camp, observe their movements and report back. Do not engage unless you come under fire. Do you understand?"

"Roger that," Justin had an ear-to-ear grin as he answered.

Adam added, "And not a word of this is to be spoken around Karen. If she gets a whiff of this, she'll never let up. Is that clear?"

Justin said, "Crystal."

Adam dropped Justin off and headed home.

# CHAPTER 17

"A strong body makes the mind strong. As to the species of exercises, I advise the gun. While this gives moderate exercise to the body, it gives boldness, enterprise and independence to the mind. Games played with the ball, and others of that nature, are too violent for the body and stamp no character on the mind. Let your gun therefore be your constant companion of your walks."

-Thomas Jefferson

Justin walked into the house and closed the door. Karen and Rene were sitting at the table.

"You two are still up?" Justin asked.

Rene said, "Yeah, we had an eventful night."

"Why? What happened?" Justin quizzed.

Rene told Justin every detail of the robbery and how they had just finished burying the bodies and getting cleaned up.

Justin hugged his wife tightly, "I'm so sorry I wasn't here. Are you all right? Why didn't you just go back to Adam's and wait for us to come home? You could have been killed."

Rene said, "Justin, you're freaking out. I'm okay and the bad guys are worm food. Relax. Everything is fine. Besides, they didn't get our food or our stuff."

Justin was still upset, "It's just stuff. It's replaceable. You're not."

Rene countered, "That's very sweet, but the stuff isn't replaceable. That's the only reason we fought it out. Society collapsed and I don't think Walmart is going to be back in business next week. That stuff is the difference between life and death for us."

Miss Mae ventured into the kitchen were everyone was congregated. It was the first time she'd come out from under the bed since the shootout. Karen got up, put a scoop of food in the bowl and said, "I was also afraid that they might hurt my cat. That might not sound like a good enough reason to kill someone, but with Matt gone...."

Karen choked up and a single tear streamed down her face. Rene came over and gave her a hug.

"They came in your house, you two had every right to do what you did, Karen," Justin said. Even with Karen getting a little choked up, he was surprised by how well the girls were dealing with the situation. He was still shook up about the way Adam had killed Michael's crew. That was a little more up close and personal, but still, taking a life is never a small incident.

Karen asked, "Did you find out anything about Matt from the guy?"

Justin looked down and started unlacing his shoes so he wouldn't have to look at her when he answered. "Nothing solid."

Karen pressed harder, "But something? Did you get some clues?"

"Not really," Justin said. "I shouldn't have gotten your hopes up. I'm sorry about that."

"I pried it out of you. You don't have to apologize," Karen replied sadly.

Justin went to get cleaned up and left the girls in the kitchen. As he was getting in the shower, Rene stuck her head in the bathroom, "I totally spaced out. I bet you're starving. What do you want to eat?"

"You've been in battle and burying bandits all night. I can fix something for myself," he replied.

Rene said, "I'm going to warm up those rabbit dumplings. Actually, I'm starving. Karen's probably hungry, too. I didn't even think about food 'til now."

"Okay, I'll have a bowl of dumplings," Justin said.

After he finished cleaning up, Justin rejoined the girls in the kitchen. They were already eating. The warm rabbit dumpling stew was just the thing to calm his nerves so he could sleep. Justin had set several snares around the garden to catch rabbits. He had caught several over the past couple of days. Those that didn't injure themselves in the snare were put in cages to breed. Those that were hurt trying to escape from the snare or looked a little too old went into the stewpot. (The recipe for the stew was simple. The rabbit was stewed with salt, pepper, onion powder and garlic powder. The meat was removed from the bones and the remaining stock was used for the dumplings. The dumplings were made of biscuit dough rolled very thin, cut into pieces and dropped into the boiling broth. Once the fresh carrots, celery, onions and garlic were available from the garden, the broth would be even better.) Although the ingredients were sparse, the rabbit made a nice broth.

After they finished eating, Justin said, "We should be getting to bed."

Rene said, "I don't think I can sleep yet. I'm still a little freaked out."

Justin asked, "Can you just come lay beside me for a while so I can sleep?"

Rene smiled, "Yes, I can do that. Are you going to be okay tonight, Karen."

Karen nodded, "Miss Mae will be with me."

Justin and Rene went to their room and got ready for bed.

Justin said, "I couldn't say anything, but we might have a lead on where Matt's being held."

Rene punched him in the arm. "Why didn't you tell her?"

"Adam made me promise. It's nearby, in what we think is a labor camp. The guy told Adam that DHS takes the hostages over there to mine coal," Justin said.

Rene asked, "Are you guys going to get him?"

Justin said, "We have to find him first. The guy said there's an attack coming on the communications hub early Sunday. Adam has to plan the defense for that. I volunteered to try to find the location of the camp and see if I can identify Matt."

"By yourself?" Rene asked.

"I volunteered you, too." Justin gave himself some space. He was unsure of her reaction.

Rene didn't get upset. "Okay, I'm up for that."

Justin grabbed his wife and kissed her. "We're going to be spies."

Rene snarked, "Yeah, that'll be fun, if we don't get executed."


The next morning Justin got things going around the farm. He had a cup of coffee, then fed all of the animals. He collected the eggs from the chicken coup, then started breakfast. There was plenty of flour and the chickens were laying regularly, so biscuits and eggs were the usual breakfast. None of the Bairs raised hogs, so ham, bacon and sausage were rare. Adam tried making a batch of venison sausage, but it had some room for improvement.

Karen came out of her room, "I really appreciate all that you and Rene do around here."

Justin shook his head. "Where would we be if you hadn't given us a place to stay?"

Karen poured herself a cup of coffee. "Still, I really appreciate it. You're such a big help. I couldn't do it by myself. Just having the company is really helpful in this tough situation of Matt not being here."

"How did you sleep?" Justin asked.

She sipped her coffee. "I didn't. Every time I closed my eyes, I started dreaming and relived that whole event from last night. I didn't think it was that big of a deal, but I can tell it's going to haunt me for a while."

Justin said, "I'm sure that's normal. Well, not normal; nothing about this entire situation is normal, but you know what I mean. I'm sure everybody has those types of dreams when they go through stuff like that."

Rene finally appeared through the bedroom doorway. She wore an old but comfortable house coat that Karen had handed down to her. She always wore her pink bunny slippers that Karen gave her. Her eyes were still squinting as they adjusted to the light. She smiled at Justin, then at Karen, and sat at the table.

"Did you get any sleep?" Karen asked.

Rene raised her hand and dipped it from side to side to signal not much.

Justin said, "Rene and I are going to look for wild mushrooms. We might be gone for a couple days."

Karen said, "Cool, can I tag along?"

Justin replied, "I forgot to tell you last night, Adam said Janice is canning some venison today and would love your help. He's planning to slaughter a cow next week and is trying to make some room in the freezer. Any other time, we'd love to have you go with us, but we need a few days of alone time."

Karen replied, "Oh, yeah. That was rude of me to impose."

Justin hated lying to Karen. "You weren't imposing at all. We'll all go mushroom hunting together someday soon."

After breakfast, Karen cleaned up the dishes. Justin and Rene packed their bags.

"You're taking a tent?" Karen inquired. "How far are you going to look? Is it safe to be out for days at a time?"

Rene stepped in, "They're easiest to find right before dark and right after sunrise, so we want to be positioned near our spot. Besides, we want to get a lot of them. You can dry them you know. Later, you soak them in water and they're ready to eat."

They all walked over to Adam's after breakfast. Justin and Rene borrowed Wesley's truck and headed toward the river valley.

Rene asked, "So, Adam thinks the camp is between Williamson and Cabwaylingo?"

"That's what Milton told him," Justin answered.

"How do you know they guy was telling the truth?" she asked.

"Adam was…pretty persuasive." Justin had no desire to get into the details of the interrogation.

"We're not driving through Pikeville are we?" she asked.

Justin replied, "No way. We're going to take a detour. We'll pass Pikeville and slip between there and Prestonsburg. Then we can take Route 3 to the river."

"That's the scenic route," Rene said.

"That's the stay-alive route," Justin commented.

Justin drove all the way to the militia border outpost in Warfield. There was no bridge, and no one was likely to cross from West Virginia into Warfield, Kentucky. It was more of an observation outpost than a checkpoint, but it was run the same way as the checkpoints.

Justin introduced himself to Jonas Lee, the commanding officer, and explained his mission. The officer called into the communications hub at Lt. Joe's to verify Justin's mission.

Jonas said, "We can drive you down River Front Road a ways. The old Nolan Toll Bridge is about six miles south from here. It's a little one-lane bridge. They don't have anyone watching it, but patrols drive up and down US 52 all the time because it's so close to Williamson. Williamson is a Yankee stronghold you know. That's why we don't have a checkpoint at the bridge. You can run across on foot and no one will ever see you. Be sure to stay off the roads and out of sight once you cross. We can slow down just enough for you to bail out. You'll have to be careful. Ya'll recruitin' ladies down in London these days?"

"Most of our team was killed or captured in an ambush near Pikeville," Justin answered.

Jonas replied, "Oh, that was you boys. I'm sorry about that. I sure didn't mean any offense."

"None taken," Justin replied.

"And I didn't mean to offend you either, ma'am," Jonas said to Rene. "You look like you can give them Yankees heck."

Rene laughed at the comment. "No problem."

"Y'all aint bringin' no rifles?" Jonas asked.

"Just our pistols tucked away." Justin raised his shirt and exposed the handle of his .45. "We hope to avoid any shootouts. But if worst comes to worst, we'll take a few with us."

Jonas Lee chuckled. "Good for you. I wish y'all the best."

Justin left his truck at the outpost and the man dropped them down the road near the bridge. The truck came almost to a complete stop and the two-person recon team bailed out and slipped into the bushes. They crept up to the bridge so they could see across the river.

"It looks clear," Justin said. "I'll take point and you follow me after I cross and find cover."

Rene nodded and Justin took off across the bridge. He motioned for Rene to cross after him. The slender bridge came out onto a side road rather than directly onto US 52. There were a couple of houses on the side road, so they tried to stay out of sight. More than likely, the residents would be friendly to the resistance, but one could never be sure.

"Should we start north or south?" Rene asked.

Justin surveyed the lay of the land. "Let's start heading north. We're only about three miles north of Williamson, and Milton said the camp was well north of there. I want to follow the river around until there is a good spot to get across US 52. At this location, the other side of the highway is a rock wall where they cut the road through the mountain. We could scale it, but we'd be completely exposed while we made our way up the hillside."

Rene said, "You lead, I'll follow."

Justin started walking, "The railroad tracks follow the river as well. We can walk the tracks where it gets too steep to walk the bank. They dip below the level of the highway, so we'll be concealed from any patrols."

The two walked several hundred feet around the river bank and alongside of the railroad tracks.

Justin said, "I'm going to climb up the side and look across the road to see what we've got."

Rene stayed put while Justin crawled up the hill and peered across the road. Justin came scurrying back down the hill. "There's a patrol coming. Two Humvees."

"Did they see you?" Rene was concerned.

Justin replied, "I'm sure they didn't, but let's get down by the river in those bushes to be safe."

The two hid out until they heard the vehicles pass right by. They climbed back to the tracks and continued their mission. Several hundred feet later, Justin went back up the hill for another look.

"Be careful this time. Don't stick your head out of the shrubs," Rene advised.

Justin came back down the hill. "It looks like the tracks snake under the road right around this next turn. That would allow us to cross under the road. The only problem is we don't know what's over there."

Rene said, "Let's scope it out. If it's too populated or looks dangerous, we'll come back here and find another place to cross."

Justin nodded his approval and they continued their trek. The track indeed snaked under US 52 which crossed over the tracks via a bridge. Rene and Justin stayed tight under the bridge so they couldn't be spotted by anyone driving over it. On the other side of the bridge and around the turn was a church. Today was Thursday and it looked completely unoccupied.

"I wonder if churches are even allowed to meet over here?" Rene asked.

Justin said, "They probably are considered militia meeting places. I'm sure Howe will find a way to outlaw church."

Rene said, "Yeah, besides, he probably wouldn't like the competition. I think he fancies himself the god of this domain."

Justin smiled at the observation and kept walking. Soon they were up in the woods and out of sight. They headed east through the hills.

Rene inquired, "Are we looking for a mine where he's working or are we looking for a prison camp?"

Justin said, "Either and both. Also any activity that might lead us to either one. If Milton knew what he was talking about, the mine should be within a five mile radius of this area."

Rene said, "That's going to be like looking for a needle in a haystack."

"Yes and no," Justin commented. "There will be activity around the mine and the camp that will be making noises. We'll see roads with DHS vehicles moving in and out. Most mining operations are going to stay close to the tracks so they don't waste fuel getting the coal loaded on the train. We can also pray that God will lead us to find Matt."

They walked most of the day and saw nothing. They walked in a zigzag pattern from east to west, then back east and gradually working their way north. Just as the sun was getting low, they came across a gravel road. "This looks like a mining road," Justin said.

"How can you tell?" Rene inquired.

Justin responded, "Look at the width of those tracks. Those are dump truck tires. And they're deep, which means the truck that left these tracks was loaded down. We can hunker down here for the night and see what drives by in the morning."

They walked back into the woods and found a secluded place to make camp. The location they chose was near the top of the hill and allowed them to observe any coming traffic on the gravel road.

Justin constructed a crude shelter to shield them from the wind and keep them somewhat dry if it were to rain during the night. They decided against making a fire which might give away their location. This meant they would be eating a cold dinner. They ate venison stew with beans and rice.

After dinner, Rene fell asleep while Justin took first watch. Hours later, he looked at his watch. Rene still had another forty minutes before her shift was scheduled, but he was nodding off and it wasn't safe. He woke her up and she took over. Rene was very nice about getting up early and Justin was soon fast asleep. When he woke, he was still tired.

"Here," Rene handed him the canteen.

He detected it wasn't just water, "What's this?"

Rene held up an empty single-serve Folgers coffee packet and smiled.

Justin took a big drink. "I love you. You're the best wife a man could have. Where did you get that?"

Rene said, "Karen had them stashed in her bug out bag. She gave them to me. It's cold, but it has caffeine."

"It's fantastic!" Justin exclaimed. They ate a few stale biscuits that they brought with them. The sun was peeking through the tree tops over the mountain to the east. Rene said, "I hear a creek running back over there. You keep a watch on the road and I'll go fill up the canteens."

Justin said, "Save the purification tablets and I'll pump the water through the Katadyn filter. Additionally, it won't taste like iodine."

Rene said, "Give me the filter, and I'll pump it straight out of the stream into the bottles. Otherwise, we'll have one water container not filled."

"Okay," he agreed, "but be sure not to get too much sediment in the filter. Generally, it's better to pump from one receptacle to the other so the sediment can settle, but I see your point about one bottle being empty."

Rene filled their various water containers and returned to the post.

"I hear something coming, lay low," Justin instructed.

They both lay prone in the leaves on the forest floor and watched for the approaching vehicle.

"It's a bus," Rene whispered.

As soon as it passed, Justin said, "Let's pack everything up and start following the trail of the bus."

They threw their packs on their backs, and started walking. They found the perimeter fence of the mine about two miles down the road from their position.

"There's the bus," Rene said.

"That's it," Justin confirmed. "I guess we'll wait for the workers to come back out and see if Matt is in the group."

"Then what?" Rene asked.

"Then we'll try to track it back to the prison camp," Justin replied.

Rene said, "The bus just got here. They'll probably be here a while. Should one of us walk back the way the bus came and check for forks in the road? If there is a turn off, we might want to know which way it goes. Maybe we could lay some twigs in the road and see which ones are broken."

Justin nodded his approval. "That's a good idea. I don't know about the sticks though. Any vehicle could cross the path and break them. I think someone would have to visually observe the bus making a turn. Why don't you follow the road from inside the tree line a few miles down the road and see what's up. Don't be gone more than two hours. Pay attention to your watch; if you haven't found a fork in one hour, turn around and forget about it. Keep your radio on, but don't use it unless you absolutely have to. I'm sure there are monitoring stations around here."

"Sounds like a plan," Rene said.

Justin continued to observe the mine through his binoculars. He took notes on how well-armed the guards were, how vigilant they were about watching out and how much time they spent goofing off. They weren't the most disciplined bunch. Justin put the battery in his cell phone long enough to activate his GPS in order to get the latitude and longitude of the mine's location. Then, he removed the battery so it wouldn't continue to produce an electronic signature.

Two hours later, Justin looked at his watch. Rene was running late. "That's not good," he whispered to himself. Fifteen minutes later, Rene snuck back up to the observation position.

"What happened?" Justin scolded.

Rene said softly, "I found a fork just below where we saw the bus drive by. I wanted to walk each of those paths for forks. I went a couple miles down each road, but neither forked in the distance I walked."

Justin said, "Good work, but two hours means two hours. I start freaking out one minute after you're not back on time."

"Awe, you worried about me?" Rene chided.

Justin rolled his eyes and said nothing.

"So now what?" Rene quizzed.

Justin said, "Head back to the fork and find a secluded observation position. I'll stay here and see if Matt gets on the bus. As soon as the bus leaves, I'll come to you and we'll start walking the side of the road where the bus turns off."

"Okay, I'll be ready when you get there," she said.

Rene headed out and Justin kept watching through his field glasses. Several hours later, he noticed the guards stand up and start paying attention to the opening in the mine. In minutes, the workers were coming out one at a time. Justin looked at each worker as the guards cuffed them to the common chain that kept them all connected. Justin looked, but didn't see Matt. He saw one prisoner come out of the mine looking very weak. Two guards took him out of the gate and walked him down the adjacent hill and out of view. Justin heard a shot ring out through the forest and the guards soon returned without the infirmed worker. The remainder of the prisoners were herded onto the bus and followed by the guards. The bus pulled out of the gate and Justin started walking toward the fork.

Rene came out of her position when Justin reached the fork. "What was that gunshot?" she asked.

He answered, "One of the workers was having trouble walking, so they took him in the woods and shot him."

"I thought one of them snuck up on you." Rene grabbed him and held him close and tears started running down her cheek.

Justin hugged her back and said, "It's alright. We need to get going, it'll be dark soon."

"Alright, they went west." Rene sucked it up and started walking with Justin.

Four miles down the road, they arrived at a huge fence topped with razor wire. "That looks like a prison camp to me. There are guards all over the place."

Rene whispered, "Yeah, but I don't see any prisoners."

He replied, "Do you see how those shipping containers are all spaced out? I bet they're using those as prison blocks."

"Should we just wait here until tomorrow and see if Matt comes out of any of the shipping containers?" Rene asked.

Justin said, "We need to know if he's here and we need to know which bus he gets in and where it goes. There are several buses over there, and I bet they all go to different coal mines. Let's head back to that creek we saw about a half mile down the road. We can fill up our water containers and take a little cat bath. We can eat dinner there, then be back here by the time it gets dark. We'll scout out two positions where we can gather the most information in the morning. We'll stay together until just before dawn, then we'll get into our separate positions and stay there until the buses leave. After that, we'll rendezvous and decide where to go from there."

Rene said, "Great plan, let's go."

They moved quietly through the woods to the little stream. They both washed up in the cool stream. It was a far cry from a hot shower, but it was still quite refreshing. Tonight's dinner was venison jerky, stale cornbread pancakes and dried apple slices.

"Look!" Rene slapped Justin's arm.

"What is it?" Justin was curious.

Rene answered, "Morel mushrooms. Right over by that poplar tree."

The wild mushrooms common to the area were unmistakable because of the sponge-like texture on the mushroom tops.

Justin said, "Oh yeah. Do you want to get a few to eat later?"

"No," Rene answered. "I want to get a lot to take back to Karen. We're supposed to be mushroom hunting, remember?"

"I totally forgot," Justin said. "Let's get as many as we can find. I was so focused on the real mission, I completely didn't think about our cover story."

Rene said, "That's why you have me."

They picked about thirty mushrooms, then moved back into their surveillance position. As the sun sank down, Justin took the first watch and Rene fell asleep.

Justin listened closely, but was never able to make out any full sentences of what was being said. He was too far away to hear what they were saying and didn't feel it would be wise to get any closer to the camp. His watch ended and he woke Rene. She took the field glasses from Justin and he drifted off to sleep.

"Wake up sleepy head." Rene tapped Justin on the back at the first sliver of morning light.

He could have used another five hours of sleep. There would be time to catch up on his sleep after his mission was complete. They ate a light breakfast of homemade granola bars that Janice made a few days ago. Rene produced two more of the instant coffee packets.

"How many of those do you have?" Justin asked.

Rene smiled. "These two and two more."

"Good," Justin said. "We'll probably be out at least one more night."

Rene said, "If we find Matt, we could head back tonight."

Justin stated, "Milton told Adam that there is a pre-dawn raid on Lt. Joe's tomorrow morning. Adam said if we couldn't get back by sunset today, we should stay away until tomorrow afternoon. We don't want to return from a successful recon mission only to walk right into an enemy patrol in our backyard."

Rene said, "That makes sense. I hope we don't get done before dark then."

Justin asked, "Why is that?"

Rene answered, "So I won't have to worry about you being in another fight over at Lt. Joe's place."

Justin kissed his wife on the forehead. "I understand."

The team parted ways and each found their observation post. Justin took the field glasses and Rene took a spotting scope to watch her area. Justin looked through the binoculars and saw two guards go in one of the containers and come out with four prisoners. He watched as those prisoners took some type of food around to each container. "I guess the containers all have prisoners in them," he whispered to himself.

A half hour later, he watched each container empty out and the prisoners get outfitted into their work clothes and boots. "Matt!" he exclaimed softly to himself. He almost didn't recognize him at first. Matt had lost enough weight to make him look very different. Justin watched as Matt's group was herded onto the bus. "645." He made a mental note of the numbers painted on the back and side of the bus. Justin watched the vehicles pull out of the camp and kept track of the direction of Matt's bus.

After all the buses left and the guards went back to their complacent state, the two spies rendezvoused at their predetermined location.

"Did you see him?" Rene asked.

Justin was excited. "Yes, I watched him get right on the bus. I know exactly which road it took. Let's go!"

They circled around through the woods to keep a safe distance from the guards in the camp. They found the gravel road and followed it. The pair walked for several miles before arriving at the coal mine.

Justin took out his binoculars and scanned the two buses at the mine. "That's it! 645. This mine has two buses. It must be a bigger operation. That means more guards." Justin took out his cell phone, replaced the battery long enough to get the coordinates of the mine and then pulled the battery back out. "Okay, let's get out of here."

Rene was worried. "You're not going to be back in time to participate in the operation at Joe's."

Justin said, "Probably not, but we still need to get out of this area. Once we're out of enemy territory, we can look for a few more mushrooms. Gotta keep our cover intact."

Rene smiled. "Yes we do."

They proceeded quietly back toward the one-lane bridge which would bring them over the river to Kentucky.

# CHAPTER 18

"Be strong and courageous. Do not be terrified; do not be discouraged, for the LORD your God will be with you wherever you go."

-Joshua 1:9

Adam pulled into Gary's drive early Friday morning and honked his horn to announce his arrival. Gary's wife followed him to the door and gave him a kiss as she handed him his assault pack. Gary placed his rifle in the truck first, got in and closed the door.

Adam looked at Gary's backpack and asked, "Did you pack us a picnic?"

Gary snickered. "You told us to always carry a get-home bag with a med kit and a couple hundred rounds of ammo."

Adam said, "I know, I'm just bustin' your chops."

Gary winked. "But there's probably enough in there for a picnic. I've got Mrs. Brewer's famous fried chicken, biscuits and some fried green tomatoes."

Adam was overly cautious today as he drove. "You've got tomatoes already?"

Gary replied, "Green ones. We started them on the back porch back in late January. A couple of them already had blooms by the time we put them in the ground.

"You look like you're expecting trouble. Is everything alright?"

Adam answered, "Just staying alert. If the attack is supposed to be early Sunday morning, there could be recon teams in the area. Keep your eyes open for anyone in the bushes on the side of the road. We also have to figure that Milton could've lied or that the timetable for the assault was changed after he didn't report back."

Gary nodded. "Roger that."

The two men soon arrived at Lt. Joe's. Gary said, "Looks like Franklin beat us here again."

Adam said, "He always does. You couldn't ask for a more dedicated commander."

Lt. Joe stepped out on the porch, "Why don't you fellas put your truck in the barn. Franklin seems to think we might be under aerial surveillance."

Adam nodded and drove the truck around to the barn. Gary jumped out to open the door so Adam could pull right in.

"Wow!" Gary exclaimed when he opened the door.

Adam looked at the huge vehicle in front of him. "Cougar with a .50 cal mounted on top. That'll come in handy."

They left the barn and walked back to the house. Franklin met them at the door.

Adam shook his hand. "That's a fine piece of machinery you've got out there in the barn."

Franklin nodded. "I had to trade out those two Hummers you took in the ambush down by Harlan. The National Guard boys over at Bluegrass Army Depot must be gearing up for something with the Coalition. They're getting stingy with handing out weapons and vehicles. I know you always take resources into consideration, but anything we can capture in this operation will be a big help."

Adam nodded. "I'll keep that in mind. I guess that means you couldn't get any other shoulder-fired weapons?"

Franklin answered, "They don't really have much. If they have anything, it's because it was scheduled to be decommissioned and was going to either be destroyed or recycled. We still have six FIM 92 Stingers."

Adam said, "They're surface to air. I wish we had something to fire at MRAPs like a Javelin. Do you think Fort Campbell might have something like that?"

Franklin replied, "Fort Campbell isn't even trading with militia. They seem to have forgotten we're all on the same team. You took out surface targets with Stingers at the 421 checkpoint ambush."

Adam replied, "We took out one Cougar at close range. Past performance is no indication of future results."

Franklin said, "We have to work with what we've got."

Adam added, "Yeah, but we need tools that match the job."

Franklin asked, "Where's Justin?"

Adam said, "We may have a lead on Matt's location. Justin went to check it out. Milton wasn't able to pinpoint the prison camp, but Justin thinks he can find it if it's in the vicinity of the area Milton gave us."

Franklin inquired, "He went by himself?"

Adam dug his notebook out of his assault pack. "His wife went with him."

Franklin's tone changed. "You sent a woman on a recon mission?"

Adam became defensive. "I'm a little short-staffed here, boss. My cousin is either killed or captured, my brother is dead and most of my team was taken out at Pikeville."

Adam was probably the most well-trained soldier in the Eastern Kentucky Liberty Militia. He respected Franklin's role as a leader, but he wasn't about to be micromanaged.

Franklin backed down and let the argument die. "Since this is a night-time raid, we can anticipate that they'll be using thermal. Does anyone have any ideas on how to evade detection?"

Gary joked, "We can drink a ton of ice-tea. That'd cool us down so we give off less heat."

The silly comment served to lighten the tension in the room that arose from Franklin and Adam's short spat.

Adam smiled and almost laughed at the suggestion. "When I was in Afghanistan, we checked out some dead insurgents after a firefight. Even though we were scanning the area with thermal, we never saw them prior to being engaged. They were using homemade thermal cloaking devices. It was a blanket with Mylar sewn on each side, then a bed sheet on each side covering the Mylar. The sheets on the outside were earth tones and camouflaged with spray paint. They work by reflecting your body heat back inside the cloak and reflecting the ambient heat back into the atmosphere. The blanket acts as an insulator to keep the heat from escaping through to the other side."

Franklin asked, "We've got around thirty-six hours. Could we get the materials together to replicate those?"

Gary said, "I've got several of those shiny emergency blankets. Would that work for the Mylar?"

Adam said, "They sure will."

Lt. Joe added, "The church brought a ton of blankets and sheets out here when the refugees from Huntington were staying at my place until they could find permanent shelters. I don't know what colors the sheets are, but we'll check."

Adam said, "That's a start. Everyone can ask around. We can trade out sheets from Joe's if anyone can find earth tone sheets or even better, those camo print sheets from Cabela's."

Gary laughed, "I've got a set of those. My wife hates 'em. She'll be glad to get rid of 'em."

Lt. Joe said, "Any thought on when we should start bringing in the rest of the men?"

Franklin said, "I'm open to suggestions, but my thoughts were to bring in the other two platoons from London Company tomorrow. We could trickle them in a few at a time through a drop off service. Everyone can stay down in the cellar until it's time to get into position."

Lt. Joe said, "If everyone is in one place, a single drone strike could take out everyone."

Adam addressed his concern. "From what Milton told me, DHS wants to gather Intel on us. They're supposed to try to take as much equipment as possible. They want to know what we know. We're basing everything on that information being reliable. If he lied about any part of it, he could have lied about all of it."

Adam could sense Franklin's stare. He knew what he must be thinking. If they'd kept Milton alive, he could have been interrogated further. But, what's done is done and there was no time for second guessing. Adam was glad he didn't have to have that confrontation with Franklin. He wasn't there and Adam had to make his decision to kill Milton on his own.

Adam continued, "Franklin, that's a good plan to trickle people in. If we're observed bringing in troops, only a few will be identified. On the other hand, the multiple runs will increase the odds of detection. If we brought in everyone at once, it would be a one-shot deal. The go-for-broke approach would only have to evade detection once."

Franklin was quiet for a moment as he thought. "Okay. Then let's do it all early tomorrow morning. There will likely be fog again, like we had this morning. It will provide a little bit of a visual shield. I'll have Manchester Company standing by. I'll position them down by the lake. We'll spread them out like campers on a fishing trip. When we break radio silence, they'll know to come running. It'll take them about fifteen minutes to get up to the house. That will bring them in as either cleanup or backup depending on how hard we get hit."

Gary asked, "Is there any sensitive information we should get out of here in case we're overrun?"

Franklin said, "Good question. Let's get everything scanned on to two separate flash drives and shred most of the originals."

Gary added, "We can encrypt the drives with TrueCrypt. It's not as secure as the TrueCrypt program on the computer, but it will password protect the drives. And it's free. I have it on all of my computers and flash drives. Super easy to learn also."

Franklin nodded. "Sounds like a good idea. I'll hide one flash drive. Gary, can you stash the other one along with a few important originals in a sealed PVC pipe and bury it somewhere? Not your property or Adam's property, though."

Adam said, "We'll take it to Eli Miller's. He won't mind. He's too old to be involved in combat. It'll give him a way to feel like he's helping out. He's wanted to take these criminals out of Washington since before I knew they were criminals. I just thought he was crazy back then. Turns out, I was the idiot."

Everyone dispersed and began their respective tasks. Adam and Gary had a full day ahead of them. They took a few of the brightly colored sheets to see if anyone in their network would be willing to trade them for earth tones, blacks or possibly even camo sheets. Their first stop was Karen's house.

Adam and Gary jumped out of the truck and Karen came to the door to meet them. "Hello," she said.

"Hey Karen." Adam shut the door of the truck.

"Any news about Matt?" Karen asked.

"Not yet," he replied. "Did Justin and Rene get back yet?"

Karen replied, "No, they said they'd be gone a couple days, but weren't very specific. I try to give them their space, but I must be crowding them."

"Or they could just be looking for mushrooms, like they said," Adam replied. He saw the look Karen gave him when he said that. She was a very perceptive woman. He had probably just tried too hard to cover up the covert mission. He changed the subject quickly. "That canned venison came out really good. Gary, what did you think about it?"

Gary jumped in. "Oh, it was fine! I especially liked the spicy batch."

Karen said, "Yeah, Matt would like that one, too."

Adam said, "I wanted to stop by and make sure you're alright, but we also have a favor to ask."

Karen said, "Tell me, I'll do what I can."

Adam proceeded to tell her what he could about the attack and the need for the sheets. He explained the primitive thermal cloaking devices and the timeline of the operation.

Karen said, "We have a set of navy-blue sheets. Will that help?"

Adam nodded. "Much better than red, pink and orange."

Karen added, "Matt bought a sewing machine at the flea market. I could help put some of the cloaking blankets together. I need something to keep me busy. Especially without Rene around, I need to keep my mind occupied. Otherwise, my imagination starts working overtime wondering where Matt is and how he's being treated."

Adam avoided the conversation points about Matt. "That would be a huge help. I'll drop off the other materials in a couple of hours."

They said their good-byes and the two men drove away.

Adam and Gary made their rounds, dropped off the materials to Karen, and headed home. Adam scheduled the carpools to get the other two platoons of London Company to Lt. Joe's the next morning. The total number of men at Joe's would be near sixty. They would be placed in various positions around the property, out buildings and outposts along the road leading to the house.

Adam tried to lay out the positions to separate fields of fire as much as possible, but if DHS troops rappelled behind the line from helicopters, the battle lines would be blurred.

Adam fashioned roadside bombs to take out the small bridge which went over the creek. That would eliminate the road as a path for the invading force. He also used the Claymore mines he was given by Bluegrass Army Depot to set up along the road leading to Joe's. DHS troops who abandoned their vehicles to approach the house on foot would be exposed to the lethal shot from the Claymores.

Saturday morning came early and Adam didn't get much sleep. He picked up Gary and three other men from London Company. Everyone rendezvoused at Joe's, in line with the battle plan. After dropping off their assigned militia team members, the drivers drove their cars to several different near-by rally points and returned to Joe's in two trucks that would stay in the barn.

Adam's last task was to collect the cloaking blankets which Karen, Janice, Shelly and a few other women had volunteered to put together. After he finished gathering them, Adam had a total of thirty blankets. In some instances, two militia men would huddle under one cloak. Hopefully, it would be enough for the men stationed outside of the house to be less detectable by thermal scopes and drone-mounted cameras.

The Cougar would be manned by a team from Manchester Company. The team consisted of three US Army vets who served in various theaters. The captain of Manchester Company, Sam Hart, served in Desert Storm. He would be the driver. Jeff Hillier served in Iraq and would be manning the .50 cal turret on top. Jeremy Pence served in Afghanistan and would be feeding ammo to Jeff and also manning communications.

Adam encouraged all of the men to hydrate well before sundown and then avoid liquids in the final hours before the anticipated raid. This would saturate their cells with fluids now and keep them from needing to relieve themselves every hour or so right before the raid.

The men began to get into their fox holes and sniper nests around the property shortly after sundown. Adam said, "Franklin, you and Joe should head on down to my house and hang out there until after the operation. There are still three other companies in the Kentucky Liberty Militia that depend on your leadership. Joe, you're one of the few communications experts we have. It's imperative to the overall mission that you stay safe."

Joe was the first to object. "Think I'm too old to shoot a rifle? I might be feeble, but I've got six pounds of pull left in my finger. This is my home, and I ain't bein' run off by no commie dictator."

Franklin added, "I appreciate your concern, but I'm staying, too. I wouldn't miss this fight for the world."

Adam threw his hands in the air. "I can't argue with you. Gary, let's get into position."

Adam and Gary walked out the door and headed down the road to the area where Adam had the roadside bombs buried. Their position was a foxhole dug out about a hundred feet back, on the east side of the road. All of the militia positions formed an angle facing either south or west. This placed approaching forces in a crossfire from the two sides of the angle and reduced the odds of a friendly-fire incident among the militia men. The claymores were also mounted on trees facing west from the east side of the approaching road.

The hours ticked by in slow motion. Gary said, "Didn't someone say that war was ninety-nine percent boredom and one percent sheer terror?"

Adam responded, "I think it was a Civil War soldier, but I couldn't tell you his name. I've seen enough of it. I think I prefer the boredom."

Gary said, "Yeah, me too. I just hate waiting for it when I know it's coming. I'd rather get it over with."

Adam looked at his watch. "4:30 AM. You won't have to wait long now."

Gary said, "And if they don't show by sunup, what do we do?"

Adam said, "Hold our positions till at least noon."

Gary joked, "So I guess I'll miss church."

Adam shot back with a witty comment. "You mean they'd start without you?"

Gary said, "Think I heard something."

Adam listened carefully. "I think I feel the vibrations in the ground. Must be MRAPs."

The two men sat quietly in their foxhole as they watched the headlights appear through the woods.

Gary whispered, "I see at least three sets of headlights."

Adam watched closely as the first vehicle approached. "It looks like four. The front one is a Cougar. The next one is a MaxxPro XL. The rest are probably MaxxPros, too. I'd rather pop the bridge under a MaxxPro, because they're chock full of agents, but that means I have to let the Cougar cross."

Gary said, "We've got our own Cougar to fight it out with theirs."

Adam waited until he saw the Cougar on the bridge to hit the ignition switch for the bomb.

BOOM! The earth rumbled beneath them and the Cougar flipped over. The second vehicle was moving too fast to stop and rolled right over the bank and into the creek. The men inside the MaxxPro weren't hurt by the accident, but the vehicle was stuck and out of commission for now. The men from the three MaxxPros rolled out and crossed the creek by foot.

Adam whispered, "Let's let them pass and hit the Claymores as they run by. We'll meet up with Manchester Company as they approach from the lake."

Gary nodded and the two men sat motionless as the DHS agents scanned the woods with a spotlight. They waited as the first two teams passed the first set of Claymores. Adam let his finger lay on the toggle switch for his detonation device until the last team reached the first set of Claymores. Adam hit the four toggle switches in rapid succession. BOOM! BOOM! BOOM! BOOM! Adam and Gary could hear the screams of the injured men. They ran out of their foxhole and headed toward the disoriented agents. Gary dropped near a tree and began firing. Adam dropped down nearby and did likewise. They soon had the men from Manchester Company behind them, aiding with the cleanup. Adam's radio screeched. "Adam, we've got several stealth Blackhawks overhead and men streaming down on rappelling ropes like rain."

"Roger," Adam answered. "Let's move toward the house. They need backup," he called out to Manchester Company.

When they made it to the house, it was overrun with agents. The firefight continued and it was very hard to see who was who in the dark. The yard and the surrounding woods were illuminated by muzzle flashes and the deafening sounds of rapid fire. Adam yelled out, "Gary, stay close to me, brother. This is a real mess."

Adam felt a sharp pain to his stomach and his chest as the force knocked him backwards.

Gary slid down beside him. "Are you hit?"

Adam fought to talk. The impact knocked the breath out of him and he could barely breathe, much less speak. Adam rubbed the area where he felt the two hits. There was no blood. He was finally able to say, "Just hit my armor."

Gary rolled over and kept shooting. The Cougar was out of the barn and the turret was spinning around trying to spot choppers and DHS agents with the spotlight. When Jeff locked a target, he quickly eliminated it with the .50 caliber gun.

Adam called out over the radio. "Does anyone have eyes on those Blackhawks?"

Someone called out, "Negative. I can't see them or even hear them. I'll hear something like wind in the tree tops and by the time I get a light up there, it's gone. They're like ghosts."

Gary said, "Adam, they're in the house."

Adam said, "Roger that." He called out over the radio. "I need Alpha platoon from Manchester on my six. We have to enter the house. DHS has taken it. Joe, Franklin and several other men from London Company are in there. Confirm your target before you take a shot."

The men from Manchester's Alpha Platoon were soon rallied behind Adam and Gary near the house. They made a stacked entry and then split into teams for a room-to-room search. They soon eliminated the hostiles inside the house. The shooting outside died down. Adam began checking for pulses among the fallen militia men inside the house. He radioed to the men outside. "What's happening? Are there still choppers overhead?"

Someone called back, "Negative, we're cleaning up out here. We have beaucoup wounded and beaucoup dead."

Adam returned, "Roger. Medics, do what you can."

Adam walked into the communications room and saw Lt. Joe slumped over near his rifle. "Joe!" Adam checked his pulse. It was faint. Blood was still spurting out of Lt. Joe's arm. Adam quickly pulled off the Combat Application Tourniquet that he wore on his sleeve and slid it over Joe's bleeding arm. He pushed it above the gunshot wound and pulled the tab to tighten it. He then spun the rod to completely cut the circulation off from Joe's arm and locked it into place in the attached clip. By the time he finished securing the tourniquet on Joe's arm, Gary had his Israeli Battle Dressing out of the packaging and was wrapping it on the wound on Joe's arm. Gary tightened the IBD and secured the cleats.

Adam called back on the radio, "I'm in the radio room inside the house. I need a medic to do a blood transfusion stat!"

A medic from Manchester Company called back, "On the way!"

The medic arrived and quickly assessed the situation. "He is going into shock! Grab some pillows to get his feet up and a blanket to cover him."

Adam ran to the bedroom as the medic started an IV for Joe.

When Adam arrived, he saw Franklin sitting calmly in the armchair with his rifle laid across his lap. Adam said, "Joe's in bad shape."

Adam grabbed the pillows and the comforter from the bed but Franklin didn't respond. Adam looked over, but Franklin was still staring out the door Adam had entered through.

"Franklin?" Adam looked down. Franklin was soaked in blood from the stomach down. Adam checked his pulse. He was dead. His lifeless eyes were still open and a serene look was on his face. Adam closed Franklin's eyelids with his fingers. He said, "Good-bye old friend," as he left the room.

The medic was able to stabilize Joe. Gary and Adam continued through the house to help the wounded and restrain any DHS agents that were still breathing so they could be questioned later.

By the time they cleared the house and went outside, the first light of dawn was glowing from the east. The team members from the Cougar were bringing water to the various wounded militia men. Adam walked up to Sam Hart. "How bad is it?"

Sam said, "We killed 'em all. You gotta take that as a win, Adam. Good planning on your part."

Adam rubbed his face. "We lost a lot of men, though."

Sam said, "Looks like about forty. We've got a few badly injured. Some might not make it. Several just have superficial wounds."

Adam said, "Franklin is dead."

Sam shook his head. "That's awful."

Adam said, "Maybe we should have just pulled out."

Sam said, "Don't go second-guessing yourself. Besides, Franklin was the one who made the final call to fight it out here. He wouldn't have pulled out, even on your recommendation. I'll talk with the captains of the other three companies, but I'd say you are the obvious choice to take over for Franklin. You'd make a good commander."

Adam shook his head. "I can't do it, Sam. I've got to find my

121

cousin. I've got a family and a farm to run when I'm not fighting this war. I'll fight to the end, but I can't be as dedicated as Franklin was."

Sam said, "No one will be as dedicated as Franklin was. You know, the fellow who wants the job might not be the best one for the position."

"Why don't you do it?" Adam asked. "You could promote Jeff to Captain of Manchester Company."

Sam loaded a fresh magazine into his rifle. "Jeff, Jeremy and I are a team. We're killers. I'm no leader."

"You've done a heck of a job leading Manchester," Adam replied.

Sam looked up from his weapon. "Those boys know what to do. I just get out front and do it first."

Adam said, "That's a leader, Sam."

Sam rebutted, "Let's see if some glory hound from one of the other companies wants the spot. If nobody else will take it, I'll talk it over with Jeff and Jeremy. In the meantime, we need to get everyone out of this area. DHS will be back, and they won't be putting boots on the ground this time. It'll be an airstrike or a missile."

The rest of the day was spent ferrying the men back to their vehicles and evacuating the wounded to the nearby Colony Elementary School which was set up as a makeshift hospital. Adam and Gary stripped the communications room of essential components and took as many of Joe's personal belongings as they could fit in Adam's truck. They stopped by the school on the way home to check on Joe's condition.

The lead medic said, "He's stable, but I want to keep an eye on him overnight."

"Then I'll be by in the morning to pick him up," Adam said.

Adam and Gary left. By the time Adam dropped Gary off, it was nearly dark. When he finally arrived home, Janice and the girls met him on the porch with tears. Adam was covered in dried blood and tried to keep his distance, but he was overpowered by the hugs of his loving family.

# CHAPTER 19

"If ever a time should come, when vain and aspiring men shall possess the highest seats in Government, our country will stand in need of its experienced patriots to prevent its ruin."

-Samuel Adams

President Howe breathed in the air of the Oval Office. He missed the darkness of the underground bunker at Mount Weather, but the Oval Office felt like his throne room and reminded him of his power. The phone rang. Howe detested it. It had to be bad news, it always was. The secretary's voice came over the speaker, "Mr. President, it's IMF Director Klauser for you."

Howe gritted his teeth. "Put him through."

Howe lifted the receiver. "Mr. Director, How is everything?"

Klauser shot back, "Not good, Mr. President. We had an agreement that the US would have this issue with secession dealt with by tomorrow. You understand that in order to have a world of peace, we need more global unity, not more division. As I told you before, the IMF will not be able to grant you any more loans until this civil conflict has reached a permanent solution."

Howe's fleeting sensation of omnipotent power was gone. "Mr.

Director, I assure you that this temporary situation will be over within a few days. I have done everything I know to show that the United States is part of the global community. I have granted full authorization for the Hangyun Corporation of China to assist with relief efforts and security on the west coast. We have sold a huge portion of our military assets to China, Russia, India and Brazil in order to raise capital and provide collateral to the IMF. You can be confident that this will be settled by the end of May."

Klauser was direct with his response. "I'm sorry Mr. President. I've done all I can do. I will make a recommendation to the UN Secretary General Boris Gavrikov to provide the US with nutritional aid. Perhaps you can invite the UN to send in their global peacekeeping force since you are unable to handle it yourself. Good day, Mr. President."

Howe was furious at the blatant insult, but he knew he had to suck it up for now. "Mr. Director, I can promise you that...."

Klauser cut him off. "I said good day."

The line went dead.

Howe slammed the receiver down, then buzzed his secretary. "Get Scott Hale in here right now." Howe breathed out, then remembered Al Mohammad's advice about treating his staff more humanely. He buzzed the secretary again and said, "Please."

The voice came back over the speaker phone, "Right away, Mr. President."

Within minutes, Scott Hale entered the oval office. "You wanted to see me, Mr. President?"

Howe had cooled off since his conversation with Klauser. "Scott, how far out are we from being ready for Operation Black Out?"

Hale answered, "The engineers are finalizing the computer models that will generate the maximum pulse and the least amount of radiation. That should be finished by the end of the week. After that, each AGM-158 JASSM will be loaded with a precise payload for its target location. Then, the missiles will be transported to their respective B-2 launch vehicles. We could launch the strike in two weeks."

"Make it one week," Howe snapped.

Scott Hale said, "I can certainly push the time table to fit your demands, Sir, but please understand that it will greatly reduce the precision of the attack."

Howe sat silent for a moment as he thought. "Scott, I appreciate what you're saying, but we've just lost all our financial support from the IMF due to these rebels. Klauser is already recommending that I allow UN troops to assist us. If that happens, I'll lose all control. We have to end this and end it now. I have a few extraordinary measures that I can use to tide us over financially for one more month, but we need to have this nation put back together by June first."

Scott Hale sighed. "Our original plan was to let the Coalition wither away over the course of three months. We don't have the soldiers or equipment to take out the Coalition forces in one month."

Howe said, "Let's institute a draft. That will solve two problems. We'll have the soldiers we need to fight the Coalition and for each one who dies in action, we'll have one less mouth to feed."

Secretary Hale responded, "The ration system has already convinced most everyone fit for combat to sign up voluntarily."

The president countered, "Not those in the FEMA camps. Let's draft everyone from age sixteen to forty-five. Also open up voluntary service to men and women from age sixteen to fifty. I'll have the rations cut in half for those who don't serve and double it for those who are drafted or volunteer. Hunger is a great motivator."

Scott Hale said, "I think it's a great idea. You're not worried about the political fallout?"

Howe laughed, "Scott, we're not holding elections anymore. I'm not putting all of this blood, sweat and tears into keeping this nation together only to hand the keys over to some fool in four years. This is an investment. And your seat at the table will always be secure as well."

Hale said, "Thank you, Mr. President."

"So we'll be ready to go in one week?" Howe inquired.

Scott said, "If you can give me ten days, I think we could still make a relatively surgical strike."

"And then how long do I have to wait for the invasion?" Howe was impatient.

Scott Hale responded, "Let's give them three weeks to run out of food and lose hope from having no electricity. After that, the Coalition will be much weaker. We'll be able to roll in with much less resistance. We'll invade on June first."

Howe poured them both a drink. The president knew Hale hated straight whiskey, but he liked to watch him gag on it. Howe handed him the drink. "Okay, but don't come back to me begging for more time."

Hale took the glass reluctantly. "You have my word, Mr. President. June first."

# CHAPTER 20

"You care for the land and water it; you enrich it abundantly. The streams of God are filled with water to provide the people with grain, for so you have ordained it. You drench its furrows and level its ridges; you soften it with showers and bless its crops. You crown the year with your bounty, and your carts overflow with abundance."

-Psalm 65:9-11

Karen sat at the kitchen table and stared out the window Sunday evening. She thought about where Matt was. She wondered if he was alive. She didn't want to give up hope, but how long could she deal with not knowing? The sun was setting and another day without him would soon be past. Karen pondered the raid on Lt. Joe's and wanted to know how it had turned out. "Maybe I should walk over to Janice's and see what she knows about the attack," she said to herself. Then she remembered the horrible ordeal of killing and burying the intruders the last time she came home after dark. The memories of the shooting, dragging the dead body out of her house and digging the shallow grave in the night were playing in her head. Just then, she caught a shadow out of the corner of her eye. Her heart jumped and she looked for her gun. "It's on the bedside table!" she whispered. She jumped up to run for the gun when the handle of the door turned.

"Karen?" Rene called as she opened the door.

"You're back!" Karen exclaimed.

"Happy to see us?" Justin inquired.

"Yes," she said. "I was just thinking about the burglars when you came home. I'm happy to see that it's you. I got a little scared for a second."

"Where is your pistol?" Justin asked.

Karen answered, "By the bed. I had just jumped up to get it."

Justin said kindly, "I can't tell you what to do, but you should really keep it with you all the time; especially when you're home alone. Just wear your holster. It might feel a little clumsy at first when you're doing stuff around the house, but you'll get used to it being there."

Karen admitted, "You're right. Matt would say the same thing. Did you find any mushrooms?"

"We did!" Rene exclaimed. "We also found some wild garlic and dandelion greens. Are you hungry?"

Karen said, "I could have a little snack."

Rene then asked, "Have you had morel mushrooms before?"

"I can't say that I have," Karen answered.

Rene said, "They're fantastic. I'll put some of that goat cheese you made with a little bit of this fresh wild garlic and a few bread crumbs on the mushrooms and you won't believe how good they are."

Karen said, "Oh, stuffed mushrooms. How delicious. Too bad we don't have any crab meat to toss in there."

Rene looked at Justin and smiled.

Karen asked, "What? Don't tell me you found crabs."

Justin said "I caught five small crayfish in the creek. I'll boil them, shell them and throw the meat in the stuffing. You'll be surprised how much it tastes like crab."

Soon, the mushrooms were ready and the three sat down to eat. Justin prayed, "Lord, we thank you for this bountiful feast. We know that you always provide for your people. You provided manna in the desert for the Israelites and you have provided so many wonderful things for us during this painful period of adjustment. We thank you for watching over us and protecting us and pray that you will soon bring Matt home as well. Amen."

Karen echoed, "Amen."

After dinner, Karen cleaned up the dishes while Rene washed the remaining morels. They required a bit more care in the cleaning because of the porous, sponge-like texture on the top of the mushrooms. Once they were cleaned, Rene used a needle and thread to string the mushrooms together so they could be hung up and dried.

Karen said, "Tomorrow is our day to take food to the National Guardsmen working at the power plant. I wonder if we could make enough of these to go around."

Rene said, "I doubt we could catch enough crayfish, but we probably could do mushrooms with just goat cheese and garlic."

Karen added, "That'll be a nice touch. I'll make a big pot of rice and beans with some of the venison I made with Janice while you were gone."

Justin took a quick shower, got dressed and grabbed his rifle. "Ladies, if you'll excuse me, I'm going to run over to Adam's and see how the assault went this morning."

Rene said, "Don't stay over there too long. We want to know what happened, too."

Justin replied, "I'll try to be back in an hour or so."

Justin left and Karen put on a pot of tea. "I wish I had seeds for chamomile. It would probably grow well around here."

Rene said, "My grandmother used to pick wild chamomile."

Karen asked, "Are all of the daisies around here chamomile?"

Rene answered, "No, chamomile has more of a ball-like center, whereas daisies have a flat yellow center. Wild chamomile just has the yellow ball, it doesn't have the little white petals."

"Could you make tea out of daisies or are they poisonous?" Karen asked.

Rene answered, "Grandma used to make tea out of daisies for coughs. She would load it with honey, so I only remember it being sweet. I don't remember what the actual daisy tea tasted like."

Karen said, "Good to know if we're ever in a pinch."

The tea kettle whistled and Karen poured them each a cup. "I'm really having a hard time. I don't know whether to keep hoping or start going through the grief process. I just wish I knew if Matt was alive or dead."

Rene hugged Karen. "I think you should keep hoping and keep praying. God is faithful."

Karen replied, "I know He is, but sometimes He is faithful to take you through the pain and grief. Shelly was only married a few weeks and God saw fit to take Wesley home. Wesley tried to do things right and God still allowed him to die."

Rene retrieved her cup and sat at the table. "I just believe Matt is going to be alright."

"Do you know something?" Karen asked.

"I know God is watching over you and He is watching over

Matt," Rene said.

Karen could tell by the way Rene answered that she was trying to feed her hope. "So you know he is alive. Rene, I cannot possibly relay the pain that I am going through right now simply because I don't know if my husband is alive or dead. If you have any information, you have to tell me. Please, Rene. Put yourself in my shoes. How would you feel if you didn't know whether Justin was alive or dead? If I knew something, I would tell you. You know I would. Rene, please!"

Rene shook her head. "Karen, you can't tell anyone that you know. If Adam finds out that you know, he'll punish Justin. I don't know how, but he'll do something. If that happens, it will put a strain on my marriage. Times are stressful enough without having any additional pressure on my marriage. If you tell anyone, Justin and I will leave. That's how important it is that you don't say anything. You've been very kind to us. I feel like we've grown to be close friends in a very short amount of time. It would be tough for us to find another place to stay, but we'll leave if you say anything to anyone. Okay?"

Karen nodded.

Rene said, "Matt's alive. He is healthy and the boys are making a plan to go get him. I'm not saying anything else, so please don't ask me. Adam is worried that if you know, you'll want to go or you'll try to push the timeline on the rescue or that something will go wrong and they won't be able to get Matt and you'll be disappointed. If you have any respect for our friendship, promise me you won't say anything."

Karen shook her head to affirm the promise. She grabbed Rene to hug her as the tears flowed and she began to sob. When she was finally able to speak, Karen said, "Thank you."

# CHAPTER 21

"The people alone have an incontestable, unalienable, and indefeasible right to institute government and to reform, alter, or totally change the same when their protection, safety, prosperity, and happiness require it. And the federal Constitution, according to the mode prescribed therein, has already undergone such amendments in several parts of it as from experience has been judged necessary."

-Samuel Adams

Paul Randall opened the door for his guests early Monday morning. Texas Governor Larry Jacobs and General Allen Jefferson attended the Coalition meeting at Paul Randall's ranch in person. They both arrived at 7:30, well before the meeting was to begin. They joined Paul at the breakfast table where Kimberly was setting out an early morning feast.

Larry asked, "Where is Sonny?"

Paul replied, "He's double-checking all of the connections and going over the security program."

Jefferson joked, "You better be paying Sonny well. If I ever hear that he's looking for new opportunities, I'd be tempted to let him name his price."

Paul said, "I couldn't do it without him. Besides being a great advisor and assistant, he's one of my best friends."

Kimberly put the biscuits on the table and sat down with the men to eat. "Does anyone need more coffee?" she started to get back up.

Paul stopped her. "Eat your breakfast, I'll get up and get the coffee."

Paul went to retrieve the coffee. When he returned, Sonny had joined the table. Paul filled Sonny's cup and topped off everyone else's.

Kimberly asked, "Paul, are you concerned that the leftist lawmakers within the Coalition States are going to take issue with our direction?"

Paul answered, "That thought has crossed my mind. A lot of the federal level senators and congressmen stayed in D.C. Most of them have completely forgotten about their states. Howe has reassigned many of them as high-level DHS officers. The rumor is that he's promised them some sort of magistrate positions over their own states after he wins the war. I suspect the state-level representatives on the left are expecting a similar reward for their loyalty. I doubt we'll hear much from any of them. They'll want to keep their distance to prove to Howe that they had no part in the secession."

Jefferson asked, "Larry, did you reach out to the state-level Democrats in Texas?"

Larry answered, "I did, but it was like Paul said. None of them responded to me. And to my knowledge, all but three of Texas's federal lawmakers stayed in D.C."

Sonny added, "And we won't have to worry about most of the neo-cons, either. They either stayed in D.C. to suck up to Howe like Juan Marcos of California or they've been disappeared by the administration."

The men finished their breakfast, then retired to Paul Randall's subterranean bunker which had a huge conference room the men had nicknamed the War Room.

The connections were established and Randall began the conference. "Gentlemen, thank you all for taking time to attend the conference today. I would like to express special appreciation to Pastor John Robinson. He is joining us via teleconference from Governor Goldwater's residence in Idaho."

Pastor John said, "Thank you, Senator Randall. I am truly honored and humbled by your invitation."

Randall continued, "Men, I'll go over my notes for your consideration as expeditiously as possible. After that, we'll allot a brief period for each governor to address any personal concerns or issues from their state legislatures. We'll take a one-hour break for lunch, then we'll finish the day. Let's remember to keep the discussions on topic. We don't want to get bogged down in the details today. Remember, this is just a glorified brainstorming session and not a constitutional convention. We'll take the topics from today back to our state legislatures for their consideration. Then, we'll come back and debate each topic in detail for as long as it takes to come up with solid proposals for the states to vote on.

"I've already spoken with many of you about adding words or language to amendments and possibly stripping some amendments completely. Article Five of the Constitution tells us that we may propose new amendments through a two-thirds vote from both houses and ratify them through the approval of three-fourths of the state legislatures. There is no process described for changing language. We may need to pass an amendment to allow us to do this, or as in the case of the Twenty-First Amendment which repealed prohibition, we'll simply pass a new amendment to repeal or replace the amendment in question.

"While we are the legitimate government of the United States and the other states are actually those in rebellion to the Constitution, I would appreciate it if some of you historians and legal scholars would consider a formal declaration that will enumerate the states of the

Coalition. I think that will help to solidify the legality of the actions we take here over the next several weeks.

"I suppose one of the issues that has been nearest and dearest to my heart throughout my time in Washington, and is the primary injustice that motivated me to get involved in politics in the first place is abortion. I don't think we can claim to have a free society when we do not protect the right to life, liberty and the pursuit of happiness for every American. I think most of you have heard my father's account of his experience in med school. He witnessed an aborted fetus being stuck in a bucket. The baby was crying and fighting for life. The physician and staff performing the abortion simply ignored the crying until it stopped. While the left may argue that life doesn't begin at conception, they are never able to give a hard and fast time when life begins. Since they cannot pinpoint when life begins, they can't say for certain that life doesn't begin at conception. I think it is our duty to establish a personhood law that bestows citizenship and all the rights of a US citizen on the unborn human at conception."

Mickey Abrams interjected, "Don't you think that could open the door for would-be immigrants to conceive children while on vacation in the US for the purpose of gaining citizenship?"

Randall said, "That may be possible, Mickey, but right now, we are in the middle of a civil war and an economic collapse. There are more people fleeing the US to Canada and even Mexico than trying to sneak in. The days of folks flocking to the states because it's the land of opportunity are far behind us. While I hope to regain those days, if they do return, they will be in the distant future. Besides, if people want to immigrate to America or the Coalition, it will be because they want the opportunity to work in a free market system and contribute. Without the welfare state, there will be no more people coming here for a free ride."

Kentucky Governor Harvey Simmons said, "I'm all for letting people come to America who want to work hard, but even hard workers bring their culture and religion which often don't coexist well with ours. The next thing you know, they outnumber us and they start writing the rules to fit their culture."

Randall sat silent for a moment. He finally said, "You're right, Harvey. We're going to have to decide how open we want our borders to be. We're going to have to figure out if we want a picket fence or a twenty-foot wall. I guess this will be a discussion we'll have to examine in-depth over the course of several days or maybe even weeks.

"To go back to the point I touched on earlier, I think welfare is something we can all agree on. I would like to have a specific statement prohibiting the Federal government from being involved in welfare at any level. My recommendation would be for the individual states to have similar language on their books, but that will be up to the individual state. Before the government got involved in welfare, the church and individual communities did a fine job of taking care of the less fortunate. They had compassion on the needy, but no tolerance for freeloaders. When the government stepped in, we made a mess of it all."

Most everyone made a small gesture acknowledging their agreement on the subject of a ban on federal welfare programs.

Randall continued, "Along those same lines, I think we can say the same for socialized medicine, socialized retirement programs and federal education programs."

North Carolina Governor Ronald Taylor said, "I would agree with banning federal agencies from being involved in education, but I don't know about that at the state level. I think schools could be a public good that everyone can benefit from. I rather like not living around a bunch of idiots."

Samuel Richards of Tennessee jumped in. "I think private corporations, churches and even community groups could provide a better school system than state governments. Government schools have done a better job of churning out idiots than if they'd been left in their natural state. At least the ignorant child is a blank slate who can be taught. The products of the public education systems often have to be stripped of all the nonsense they get through Common Core before they can be taught anything of value. It is worse than ignorance."

Randall said, "The education debate is a healthy disagreement. I know I made a recommendation for states to ban government welfare programs, but in the end, it will be up to the individual state. Let's keep in mind that we're not here to dictate to the states. Our purpose is only to place strict limitations on the size and scope of the Federal Government. When it comes to education and roads, what may work for North Dakota may not work for South Dakota. I think our founding fathers, especially the anti-federalists who we'll be looking to for guidance through this process, intended for each state to be its own individual experiment in freedom.

"Another thing I think we can all agree on is banning a central bank. We just witnessed a tectonic failure from allowing a private central bank to manipulate interest rates and the money supply. The Federal Reserve was the institution that enabled all of the bad behavior of the Federal Government. Everything from an overstretched military to insane levels of welfare spending which enslaves and buys votes from the poor was facilitated by this evil beast."

Wyoming Governor Jacob Schmidt asked, "And what about Federal debt? Should we ban borrowing?"

South Carolina's Governor Hayden said, "If we don't outright ban a national debt, we should at least restrict it to a manageable level. We should also enumerate the types of things that could be purchased through debt. In my personal life, I had no problem taking on debt for an asset that produced income or some other benefit such as shelter, but I never took on consumer debt to go out to eat or go on vacation."

"Good point," Randall acknowledged.

Sonny Foster spoke. "Paul, you wanted me to remind you about the amendments to the Constitution."

Randall said, "Yes, thanks, Sonny. I think we should look at each individual amendment and determine if it stays or if we need to throw it out or revise it. We have a divine opportunity, men. I pray our nation will never have to go through this again. Let's do this right. Let's start with the first ten. Does anyone have any issues with the Bill of Rights?"

Montana Governor Mark Shea spoke. "I don't think any of us would disagree that the Bill of Rights should be left intact. My only issue with the Bill of Rights is that the language doesn't go far enough. Many of those same principles that were listed in the Articles of Confederation had much more evident language of the intentions. I would support additional language that would clarify and safeguard those rights. We may also need to consider a separate piece of legislation that declares attempts to circumvent those rights as treason. I think a noose makes a fine deterrent against tampering with the Bill of Rights.

"The Second Amendment is a perfect example. I don't know how it could be made any clearer. It reads, 'A well-regulated militia being necessary to the security of a free state, the right of the people to keep and bear arms shall not be infringed.' What else can you add to that to tell lawmakers not to infringe on the rights of the citizen? I think the only thing you can do is put teeth to it by imposing swift and harsh punishments. I'm sure if Senator Dena Fitch thought her life would be in jeopardy, she'd never have considered her legislation that sought to nullify the Second Amendment. Since there were no consequences, she and many like her have had nothing to lose.

"I would recommend a blanket bill that would cover the entire Bill of Rights. That would put the fear of man, if not the fear of God into lawmakers who sought to trample on the Second, Fourth or any other amendment in the Bill of Rights. If these enemies of freedom thought their neck was the one that might be stretched out, we would have never seen the Patriot Act, the 2012 NDAA Indefinite Detention Clause, Prism or many of the other gross violations that have been pushed through because Congress and the executive branch have had no consequences for their treasonous behavior. That does not represent the rule of law nor the society our forefathers fought and died for."

Applause broke out amongst everyone attending the conference. When the clapping finally began to die down, Randall said, "It sounds like everyone is in agreement with you, Mark. I'd like to appoint you to put together a committee that will draft a bill to safeguard our Bill of Rights through swift punishments for lawmakers who seek to violate the first ten amendments through legislation. I'm not sure how I feel about capital punishment at the federal level. Life-long prison sentences may be an adequate deterrent. I think capital punishment should be up to the individual states for their own laws, but I have some reservations at the federal level. I think this might be a good issue for us to hear from Pastor Robinson."

John Robinson said, "Thank you, Senator. Capital punishment is biblical. In the Old Testament, the book of Leviticus lays out several crimes which are punishable by death. On the other hand, in the New Testament, we see Jesus grant mercy to the woman caught in adultery. I think there were other things going on in that story. The Pharisees who were asking Jesus if they should stone the woman were trying to get him in trouble with the Roman authorities which did not permit the Jews to execute anyone. I suppose, from a biblical standpoint, you could take either side. I think for crimes like murder and rape, execution makes a good disincentive for the criminal. I suppose you could argue the same for treason.

"It is certainly something that should be very well spelled out in the law. We should remember, we even had proponents of freedom like Glenn Beck calling for the execution of Julian Assange many years ago. I'll admit the work done by WikiLeaks was a grey area between letting the people of the United States know the atrocities being committed by their own government and releasing government secrets. Many conservative pundits and lawmakers called for the execution of Edward Snowden even though he was the only one willing to stand up and tell America about their Fourth Amendment violations. On the contrary, National Intelligence Director James Clapper lied about the same subject, under oath, which is obviously a crime, yet faced no charges whatsoever.

"Another issue is that the courts favor the rich. If one has the means, like OJ Simpson, he is unlikely to be convicted even if he did commit the crime. On the other hand, a poor man who did nothing wrong can easily be convicted by an overzealous district attorney looking to make a name for himself. It's a double-edged sword. And it's a question that I can't give you a quick, easy answer for."

Paul Randall said, "You've certainly given us some things to consider while coming up with the penalties for treason. Thank you, Pastor."

Robinson added, "If I may add one other thing."

"Absolutely, go right ahead," Randall replied.

John Robinson stated, "I'd like to read some comments written regarding the First Amendment and the Constitution written in 1833 by Supreme Court Justice Joseph Story.

'Probably at the time of the adoption of the Constitution, and of the amendment to it, now under consideration, the general, if not the universal, sentiment in America was, that Christianity ought to receive encouragement from the state, so far as was not incompatible with the private rights of conscience, and the freedom of religious worship. An attempt to level all religions, and to make it a matter of state policy to hold all in utter indifference, would have created universal disapprobation, if not universal indignation.'

"By failing to include such language and assuming all subsequent generations would see America as a Christian nation, our founders left a crack for the enemies of God to work their black magic against our heritage. The leftists, atheists and non-Christians have fought everything from prayer and Bibles in school to disallowing nativity scenes in public spaces and government buildings. I think now that we are all Christians...."

Mickey Abrams of North Dakota interjected, "And Jews."

Robinson continued, "I apologize, Governor Abrams and Governor Goldwater. And Jews."

Terry Goldwater of Idaho said, "I'm a Messianic Jew, Pastor. I am a Christian. But please continue."

Robinson said, "Since we are all Christians and Jews, perhaps we should try to find a means of including Justice Story's description of our founders' intentions into the First Amendment. Something that states that the government ought to encourage Christianity, which finds its roots in Judaism."

Abrams spoke out. "I'm not particularly comfortable with that. My people have had some pretty hard times throughout the ages. Any language I would support would have to expressly include Judaism. This is the problem with bringing clergy into the legislative process. I appreciate that many of our founders were Christians, but I think the First Amendment is fine just the way it is. Once we go down that path, then some Evangelicals don't consider Mormons or even Catholics as Christians."

Randall nodded. "Mickey, could you support language that stayed very vague, but stated that the state encouraged the worship of Jehovah? That pretty much covers us all but keeps the atheists from telling us we can't have a nativity scene."

Mickey Abrams said, "Or a menorah. I could support that."

Larry Jacobs added, "I like that idea. There has been a lot of fear that the First Amendment would be used as a back door for radical Muslim groups to try to institute Sharia law in their states or municipalities. I don't have any problem with other folks worshiping whoever they want, but I'll tell you that there is no Muslim country on Earth where Christians are free to worship and proselytize and Muslims are free to convert. I don't want to sound phobic, but that fact is evidence that it's something we have to safeguard against."

Randall said, "I really like what Pastor Robinson read for us. I think that was very well put. I don't want to get bogged down all day on the appropriate relationship between church and state. It's a very important topic, and one that needs a lot of attention. I recommend that Pastor Robinson and Mickey Abrams form a committee consisting of legislators from each state to come up with some proposals to ensure that the worship of the God of Abraham has an elevated status of protection over other forms of religion."

Governor Goldwater said, "I'll second that motion."

Governor Jacobs said, "I don't want to rush ahead, but while we are on the Bill of Rights, I'd like to propose that we insert the word 'express' into the Tenth Amendment. There was a lot of debate between the federalists and the anti-federalists over that one little word. The federalists won the day, but seeing how there are none with us today, we could spare our posterity much grief by including it now."

Paul Randall said, "Then the Tenth Amendment would read 'The 'express' powers not delegated to the United States by the Constitution, nor prohibited by it to the States, are reserved to the States respectively, or to the people.' Is that what you're proposing?"

Jacobs said, "That's right. That would put strict limitations on the Federal Government. They would only be allowed to act in the powers specifically enumerated in the Constitution. There would be no more 'implied powers' for the Federal Government."

South Carolina Governor Hayden said, "I'll second that motion."

Everyone voiced their support of adding the word to the Tenth Amendment. It was now well after one o'clock.

Paul Randall said, "Gentlemen, it looks like we could go on and on, but we need to take lunch. We'll reconvene in one hour and try to get through as many of the remaining amendments as possible today."

The men approved of the timing and broke for lunch.

# CHAPTER 22

"The peaceable part of mankind will be continually overrun by the vile and abandoned while they neglect the means of self-defense. The supposed quietude of a good man allures the ruffian; while on the other hand, arms, like laws, discourage and keep the invader and plunderer in awe and preserve order in the world as well as property. The balance of power is the scale of peace. The same balance would be preserved were all the world destitute of arms, for all would be alike; but since some will not, others dare not lay them aside."

-Thomas Paine

Justin woke to his wife gently nudging him.

"Time to wake up," Rene said.

Justin joked, "Am I late for school?"

Rene smacked him with a pillow. "No, but it's afternoon already. What time did you get home from Adam's?"

"Late," he replied.

She asked, "Did you come up with a plan?"

Justin answered, "Adam is going to finalize it with Gary, but the rough idea is that we'll cut down a tree in the road right before they bring the prisoners back from the mine. When the guards get out of the bus, we'll snipe them off from the trees."

Rene whispered so Karen wouldn't hear her. "What if the guards decide to execute the prisoners?"

He answered, "They can shoot the prisoners or try to defend themselves against the attack. They can't do both. I'm counting on their good sense of self-preservation."

"Who's going on the raid?" Rene inquired.

Justin replied, "Not you, if that's what you're hinting at."

"Why not?" she demanded.

Justin shook his head. "You've seen enough action this week. I don't want you getting PTSD."

"Because I'm a girl?" she asked.

Justin knew better than to get into this argument. "Did you already eat breakfast?"

"We've already had lunch," she said. "Don't change the subject. I've proven I can function under stress. Karen and I took on two armed men in the house. I went on the recon mission with you, so I know the area."

Justin said, "I need you to watch out for Karen while we're gone."

"You're just trying to push me to the side. Make your own breakfast…and lunch." Rene slammed the door as she left the room.

Justin stretched and rolled out of bed. He had been running on very little sleep for several days. It felt good to get caught up. His muscles were stiff from sleeping so long. He stretched a little more and got dressed. He made his way to the kitchen and started a pot of coffee. He put a scoop and a quarter of coffee into the French press. Normally, he would have put two big scoops, but coffee was rationed. Matt and Karen had brought several pounds when they moved up from Florida. Adam bought an entire pallet of coffee before the crash. Even though they had a substantial amount, it was a valuable barter item in addition to being available for their personal use.

Karen was preparing several containers of food to take to the power plant. "I left a pan of beans and rice for you on the stove for whenever you're ready to eat it. Rene and I will be back in a couple of hours."

"Thanks," Justin said. "Be sure to take your rifles and a side arm."

"We will," Karen said as she carted a load of food to the truck.

The girls left and Rene didn't bother to say good-bye. Justin knew she'd be over it by the time she got home, so he didn't let it bother him. Justin unloaded his pack and cleaned up everything that was dirty. He replaced the items he used up on the recon mission and began loading it for the rescue mission. He cleaned his weapon and oiled it thoroughly. He replaced several of the magazines he had removed for the recon mission. His pack had been more for food and sustaining him for several days rather than ammunition on the recon trip. The rescue mission would be much shorter and a firefight was inevitable. He adjusted his gear accordingly.

Once finished with loading his gear for the next mission, Justin considered going out to check the garden and animals. He was just too tired, so he sat down on the couch and listened to the news radio station out of Lexington for a while. There was a complete media blackout in many of the worst cities around America, but a refugee who had made it from New York City to Kentucky was giving an account of the conditions in New York and of his trip to his daughter's house in Kentucky. Justin adjusted the antenna to get the best reception and turned the volume up slightly.

The man on the radio spoke with a heavy New York accent, "New York is a mad house. I've never seen anything like it. There are no police, no emergency services, no hospitals, no food and no sanitation. It's like nothing you could imagine. Death, everywhere you look, it's death. I don't know how else to describe it."

The reporter asked him, "Is it like 9/11 or is it like a third-world country?"

"None of that," the man responded. "This is so much worse than 9/11 or anything you've ever seen on television. There is human waste all over the streets. People are dying of starvation, the city is riddled with disease. People are walking around with huge boils on their faces and arms. People have nowhere to put their dead. They just drag their dead family members out in the street and leave them there."

"And they just decay in the street?" the reporter asked.

"No," the man's voice cracked. "People come take the bodies...because they ain't got nothin' else to eat."

"Oh...no!" the reporter's voice sounded shocked. He sounded as if he might not be able to continue the interview.

The reporter was silent for a moment, then finally asked, "Why are the people staying in the city?"

He answered, "We kept hoping the government would come. We keep thinking that FEMA would be there with food, with water. But they never came. By the time we figured out they weren't coming, most people were too weak to even leave. Most of them didn't have anywhere to go and no way to get there even if they did. My wife and I decided to set out walking. We figured it would be better to die out in the wilderness than cooped up in the city. You can't believe the smell in the city. The stench is so strong. It is physically painful to smell.

"We started walking towards my daughter's home down here in Kentucky. She lives here with her husband. We didn't have a car. We always took taxis in New York. I had a good job when the crash came. I had money in the bank, a good portfolio and credit cards out the ear. None of that mattered after the crash. We did everything right and now I've got nothing to show for it. It's all gone. All of it. My wife slipped in the mud one day while we were walking here. We were about halfway through Pennsylvania. She cut her arm on a rock. By the time we got to the southern border of Pennsylvania, her arm was really infected. She got real sick and died shortly thereafter. I stayed in the woods by her body for two days. I buried her with rocks near the place where she died. I feel so terrible that I couldn't give her a proper funeral."

"I'm so sorry for your loss," the reporter commented. "You've been through a lot. Are you alright to keep the interview going?"

"I need to talk about it," the man replied. "People need to know what's going on out there also."

"What did you eat?" the reporter's voice sounded hesitant, as if he were afraid of what the answer might be.

"Some of the guys from the office had talked me into going duck hunting in upstate New York about a year ago. We only went one time, but I bought all of the stuff. I bought a single-shot 20 gauge shotgun and a few boxes of shells. If it hadn't been for that shotgun, I'd have never made it. It provided security to get out of the city and once we made it out, I shot birds, squirrels, whatever I could find. I also ate acorns. I found some berries, but they made me sick for three days. That was after Linda died. I thought I was going to die too, but after three days, I started getting better. I kept drinking water to try to flush out the poison. I suppose it worked."

"That was a horrible experience. I'm glad you made it," the reporter said.

"It ain't over yet," the man replied. "It's a lot better here, but things are still tough and we still got this war we gotta live through."

Justin switched off the radio. He'd turned it on in hopes of escaping for a moment. There would be no escape today. He heard Adam's truck pull in the drive and went to the door to greet him. Shelly was in the truck with Adam.

"Howdy," Justin said.

"Hey, man," Adam replied. "Can you be ready at four o'clock in the morning?"

"I'll be ready," Justin said.

"We're going to be a small team. Bring lots of ammo," Adam said.

Justin looked at Shelly and back at Adam as if to ask if he realized that she was standing there.

Adam caught the look and said, "Shelly is going with us. She won't take no for an answer. She's a good shot."

Justin said, "Please don't let Rene find out about this. I'll never hear the end of it. She's mad right now because I said she couldn't go."

Shelly said, "I need this. I'm not trying to prove anything, but these people took my husband from me."

Justin said, "Revenge isn't going to make you miss Wesley any less."

Shelly said, "It's not revenge. I don't know what it is. Maybe it's resolve, but it's not revenge."

Justin nodded. "Who else is coming?"

Adam answered, "Gary and three guys from Manchester. I fought beside them at Joe's. They've got some fire in their bellies, too. I think you'll like them. They're all three ex-military. Get some rest. Tomorrow is going to be a long day."

Justin said, "Yeah, I'm getting used to those."

Adam and Shelly pulled away and Justin went back in to double-check all of his gear. He put together a few things to eat. He packed some jerky and decided to make a pan of cornbread. "Matt and his buddies might be hungry. I better pack a little extra," Justin said to himself. Once he was confident that everything was ready, Justin laid down on the couch. Tomorrow was going to be a big day. He had better get as much rest as possible.

# CHAPTER 23

> "A democracy is nothing more than mob rule, where fifty-one percent of the people may take away the rights of the other forty-nine."
>
> -Thomas Jefferson

Paul Randall and the other men reconvened after lunch Monday afternoon.

Randall opened the meeting. "I hope everyone enjoyed their lunch. We're going to jump right back into the meeting, because we have a ton of material to cover. It is very unlikely that we'll be able to even touch on all of our concerns today, so we'll just focus on the main topics and revisit the details in subsequent forums. I'd like to focus on just three of amendments eleven through twenty-seven today.

"I'll start with the Fourteenth Amendment, because it is a small word change that I would like to propose and I hope we can all agree on it. I believe it would be a perfect place to ensure the personhood of the unborn. Currently, section one of the Fourteenth Amendment reads,

'All persons born or naturalized in the United States, and subject to the jurisdiction thereof, are citizens of the United States and of the

State wherein they reside. No State shall make or enforce any law which shall abridge the privileges or immunities of citizens of the United States; nor shall any State deprive any person of life, liberty, or property, without due process of law; nor deny to any person within its jurisdiction the equal protection of the laws.'

"I propose that we add the word 'conceived.' I know some of you have voiced concerns over the possibility of 'citizenship tourism' where immigrant hopefuls will visit America only to conceive a child that will give them a path to citizenship. I don't think it will significantly increase the amount of people who are already using the amendment for this purpose by having their children born in America. And given the two evils, I would say murder of over a million unborn babies a year through abortion is certainly the more egregious."

Sonny spoke next, "So, just to clarify, the first sentence of section one would read, 'All persons, conceived, born or naturalized in the United States, and subject to the jurisdiction thereof, are citizens of the United States and of the State wherein they reside.'"

Paul affirmed, "That's correct."

Schmidt of Wyoming said, "I'll gladly second that motion."

The men discussed the proposal for roughly an hour. Some did have concerns over citizenship tourism, but those concerns were quickly put to rest. Each state would be allowed to enact and enforce its own immigration laws. With this solution, everyone eventually came around to Paul's proposal.

Paul said, "Another proposal I hope we can all agree on is repealing the Sixteenth Amendment. It was originally derived from the 1894 Wilson-Gorman Tariff Act which sought to impose a two percent tax on incomes above $4,000. If you equated that to the purchasing power of the dollar before it finally crashed, we would be talking about annual incomes over $150,000. Few people made that much money, so why not tax the rich? Little did they know, once the camel gets its nose under the tent, it will soon be in the tent and wreaking havoc. That two percent quickly grew to a top rate of thirty-nine and a half percent, not to mention Social Security, Medicare and capital gains taxes.

"Many tax protestors have argued that the Amendment was never ratified or that there is no law requiring most Americans to file. Repealing this amendment and banning federal personal income tax will put this to rest once and for all."

Donald Barlow of South Dakota asked, "How do you propose the Federal Government to collect revenue to fulfill its constitutional obligations?"

Randall said, "We managed to do that through tariffs all the way from the birth of our country until 1913. I don't see why we couldn't do it again. Especially now that the obligations of the Federal Government are going to be so restricted."

General Allen Jefferson spoke. "I'm not trying to sway your opinions one way or the other, but we will have a much smaller military than we have now. Tariffs are very limited in the amount of revenue that they can generate. If tariffs get too expensive, people will simply do without the product or find a way to produce it domestically. It may be nearly impossible to maintain a standing army. I know the Jeffersonians were against a standing army, but we do live in a different global landscape than they did."

Governor Shea of Montana stated, "We do live in a different world, but there are several very civilized countries, even now, that do not maintain a military that remotely resembles ours. Switzerland's military is made up of only five percent professional soldiers and the rest is a militia. They mind their own business and have no need of a global dominating force. We have to remember, the main proponents of the income tax were, of course, the liberals who sought a method of wealth redistribution, but we also had the predecessors to the neo-conservatives: Teddy Roosevelt and the Progressive Republicans who wanted a global military. The neo-cons were every bit as responsible for the collapse of the dollar as the leftists."

Jefferson said, "I agree with your statement, Mark. I just want everyone to know what they are signing up for. I would recommend including a cap on tariffs to prevent their abuse as an income stream."

"Any thought on how you would structure the limits?" Randall asked.

The General replied, "I haven't really thought about it. Perhaps something like ten percent on items that could be produced domestically. That category would be things like computers, appliances and automobiles. It would make it tougher to import goods that take away American jobs. Maybe five percent on items that can't be produced in sufficient quantities for American consumption. We can grow a few bananas in South Carolina and Texas, but even if we are able to incorporate Florida into the Coalition, it would probably never keep up with demand. I would reduce the tariff to one percent on things we simply can't produce in any significant quantity. That would be things like coffee."

Randall said, "I think that is a very good recommendation. We'll discuss tariff categories and maximum rates in depth at a later date. General, I know you are fighting a war right now, but would you consider being on a committee to explore the economic factors of tariffs? It sounds like you have a good understanding of how they could affect us."

Allen Jefferson replied, "I appreciate your offer, but I'll have to decline at the present time. Why don't you put Sonny on that? He's as well versed in economics as any of us."

Paul said, "Great idea. Sonny, will you accept?"

"I'd be honored," Foster replied.

Property Tax

Governor Schmidt of Wyoming said, "While we're on the topic of taxation, I'd like to request that we ban property taxes on the state and federal levels. Property taxes create a sort of serfdom where you never really own your land. If you fail to pay your taxes, you are at risk of losing your home or land to the state. The effect is that you are little more than a renter of your own land."

North Carolina Governor Taylor said, "That's a grand concept, but we do a lot of good things with the revenues from property taxes. It seems most of you are against public schools, but still, there are fire departments, police, code enforcement, libraries and many other public services funded by property taxes. Are we willing to go back to the pioneer days where there are no public services?"

Jacob Schmidt responded, "I don't have a problem with fire departments, police departments or even code enforcement if a community decides they want those things. I would argue that they could all be provided through the private sector or by volunteers, but even if you want them provided through states or municipalities, it could be done through a sales tax. If the state or municipality raises taxes to an uncomfortable level, residents are free to move to a place where services and taxes better meet their needs."

Paul Randall said, "Your point is valid, Governor. We'll definitely discuss it further.

"Gentlemen, the last item on today's agenda is the Twelfth Amendment. I saved this until last, because I think we may have more varied views on this subject than most of the others we've discussed today. I don't anticipate that we'll get it completely hashed out today, but I would like to give you a few things to think about until we get back together, hopefully the same time next week.

"The current Electoral College system is a real mess. It's defined in Article two of the original Constitution. Senators and representatives are barred from being electors, but I feel they are the very people their constituents sent to make decisions for them. Our founders set this country up as a republic. The current Electoral College is directed to choose a presidential candidate through a democratic process. What this has done is turn presidential elections into popularity contests and a means to vote for the person with the most handouts. The campaigns are often funded on both sides by the same banks and corporations. No matter who wins, they are beholden to those corporate and banking interests. This should not be the case in a republic. Once this new American Idol is elected by mostly low-information voters, they select Justices to fill the vacancies in the judicial branch of the Federal government. Thus, the banks and corporations have effectively hijacked two thirds of our entire government through the supposed democratic process. For generations, we've done it this way and now our country is ripped apart, broke and people are resorting to cannibalism all around the nation. I think we need to make a fundamental change to the presidential election process.

"First and foremost, I recommend taking a step back to being a Constitutional Republic. I recommend that the House and the Senate be the ones who select electors and instruct the electors on who to vote for in the presidential and vice presidential elections. This maintains the integrity of the Constitution and restores the Republic. Senators and representatives would still be elected by popular votes from their states and districts, but in order to vote, citizens must pass a basic test that shows they understand the process, our history and our founders' intents. We require this simple test of new citizens who wish to immigrate to this country. Why shouldn't we make this simple requirement of those who wish to participate in the election process? For those who are content to remain slack-jawed imbeciles, that's their choice, but they should not be allowed to vote."

North Dakota Governor Abrams spoke up. "Requiring a test will dissuade many people from participating in elections. I think it will have a disparate effect on the poor who don't have time to study or take the test."

Jacob Schmidt said, "It will only have a disparate effect on those who don't care enough to take the test and study the material. We don't use that argument when it comes to drivers licenses, yet selecting our country's leaders is a much higher calling than driving a car."

Mark Shea added, "I liked Senator Randall's term, 'low-information voter.' I think it was probably too kind. Perhaps 'no-information voter' would be more accurate. The disparate effect of allowing those with no knowledge and no understanding to elect our government officials has been the absolute and complete destruction of this country and our monetary system. I think this is the most important point that has been raised all day. I agree with Senator Randall emphatically."

Governor Harvey Simmons of Kentucky said, "It's a lot to think about. I suppose I'm used to the way things were, but like Governor Shea pointed out, that's not working for us. I'd like to take the week to think that one over before I issue my verdict."

Sam Richards of Tennessee said, "I agree with Harvey. I'm used to thinking of America as a democracy. I suppose that is what I've always thought we were supposed to be. I'll have to go back and read over some history with Paul's comments in mind."

Paul Randall made his closing comments. "Thank you, gentlemen, for being open to these suggestions. I know they appear very radical, but so were our founders in their day. Please consider everything we've talked about today, and we'll plan to reconvene next week."

The men said their farewells and agreed to meet again in seven days' time.

# CHAPTER 24

"The constitution ought to secure a genuine militia and guard against a select militia, all regulations tending to render this general militia useless and defenseless, by establishing select corps of militia, or distinct bodies of military men, not having permanent interests and attachments to the community ought to be avoided."

-Richard Henry Lee, Virginian
Delegate to the Continental Congress

Justin's alarm went off at three in the morning. He shut the alarm off and felt the heaviness of his eyelids as they began to close. He knew better that to lay there for one more second. He looked over at his wife beside him. Her eyes were open. She reached over and touched his arm.

"Be safe," she said.

"I will." He kissed her on her head and her eyes closed.

Justin got dressed and headed for the kitchen. He used three scoops of coffee this morning. He never violated the coffee ration limits, but today was different. He was sure everyone would understand. He made a batch of pancakes. They were high in carbs and would keep him full for a while. The leftovers could go in his assault pack and could be eaten by hand while they were hiking to the ambush site.

Justin checked his gear for a third time. Adam would do a pre-combat inspection once all the team members were assembled, but it would be too late to get anything from the house. Justin decided to put together a second Individual First Aid Kit or IFAK. There was the possibility that Matt or his fellow prisoners could be injured in the firefight. Justin's personal blow-out kit contained an Asherman chest seal (to address sucking chest wounds,) a packet of Quickclot, an Israeli Battle Dressing or (IBD,) EMT shears, a TK4 tourniquet and a selection of gauze and bandages. It was all contained in a small MOLLE pouch that affixed to the MOLLE straps on the back of his assault pack. While he was digging through the medical supplies closet, Karen came out of the bedroom.

"Good morning," she said.

Justin hadn't expected her. "Sorry, did I wake you up?"

"I'm a light sleeper these days. What are you looking for?" she asked.

"Do you have an extra IBD or any extra Quickclot?" Justin knew the Bairs were preppers prior to the crash and assumed they had more trauma supplies than what Matt was carrying when he was captured.

Karen rummaged through the closet and produced two of each item Justin requested. She didn't ask any questions. "Here are two Combat Application Tourniquets. Can you use these?"

Justin said, "Wow. That'd be great." He figured she must have some idea of where he was going, otherwise she'd be quizzing him on why he needed all of this stuff.

They returned to the kitchen and Karen assisted him in packing the extra supplies into his assault pack. "Aren't you wearing your body armor today?"

Justin shook his head. "I have to be light today. It weighs too much for the…. We're doing some training and we have to cover a lot of ground."

Karen said, "Then we'll just have to pray that God will be your armor today." She picked up her Bible off the table and turned to Psalm 91. She read out loud.

"He who dwells in the shelter of the Most High will rest in the shadow of the Almighty. I will say of the LORD, 'He is my refuge and my fortress, my God, in whom I trust.' Surely he will save you from the fowler's snare and from the deadly pestilence. He will cover you with his feathers, and under his wings you will find refuge; his faithfulness will be your shield and rampart. You will not fear the terror of night, nor the arrow that flies by day, nor the pestilence that stalks in the darkness, nor the plague that destroys at midday. A thousand may fall at your side, ten thousand at your right hand, but it will not come near you. You will only observe with your eyes and see the punishment of the wicked. If you make the Most High your dwelling—even the LORD, who is my refuge—then no harm will befall you, no disaster will come near your tent. For he will command his angels concerning you to guard you in all your ways; they will lift you up in their hands, so that you will not strike your foot against a stone. You will tread upon the lion and the cobra; you will trample the great lion and the serpent. 'Because he loves me,' says the LORD, 'I will rescue him; I will protect him, for he acknowledges my name. He will call upon me, and I will answer him; I will be with him in trouble, I will deliver him and honor him. With long life will I satisfy him and show him my salvation.'"

Karen laid the Bible back on the table and put her hand on Justin's shoulder. "Father God, I pray that you will watch over Justin and the other men today. I pray that you will find it in your heart to return my husband to me safely. We love you and always seek to accept your will, but please bring Matt home to me, God."

Justin looked up. He smiled at Karen and gave her a nod. He heard Gary's truck pulling into the drive and saw the headlights shine through the window.

"I gotta go," he said.

Karen said, "I'll be praying. All day. I'll be praying for all of you."

"Thank you." Justin grabbed his gear and headed out the door.

Justin closed the truck door. "You ready?"

Gary responded rhetorically, "Do turkeys get nervous at Thanksgiving?"

"Then let's go get Matt," Justin said.

Gary put the truck in gear and they headed to Adam's.

When they arrived, Shelly, Adam and the three men from Manchester Company were sitting around the picnic table outside.

Adam introduced Justin to the men from Manchester. "Justin, this is Sam, Jeff and Jeremy. These are the guys from Manchester Company that fought alongside us at Lt. Joe's. They're all military veterans and have the experience we need for this operation. Sam, Justin was on the recon mission while we were getting hit at Joe's. He brought all the pictures and helped us piece together the maps for the raid. If you need more details, he is the one to ask.

"My plan is to wait until after Matt's shift. We'll hit the buses on the way home. By the time the prison camp figures out that the buses aren't returning, they'll only have a couple hours of daylight left to search for us. I don't know if they'll chase us into Kentucky or not. I spoke with the Warfield militiamen who have been guarding the section north of the border where we'll be crossing. They've offered us their full support once we cross back over. They're ready to fight. I had to talk them out of coming with us on the rescue mission; but we need to keep this team small and agile."

Adam arranged some sticks and rocks on the table which represented the buses and the rescue team.

"I'd like to find a decent-sized tree that looks a little rough and cut it to fall in the road. We'll have to use a chainsaw which is going to make a lot of noise, so it will have to be a good distance away from the mine and the camp. I want it to be a small tree so they'll get out and move it themselves rather than call for assistance. That's when we hit 'em.

"We'll eliminate the hostiles from the cover of the trees, then free the prisoners. We'll turn the buses around and head back toward the border. We have pictures of the one-lane bridge where we'll be crossing. I don't trust rolling a full bus over that small bridge. Besides that, the buses would be too easy to spot by aerial surveillance drones. If we can get there without being detected and if everyone is still in good enough shape to run, we'll ditch the buses under this overpass and run like heck to the border. Once we cross, we'll take up positions with the militiamen on the other side of the river. If we're pursued, we'll engage there. If not, we'll pull back to Warfield which is about six miles north of the bridge. We'll wait it out in Warfield 'til morning. If they haven't hit us by first light, we'll head on home.

"Sam, you and your boys will take this side of the road about fifty feet up from the ambush site, Shelly and I will be here. Gary, you and Justin will be up the road from us. Our positions form an angle, so everyone has to be very aware of where they're shooting. You have to focus on the targets in your sector. If you pivot your line of fire too far, you could be endangering other team members. Any questions before we roll out?"

Gary inquired, "Why isn't there a checkpoint at that bridge?"

Adam answered, "It's only two miles outside of Williamson, West Virginia. DHS is using that town as a forward operating base. They have patrols running around the area non-stop. It would be asking for a fight to put a checkpoint there and the local militia men don't have the strength, so they just maintain the outpost in Warfield."

Justin said, "We have to drive the buses right back by the mines to get on Route 52. There are about four guards stationed at the mine."

Adam answered, "If we have to fight them, we have to fight them. There's no other way back to the main road."

Justin asked, "Could we send in a sniper team and try to pick them off?"

Adam said, "The guards on the trucks will have already called in the ambush. We'll be racing against the clock to get back to the bridge before backup arrives from the camp. If they see us, we'll kill as many as we can while we're driving by."

Sam Hart said, "They'll be on the same radio channels. The guards at the mine will be waiting for us. We'll just have to ride straight through and shoot as many as we can, like Adam said. If they block the road with vehicles, we'll have to ram them."

"Any other concerns?" Adam asked.

Everyone confirmed that they understood the overall plan. Justin knew it wasn't fool proof. It was going to take some divine intervention if they were to pull it off. He was glad that Karen was going to be praying for them all day.

"Okay," Adam said. "Let's go."

The rescue team loaded into two trucks and headed toward the militia outpost in Warfield, Kentucky.

When they arrived, Commander Jonas Lee welcomed them. He recognized Justin and asked, "Where's that pretty little wife of yours?"

Justin laughed. "She's holding down the fort. She's actually very good at that."

Jonas said, "Well, you tell her I said hello."

Justin answered, "If we make it back, I'll tell her."

Jonas slapped him on the shoulder. "You'll make it back. You have a tough crew here. I spoke with Adam. He knows what he's doin'. Y'all will be just fine."

Adam's team left their vehicles at the Warfield outpost. Jonas and another man ferried them to the bridge. When they arrived, they jumped out of the pickup truck beds and went straight to the cover of the brush on the roadside. They crossed the bridge undetected, and Justin led them along the river bank to the railroad underpass which was less than a mile north of the bridge on the West Virginia side. They travelled through the woods in a straight line to the road where they would be setting up the ambush. When they came to a small country road, Justin whispered to Gary, "This is the road that we'll be taking back to US 52. That way goes to the mine where Matt works, and this direction goes to the main road. The team crossed the road slowly in pairs being cautious to check for patrols.

Once on the other side, Justin tapped Adam and pointed to a spot on the map. "If we go straight, we'll hit the road that runs from the mine to the camp. Up this hill, the road runs through a thick patch of woods that will buffer the sound of the chainsaw. It's a good three-quarters of a mile from the mine, I doubt they'd hear anything from there. That might be a good spot."

Adam agreed and they continued on. They arrived and set up their positions. It was now 11:00 AM. They still had several hours before the ambush, so they waited until a half an hour before to cut down the tree. This would prevent other vehicles from locating the downed tree and removing it.

Everyone was set, now the only thing left was the anticipation.

# CHAPTER 25

"The very atmosphere of firearms anywhere and everywhere restrains evil interference—they deserve a place of honor with all that's good."

-George Washington

Matt could feel himself getting weaker. He'd only been a prisoner for two weeks now, but he'd lost a lot of weight. A week ago, he looked trim. Now he was starting to look skinny and it was beginning to eat away at his muscle. The days in the mine were long, but Matt usually had the stamina to get to the end of the day. He kept going, because he knew the moment he was no longer considered useful, he'd be sent to the infirmary.

Doc gave a short talk and reminded everyone in the mine that they should work just enough to not draw attention to themselves. They had to conserve their calories. The way the men were fed, they wouldn't last long if they worked hard.

The day was nearly over. Matt asked Doc, "How long do you think we have until we start getting too weak to fight or run?"

Doc looked around. "Some of these guys are getting close to that point right now. It's different for everybody. If they don't up our calories, you and I probably have about two weeks left at full steam."

Matt replied, "Then we need to start thinking up a plan. I don't think our golden opportunity is going to present itself."

Doc whispered, "What do you have in mind?"

Matt said, "Everyone seems to be on board with pulling something. We'll just have to pop our cuffs and jump the guards. Some guys are going to get shot. We won't all make it if we have to overpower them with our bare hands. I suppose we'll have to draw straws. If we do nothing, we'll all be dead within a couple of months. The shipping containers they keep us in have no ventilation. They stink now, but they'll be ovens once the heat of summer really gets started."

Doc said, "Yeah, that will kill folks as quick as starvation. Let's start getting an escape plan together for next week. We'll plan it for a morning on the way to the mine. Everyone will be fresh and have the most energy."

Matt agreed. "Okay, next week then. There are twenty of us on each bus. That's forty of us against eight of them. At least some of us will make it. We've got no other choice."

Matt continued his task before he drew attention for not working. Soon the day was over and they were returned to the surface and loaded into the bus.

On the way back to camp, Matt looked at the trees and the beautiful sky. He cherished the bus rides to and from the mine. They were the only time he got a chance to look at the magnificence of God's creation. His days were spent underground in the mine, and his evenings were spent locked up in the dark shipping container which was used for his prison.

Matt's bus was in the rear, so he couldn't tell why the bus in front had come to a stop. Two of the guards got off the bus. Matt saw the opportunity. He quickly pulled the wire out of his mouth and popped his handcuffs open. He looked at Doc who was doing the same thing. There were two guards still on the bus. The driver and one other gunman.

A low murmur was growing among the other prisoners.

The gunman turned toward the back of the bus, raised his rifle and said, "Everyone shut up. We'll be back on the road in a second."

Matt heard a pop from outside and saw blood begin to spurt out of the gunman's neck. Matt and Doc jumped up and hopped over the chain that kept the other prisoners connected. Matt could see the others fighting to get their cuffs off. Before he reached the rifle of the gunman, the driver was up and had his pistol leveled at Matt's head. Doc grabbed the man's pistol and pointed it toward the roof. Matt spun the driver around, put his arm around the man's neck and placed him in a sleeper hold. Before the man went out, he grabbed his knife and thrust it backwards into Matt's leg. The pain shot through his body, but he willed himself to keep squeezing until the driver fell unconscious.

Matt was focused on his own conflict with the driver, but all the while, he could hear gunfire coming from the trees around the two buses. The man fell unconscious and Doc wrestled the pistol from his hand.

Matt fell to the floor from the pain of the knife still lodged in his upper thigh. "Shoot him!" he yelled.

Doc put the pistol to the unconscious guard's head. His hand shook as he tried to put pressure on the trigger.

Matt said, "Doc, he's just out for the moment. When he comes around, we'll have to fight him again. We've got other guards out there we still have to fight. Shoot him now!"

Doc focused but was unable to fire the pistol. He shook his head and said, "I can't. I'm sorry."

"Give me the gun!" Matt yelled.

Doc handed him the weapon and Matt stuck it against the driver's temple and pulled the trigger. The close range shot made a mess all over the floor of the bus. Matt dropped the pistol and grabbed the knife to pull it out of his leg.

"No!" Doc yelled. "If the blade severed an artery, that knife might be the only thing keeping you alive. We have to cut off the blood flow before we pull it out."

Matt understood what Doc was saying and left the knife in his leg despite the debilitating pain. By now, the other prisoners were out of their chains and off the bus. The first one grabbed the rifle of the guard and the second grabbed his side arm. Another asked Doc if he could pass him the driver's pistol lying on the floor of the bus by Matt's leg. Doc handed it to the man who wiped the blood off of the weapon and ran out the door of the bus.

The gunfire soon dropped to only a couple of exchanges, then all was silent. As the adrenaline wore off, the pain in Matt's leg grew more severe. Matt could feel his head getting light. Doc took off his shirt and rolled it up under Matt's neck. He pulled the belt off of the dead driver and put it around Matt's thigh and pulled it tight to cut off the circulation. Even with the knife still in his leg, Matt was bleeding badly. Matt felt his body getting cool. Someone else was coming up the stairs of the bus. Was it more guards? They had done all they could do. If he were to die, he would die knowing he had done his best. Matt was barely conscious when he saw the face of the man who had just boarded the bus. Justin? It couldn't be. Everything went black.

# CHAPTER 26

"He lifted me out of the slimy pit, out of the mud and mire; he set my feet on a rock and gave me a firm place to stand."

-Psalm 40:2

Justin put two rounds into the guard that was running into the woods in his direction. He looked at Gary, "I think that was the last one. The prisoners have a couple of weapons. Looks like they've done a pretty good job at cleaning up. I'm going in, cover me."

Gary said, "Identify yourself to the prisoners. They're a little shook up. You don't want to get shot by the people you're rescuing."

"Good point," Justin said.

Justin yelled out, "Hold your fire. I'm a friendly. I'm with the militia and we're here to take you boys home."

He walked out from his cover with his hands up and his rifle hanging by the single-point sling in front of his chest. The prisoners lowered the weapons they had captured from the guards.

Justin asked, "Does anyone know Matt Bair?"

One of the prisoners pointed at the bus in the rear. Justin began walking towards that direction. Adam came out of the woods and began briefing the prisoners on the evacuation plan.

Justin walked up the stairs of the bus and saw a man helping Matt, who had a knife in his leg. Matt's eyes were barely open, then they closed completely.

The man helping Matt asked, "Do you have a med kit?"

Justin dropped his pack on the seat of the bus and ripped off the IFAK pouch. "Are you a doctor?"

"Yes," the man said. "Do you have a tourniquet in your kit?"

Justin answered, "Yes, but take this one on my arm. It's better than the one in the kit."

The man took the C-A-T and wrapped it around Matt's leg. He spun the rod to tighten and locked it into the clip. He removed the belt that was on Matt's leg and started looking at the supplies he had to work with in the first aid kit.

He took out the EMT shears and cut the leg out of Matt's pants. He used the hand sanitizer to sanitize the hemostats and his own hands, then slowly removed the knife. He probed the wound and said, "It's not the artery."

Justin asked, "Then why did he pass out?"

The man answered, "They feed us almost nothing, then work us like animals. None of us are in very good shape to begin with. The amount of blood Matt lost was just enough to knock him out, I guess. I'm sure the pain was pretty intense, also. He was coming off a pretty big adrenaline dump on top of everything else. I'm Doc, by the way. Matt is in the cell next to mine."

Doc opened a packet of Quikclot and pressed it to the wound.

Justin said, "I'm Justin. I was with Matt when he was captured."

Doc replied, "Matt told me all about you. It's nice to meet you. I'd shake your hand but...."

"It's okay. You keep working," Justin said.

Adam and Gary climbed on the bus and looked down at Matt.

"Is he going to be alright?" Adam inquired.

Doc said, "He'll be fine, he's just weak."

Adam asked, "Can we move him to the back of the bus? We need to get loaded up and get out of here. We still have a ways to go before we're home free."

Doc answered, "Sure." He quickly put the Israeli Battle Dressing around Matt's leg, then he and Justin moved Matt to the rear of the bus.

Everyone was soon loaded on the bus and they were on the way back to the mine. Sam and his guys manned the front bus and Adam and his crew took the rear bus. Of course, once turned around, Adam's bus was now in the lead.


Shelly listened in on a radio that she took off of one of the guards. "They don't seem to know what's going on yet. They know something happened and they're sending guys from camp, but I don't think they'll be looking for us when we pass the mine."

Adam replied, "That helps a lot. Keep listening and keep me updated. Get ready to kill any guards you can hit when we roll by the mine."

"Roger that," Shelly said.


Matt finally came around. Justin offered him some water from his canteen. Matt took a sip. "Who's here?"

Justin replied, "Gary, me, Adam, and Shelly's here, too."

"How is Karen?" Matt inquired.

"She misses you." Justin smiled as he held the water for his friend to take another sip.

"Is Wes here?" Matt asked.

Justin said, "He was shot at Pikeville. He didn't make it."

Matt winced with sorrow.

Justin pulled out the bag of leftover pancakes. "You hungry?"

Matt said, "Yes, please."

Justin offered one to Doc as well.

Doc tore into it. "You have no idea how good this is. The slop we've been eating for the past two weeks is miserable."

Gary asked Doc, "Is Matt going to be able to walk?"

Doc answered, "In a week or two, sure, he should be fine."

Gary said, "I meant right now. We're dumping the buses about three quarters of a mile away from our pickup point."

Doc said, "We'll have to figure a way to carry him. We could have a guy on each side and let him hop on one leg, but I don't think that is a very good way to travel that long of a distance."

Justin said, "I've got some paracord. I can lash together a few saplings to make a quick stretcher. I'll make it like an Indian stretcher. They'd lash two poles together, put their load on it and let the back end drag on the ground."

Gary asked, "Could we put a crossbar on the top so two of us could pull it at the same time? It'd be sort of like a team of mules."

Justin joked, "Or a mule and a thoroughbred."

"I walked right into that one," Gary said.

Adam yelled out from the front of the bus, "Justin, Gary, look alive, we're rolling up on the mine."

"Roger that," Justin called back.

As they approached the mine, they could see only one guard standing out front. Shelly had the volume all the way up on the commandeered radio. The voice over the radio said, "Here come the buses. It looks like they're alright. I don't know why they'd be coming back to the mine."

Shelly lined up the shot and took out the guard by the mine. Two other guards came running out of the guard house as they passed. Someone from the bus in the rear shot one of the guards, but the other guard took cover.

"They know what's happening now," Adam declared.

They drove as fast as they could on the winding gravel roads. They soon reached the underpass and ditched the buses. Justin and Gary quickly found some saplings and cut them down. Sam and his team started moving the rest of the freed prisoners ahead and Adam's team worked together to get Matt mobilized. They quickly loaded him onto the make-shift stretcher and took turns pulling it along. Adam's team worked their way along the river bank and reached the bridge without incident. Once over the bridge, the militiamen from Warfield ferried everyone back to the outpost.

Adam said to the freed prisoners and the rest of the rescue team, "We've got to keep an eye open to see if they are going to hit us tonight. If they are, this is as good of a place as any to make a stand."

The militia worked to get the prisoners something decent to eat. They were all very appreciative. As the sun set and evening came, it appeared they were not going to be pursued back across the river.

Matt asked Justin, "So who else died at Pikeville?"

Justin told him the details of Pikeville, then filled him in on how they had taken care of Michael and extracted Matt's location from Michael's brother-in-law.

After Doc finished the huge meal the Warfield militia had provided, he worked on making Matt a rudimentary set of crutches. He stitched up Matt's leg and changed out his bandages.

Adam came around and sat with Matt for a while. "It's really good to see you alive."

"I'm so sorry to hear about Wes," Matt said.

"We'll miss him," Adam said. "Somebody's been missing you." I'm going to have Shelly and Justin take you back tonight. I just wanted to make sure we weren't going to get hit during the retreat."

Matt said, "Thanks. I've been going crazy wondering if Karen was okay. And my cat. I miss my cat. And you and the girls, of course."

Adam joked, "But you missed the cat more than me."

Matt was weak but he still had his wit. "You're not as petable. Bring Doc back with you when you come. I'll make a place for him at my house. He's from West Virginia. He won't have anywhere to go home to."

Adam nodded.

The militia men loaded some spare blankets in the back of the truck to make Matt's ride home as comfortable as possible and they headed home.

Matt breathed in the fresh air and looked up at the uncovered night sky. Out in the country, the stars were as numerous as the sand on the seashore. He thought what it would be like to be home and sleeping in his own bed next to his wife and to have his cat curled up on the pillow above Karen. Matt said a prayer to thank God for sending Adam and the others to rescue him. Only hours ago, he had wondered if he would ever see Karen again. Now she would be in his arms in a couple of hours.

They finally arrived home and Karen ran out to meet them. Rene stood on the porch.

"Is he okay?" Karen asked Justin as they pulled up.

Justin motioned toward the bed of the truck, "He's fine. He has a bum leg, but he'll be just fine in a few days."

They got Matt into the house and Karen asked, "You lost so much weight. What do you want to eat?"

Matt answered, "The militia fed us before we left. That was about three hours ago, but I could probably have a little snack."

Matt got cleaned up and put on some fresh clothes. After dinner, they all sat around and got caught up on what had happened since Matt was captured. Rene told the story of the burglary. Shelly told Matt how beautiful Wesley's memorial service had been. Karen and Matt held each other tight the whole time. Miss Mae sat in Matt's lap. She seemed especially glad to see him.

Shelly said, "I need to get home and let Janice know that everything turned out well. I'm sure she and the girls will want to come say hello to Matt in the morning. We'll let you get some sleep tonight."

Everyone said good-bye to Shelly. Matt thanked her for her part in the rescue.

Rene gave Justin a stern look. "I thought this mission was no girls allowed."

Justin replied, "That's Adam's department, you'll have to take that up with him."

Matt jumped in, "Justin tells me that you headed up the recon mission to locate me. Thank you very much, Rene."

Rene said, "You and Karen have been so good to us, I wish I could have done more."

Everyone got ready for bed, said their good nights and turned in.

# CHAPTER 27

"Sir, I trust I have long since made my peace with the King of kings. No personal consideration shall induce me to abandon the righteous cause of my Country. Tell Governor Gage it is the advice of Samuel Adams to him no longer to insult the feelings of an exasperated people."

-Samuel Adams

Paul Randall returned from his morning walk Friday morning. While his security detail requested that he stay on the ranch, he could at least walk around his own property to get some fresh air and exercise. He would often take yet another walk in the early evenings with his wife, Kimberly, but he reserved the mornings for clearing his head and prayer.

Sonny met him at the door. "Sir, Governor Simmons of Kentucky is really pushing for Coalition assistance in getting DHS out of Pikeville. He says he'll do it alone if he has to, but he really wants the Coalition to help out."

"Thanks, Sonny," Paul replied. "Can you set up a conference between Simmons, the other Southern Coalition governors and myself?"

"For what time?" Sonny asked.

Randall answered, "As soon as possible. Jefferson should be in the conference also."

Sonny replied, "I'll see if everyone can meet at eleven if that works for you."

"Eleven is great," Paul went upstairs to get a quick shower. He hadn't worked up much of a sweat on his walk, but he liked to start the day fresh. Once the day started, it was hard to say when it would end. Reviving a lost republic was no small task. Once dressed, he headed straight for his office. He settled into his chair and began checking his email.

There was a light rap on his office door, then it opened. "Dad!" Ryan stuck his head in the door.

"Ryan, what a surprise!" Paul jumped up and embraced his son. "Does your mom know you're here?"

"Not yet," he replied. "I just snuck in. I brought her flowers. I want to put them in a vase before she sees me."

Paul asked, "How long are you here?"

"I have to be back on base Sunday night," Ryan said.

"So most all weekend. We'll take what we can get. Your mom will be thrilled." Paul gave Ryan's shoulder a squeeze. "You're putting on some muscle. I guess you're eating well on base."

Ryan said, "Yeah, we do a lot of PT, plus I spend a lot of time in the gym. When I close my eyes at night, I see Robert's body lying there in that pool of blood. Being physically tired seems to help me fall asleep. Otherwise, I just toss and turn all night."

Paul nodded. "We all miss him. No parent ever wants to lose a child. I'm sure it's tough to lose a twin sibling."

Ryan replied, "Yeah, well, I'm going to go get these flowers in a vase and track mom down. Don't tell her I'm here if you see her first."

"You're secret is safe with me," Paul said.

Ryan left the room and Paul clicked the folder icon in his computer labeled "Family Photos." He opened the folder inside containing the pictures from the previous summer. Every time he looked at Ryan, he saw Robert as well; even though the two looked very different to Paul. He sighed as he scrolled through the pictures of the four of them cooking out on the deck. Paul thought, *What simple times. We had no idea how good things were. We could go to the store anytime we wanted, the country was still in one piece and we were all together. If only I hadn't ran for president. I would have spent so much more time with Robert and none of this....* Paul changed the channel in his mind. He knew going down that road would get him nowhere fast. Self-loathing and regret took up too much space in his head. There was much to do and it took his full concentration.

Sonny knocked before entering. "Sir, General Jefferson wants to be here in person. Can we make the conference at twelve to give him time to arrive?"

Paul closed out the window on his computer with the family photos. "Does that work for everyone else?"

Sonny answered, "Everyone is good with twelve. You and the General should have some snacks. The Southern Coalition will have already had lunch. It will be one o'clock for them."

Paul answered, "We can eat an early lunch. Ryan is here for the weekend; I'm sure Kimberly will be cooking up a storm. I'll let her know that we'll have the meeting at twelve. Will you be ready for lunch soon?"

Sonny answered, "I could eat. I'm flexible."

Paul went to find Kimberly and inform her of the meeting time. He walked into the kitchen and found her and Ryan hugging. Ryan's flowers were beautifully arranged in the vase. He didn't want to interrupt the moment, but they ended their embrace.

Paul squeezed his wife's hand and told her about the meeting time.

Kimberly asked Ryan, "Will steak be alright?"

Ryan replied, "Absolutely, we never get steak on base. Living on a cattle ranch sure has its perks."

Kimberly told Paul, "I won't have time to bake potatoes, will mashed be fine for everyone?"

"Even better," Paul said.

"And will Sonny eat mashed potatoes if I leave the skins on?"

"He will now. He's gotten past a lot of his quirks." Paul took out the steaks and seasoned them. He took an extra one, just in case Allen arrived in time for lunch. He fired up the grill on the deck while Kimberly got the water boiling for the potatoes.

At lunch, everyone wanted to know how flight school was going for Ryan. He told them everything he was learning and all about his training. Allen Jefferson arrived about halfway through lunch. Paul got up and threw his steak back on the grill.

"We made you a plate. Medium rare on your steak?" Paul asked the General.

"Medium would be great," Jefferson replied.

Ryan had several questions for the general while they finished lunch.

Jefferson asked, "Is Ryan going to be sitting in on the meeting with us?"

Paul was caught a little off guard, "Um..." He looked at Sonny, then Ryan. "Do you want to sit in, Ryan?"

"That'd be awesome!" Ryan replied.

Paul said, "Sonny, will you ask if anyone has any opposition?"

Jefferson added, "And Sonny, make sure you tell everyone that Ryan is being groomed for a leadership position in the Coalition Armed Forces."

"I'll convey that message, General," Sonny answered.

Kimberly shot Paul a look as if to ask, "What's this all about?"

Paul threw his hands in the air to let her know that it wasn't his department.

Allen knew when to practice diplomacy. He excused himself to prepare his notes before Kimberly had a chance to engage him about her son's "leadership position."

The men met in the war room and Sonny confirmed that the governors of the Southern Coalition had no issues with Ryan sitting in on the meeting.

Paul started the meeting. "Gentlemen, I had hoped that the terrible circumstances in the Federal States would have been enough to keep Howe occupied, but evidently it wasn't. It seems his sights are set on Kentucky. I'm sure the invasion of Pikeville is to establish a foothold in the Southern Coalition with the intent of taking more ground. Governor Simmons, what efforts have you made in dislodging Federal troops from Pikeville?"

Harvey Simmons said, "We've tried to cut off their supply lines multiple times, but they keep cutting down the blockades. If we take them head on by ourselves, we'll have to pull men off the borders which will open us up to further infiltration. Tennessee has offered their support, but they're limited on what they can provide."

Tennessee Governor Richards said, "We've got the men; we're just short on heavy artillery. We really need armored vehicles from Texas."

"What about Fort Bragg?" Randall asked. "Do they have vehicles and weapons that could support your mission?"

General Jefferson said, "Harvey, tell me if I understand your predicament correctly. Kentucky would have no issues dislodging the enemy forces in Pikeville. The problem is that for every man or tank you can put in Pikeville, D.C. can match it and raise you. What you need is a deep strike, to stop the flow of weapons and supplies moving across the West Virginia border."

Simmons answered, "That's right, General. They only have a couple thousand troops in Pikeville. We could take that with no problem, it's the infinite supply of troops, supplies and weapons moving in that we can't contend with. The other problem is that Pikeville citizens are being used as human shields against airstrikes. They've had their weapons confiscated in house-to-house raids and are essentially prisoners of war."

Governor Hayden of South Carolina said, "Anything we can do to help, you let us know. We're all in this together."

Taylor of North Carolina said, "Same here. Whatever we can do. We're here for ya."

Allen Jefferson said, "I think Pikeville, in and of itself, is just going to be a never-ending battle. We've seen the amount of resources an ongoing conflict like that can consume. In Iraq, it was like cutting weeds with scissors. By the time you get the whole yard cut, the weeds you started with have re-appeared. I think the only thing you can do is attack this problem at the root. I think we have to hit D.C. It will take more effort to get to the capital, but once it's done, it's done."

Randall shook his head. "No, I have said from the beginning that I won't fight an aggressive war."

Jefferson shot back, "Paul, that is a defensive maneuver. We have to cut the head off the snake that's attacking Kentucky. If we don't, they'll eventually take the whole state. Tennessee will be next and then the Carolinas."

Randall just shook his head. "That's not what I had in mind at all."

Nicholas commented, "I'll have to agree with the General. It'd be a resource dump to fight a constant trickle over the West Virginia border. We should go in for the kill."

Randall said, "I appreciate what you're saying, but it's not that simple. General, you spoke about Iraq. You remember the cases of soldiers doing house-to-house sweeps to fight the insurgents. The number of civilians killed in those raids was astronomical. Those boys didn't know who was going to kill them and who wasn't. Many of the ones who waited long enough to assess their targets were killed. It was a complete mess. That added to the suicide rates after the surge. A lot of that was from seeing women and children killed. We'll have Federal troops embedded with civilians if we go to D.C. I know Howe will pull that trick. He wouldn't give two cents for his civilians. He'd sacrifice them in a second. I'm not willing to send Coalition forces into those types of conditions. When you're fighting a defensive war, you know who your enemy is. Anyone who comes over that line has earned a bullet and our soldiers can sleep well knowing they did the right thing."

Governor Taylor of North Carolina interjected, "We can stand on the moral high ground or we can do what we have to do to win. We may not have the luxury of both."

Simmons said, "I'm sorry Senator, I'll have to agree with the General."

Paul said, "Sam, where does Tennessee stand on this?"

"I'm not a military man, Paul," Richards replied. "I'll have to defer to the recommendations of General Jefferson."

Randall took a deep breath and exhaled. "That's unanimous. I don't like it. I don't think I'll be a productive participant in the planning process, so I'll excuse myself and let you men do what you have to do. Allen, please let me see whatever you draw up. I won't stand in the way if you men have so decided that this is the right course. Ryan, Sonny, you guys come with me."

Jefferson and the governors of the Southern Coalition didn't say anything as Randall left the room.

In the stairwell back to the surface, Paul was angry. "Can you believe that, Sonny?"

Sonny replied, "You made a very valid point, sir."

Ryan didn't say anything.

181

Paul said, "These men are going to be sending Coalition soldiers into a battlefield where they won't be able to distinguish combatants from civilians. The psychological toll is too high. It's an unreasonable request to ask of anyone."

Ryan spoke up, "It's war, dad. We didn't ask for it. We only asked to be left alone. That request has been denied. Speaking for myself, I'll fight in any condition rather than live under oppression. No one cared about our psychological toll when they sent a kill team in to assassinate our family. No one cared about mom's psychological toll when Robert was murdered by the animals in Washington."

Paul said, "But we're different than them, Ryan."

"Yeah," Ryan said. "We abide by the law of the Constitution. These people asked you to lead them in defending the last remnant of our republic. If you can't do it, you should get out of the way and let someone else do it."

"That's enough, Ryan!" Paul shouted.

"You're right. It is enough. I'm going to get my things and head back to base," Ryan said.

Paul said, "Please don't do that. I know you think you're punishing me, but your mother is the one who'll get hurt. Just stay the weekend…for her."

Ryan said, "I'll stay for mom. But leave me alone."

"Fair enough," Paul said.

The two Randall men went their separate ways and Sonny found something else to do as well.

# CHAPTER 28

"I rejoiced with those who said to me, 'Let us go to the house of the LORD.'"

-Psalm 122:1

Matt woke early Sunday morning. He looked over at his wife lying next to him and gently took her hand to hold. He had been home for the better part of a week, but he was still elated to be in his own bed with his wife. The soft sheets, the firm mattress, his pillow that he had taken for granted; they were luxuries he held a new appreciation for. Matt looked at the pillow above Karen's head. Miss Mae was awake and looking at him as she gently purred. Matt pulled his hand from Karen's who was still sleeping and scratched the little cat under her chin. "It's good to be home," he said.

Karen stirred and eventually opened her eyes and smiled. "Good morning."

Matt smiled back. "Good morning, my love."

"Do you feel like going to church?" she asked.

"Yeah, I want to go. I've got a lot to be thankful for today," he answered.

"Can you walk on the crutches Doc made?" she inquired.

"I'm sure I can," he replied.

"What will Doc say?" she asked.

"He'll be fine with it," Matt said.

"Shouldn't we ask him? He's staying in our office, it's not like we can sneak past him," Karen said.

Matt responded, "We'll take him with us. He'll enjoy it. And thanks for letting him stay. I know the house is getting to be like a hotel. You've been very gracious about all the extra boarders."

Karen remarked, "I would have gone nuts if Rene and Justin weren't here. There is no way to put a price on their companionship. They're no bother at all. Besides that, they were the ones who found you. Justin helped bring you home and Rene…Matt, you should have seen her the night the burglars broke in. She was like a professional soldier."

Matt stroked Karen's hair. "From what I hear, you were pretty lethal yourself."

Karen answered, "Yeah, when I had to do it, everything you taught me came back to my memory."

Matt said, "But thank you for letting Doc stay. He was my only friend when we were inside."

Karen replied, "He's taking care of your leg. You might have lost it if it wasn't for him. That was a deep cut."

"It's nice to have a doctor around," Matt commented. "He's also been taking good care of Lt. Joe's arm. He had some deep damage from the bullet he caught in the raid."

Karen asked, "Where is Joe going to stay?"

Matt said, "Since his home was hit by a missile after the raid, he'll be staying with Adam for now. Adam promised to help him rebuild when this is all over, but who knows when that will be."

They got dressed and met everyone for breakfast. Doc agreed that it would be alright for Matt to go to church if he promised to stay off his leg for at least another week. After that, he could start using the crutches to get around and putting light pressure on the leg.

Gas was getting harder to come by, so everyone carpooled for their monthly trip to the local church. On the other Sundays of the month, Adam would lead a small-group Bible study if he wasn't engaged in a battle. The front seat of Adam's crew cab held himself, Janice and Karen. Carissa sat in Karen's lap. Mandy, Shelly, Rene and Lt. Joe sat in the back seat. Justin, Doc and Matt rode in the bed of the truck. This allowed Matt to keep his leg straight as per the doctor's recommendation. They were a hodgepodge of a family rolling into the service, but they were happy to be there and happy to be together.

After service, Janice invited the whole bunch over for lunch. Adam killed five chickens to be sure they'd have plenty to eat. Janice, Shelly and Mandy made cornbread, fried chicken and fresh mustard greens which were one of the first things in the garden to be ready to eat.

After dinner, Matt asked Adam and Shelly to walk him up to see Wesley's grave. They agreed. Adam and Shelly each took an arm to help Matt navigate the rough terrain on his crutches. They helped Matt take a seat on the large protruding tree root by Wesley's grave site.

"He was a good guy. He loved his family and his country," Matt said.

"And his God," Adam added.

Shelly looked sad, so Adam pulled her close for a hug.

Adam said to Matt, "We put all of Joe's communications gear in your shed. We haven't set it up because we figure they'll be scanning the area for a new comms hub. I'm thinking we'll wait to set it up until we need it, then move it around every so often. Would you mind if we set it up first at your place?"

"That'd be great," Matt answered. "I'm not going to be back to full strength for probably six weeks or so. I'd love to learn how to operate all of that stuff if Lt. Joe will teach me."

"I'm sure he'd love to show you how to operate everything," Adam replied. "You may get your chance soon."

"Why's that?" Matt inquired.

"The Coalition is making a move this Friday night." Adam responded.

Matt looked for clarification. "Is the Kentucky National Guard finally going into Pikeville?"

"Not exactly," Shelly explained. "They're hitting D.C."

"This Friday night?" Matt was stunned.

Adam answered, "Allen Jefferson is taking the fight to them. Tennessee, North Carolina and South Carolina are dedicating all of their resources in an all-out assault on D.C. The general has intel that over half of D.C. is drunk by the time the sun goes down every Friday night. I suppose the culture of debauchery has even penetrated the security forces and military personnel in and around the capital."

Matt asked, "What about Kentucky? They're not going in?"

Adam said, "The plan for Kentucky forces is for the militia to hit Pikeville Saturday morning. The Kentucky National Guard and supporting forces from Fort Campbell will be hitting Huntington, West Virginia."

Matt asked, "How are you getting all of your info with Lt. Joe's communication hub out of commission?"

Adam answered, "The Coalition is putting out regular mission updates over shortwave. I'm picking it up on my single-side-band shortwave radio."

Matt was puzzled. "But can't the Feds intercept the messages?"

Adam responded, "The message is going out in PSK31. Anyone

picking it up probably wouldn't even know what it was. Franklin had us install PSK31 in all of our laptops and mobile devices a while back. Once we translate the PSK31 message into text, it's in a book cypher."

Matt asked, "What book are you using for the cypher?"

Shelly interjected, ("My Utmost for His Highest.")

Matt inquired, "By Oswald Chambers?"

Shelly confirmed Matt's guess. "Yeah, because it's a daily devotional, it has dates rather than page numbers. It wouldn't matter which printing or type size you had as long as it's a classic edition. And, it's widely available. Another upside is that very few of the liberals in Howe's camp would have ever heard of the book. Being Christian devotional literature, they'd be quite unfamiliar with it."

Matt commented, "That's ingenious. I hope my leg is good enough to roll with you by Saturday."

Adam said, "Not a chance, cousin. We're going to need two people here. I need you and Joe to run the communications hub for the operation. I'm going to try to replicate the old situation room from Joe's in your shed, if it's okay with you, that is."

Matt nodded his approval.

Adam continued, "You and Joe will be battle tracking. We'll be feeding intel to you two. Joe will work the radio, and you'll be plotting locations on the map. If anyone needs info on another team's location or the location of enemy forces that have been spotted, you'll be responsible for feeding it to them. That's what Franklin was doing."

"I can handle that," Matt said.

"It's tougher than it sounds," Adam responded, "but I'm confident that you can do it."

"Shelly, you're going to Pikeville?" Matt questioned.

Shelly placed her hands on her hips. "Can't stop me."

Adam shook his head. "Can't stop her. She's like an animal. Once she's tasted blood...."

Shelly slapped him playfully in the back of the head.

"What about Doc?" Matt asked.

Adam considered the question. "You said he has no training or combat experience, right?"

"None," Matt said.

Adam thought for a moment then made a suggestion. "Can you talk to him about going along as a medic? He could stay in the rear of the action and be there for folks that get injured. I'd still like to get him out and work with him for a day with the pistol. He should at least have a side arm if he decides to go."

Matt agreed. "I'll mention it to him tonight. I'm sure he'll want to help out in any way that he can."


Shelly bent over the grave as if to say farewell to Wesley.

Matt commented on the selection of the grave site. "It's certainly a serene spot that you picked."

"It is," Shelly concurred. "This is where I want to be buried; right next to Wes."

Adam gave her a squeeze on the shoulder. "God still has work for you down here. You still have a life to live."

Shelly said, "But I sure do miss him."

"We all do," Adam added.

The three of them headed back to the house. Matt felt guilty that he wasn't in fighting condition, but he knew Karen would be glad to hear that he would be serving away from the front line.

# CHAPTER 29

"Woe to those who call evil good and good evil, who put darkness for light and light for darkness, who put bitter for sweet and sweet for bitter. Woe to those who are wise in their own eyes and clever in their own sight. Woe to those who are heroes at drinking wine and champions at mixing drinks, who acquit the guilty for a bribe, but deny justice to the innocent. Therefore, as tongues of fire lick up straw and as dry grass sinks down in the flames, so their roots will decay and their flowers blow away like dust; for they have rejected the law of the LORD Almighty and spurned the word of the Holy One of Israel."

-Isaiah 5:20-24

Late Tuesday night, Anthony Howe sat in the White House theatre room watching a documentary on the Holocaust. On this rare occasion, Jena, his wife, sat with him.

Jena said, "They say those who don't know history are doomed to repeat it."

Howe answered, "That's true. Adolf's weakness was that he failed to sell his idea to the world. I'm not saying I approve of his motivation, but I do admire the man for his passion. He understood that one must rule with a strong hand."

Jena shook her head. "I can't believe you admire Hitler."

Anthony rebutted, "I'm giving him credit for his management style. I didn't say I admired his principles or share his particular view of a utopian society. Give me some credit. I have my own ambitions about the way the world should be."

Jena said, "Our daughter was in the *D.C. Star* again this week."

Howe said, "Good."

"Good?" Jena snapped. "It's a picture of Elizabeth snorting heroin in a bathroom at the Columbia Country Club. How is that good?"

Howe shot back, "I didn't know it was a bad picture. Don't bark at me. Besides, she's young. She'll grow out of it. No one pays any attention to the *D.C. Star*. Everyone gets their picture in there once in a while. If memory serves me, you had your picture in there, passed out drunk at a state dinner."

Jena screamed, "And then there was your picture coming out of a hotel with that whore."

Howe got up and grabbed his drink. "I knew this was a bad idea. Make sure you stay on your side of the house. If you're going to use any common areas, check with facilities first and make sure I won't be using them."

Howe removed the video disk and headed towards his study to watch the rest. His phone rang. "Yes?"

It was his Chief of Staff, Alec Renzi. "Hale and the Joint Chiefs are ready for you in the Woodshed, sir."

The president answered, "Okay, make sure there is scotch on the table. Have them put the Blue Label by my chair and put whatever in the middle of the table. Put them both in decanters so no one thinks I'm handing out the swill while I drink top shelf."

Howe stopped by his room and threw on a pair of jeans and a knit top, then headed down to the West Wing. Anthony Howe entered the conference room and said, "Show me some pictures."

Hale queued the slide show to display on the screens all around the room. "The AGM 158 JASSM-ERs were outfitted with their nuclear warheads at Nellis Air Force Base in Nevada late last night. B-2s flew out of Whiteman Air Force Base in Missouri to Nellis this morning. The planes that will be launching the missiles at the Southern Coalition returned to Whiteman this afternoon. The planes designated to attack the North Western Coalition and Texas will take off from Nellis. They are armed, refueled and will be taking off at four o'clock in the morning. This image shows the scheduled location of each plane where they are to launch the missiles. The planes will never leave federally controlled airspace. The JASSM-ER is an extended range version of the original AGM 158 JASSM. They will be able to reach their intended target areas with little threat of detection. This next slide shows the scheduled detonation site of each missile. The effective range of the electromagnetic pulse from each missile overlaps and ensures a high rate of electromagnetic destruction."

Howe asked, "And that will wipe out the grid, automobiles, and all electronics?"

Hale replied, "The grid will absolutely go down. Even in the areas where you see gaps between the effective zones, the grid will suffer a cascading failure. DOD ran several tests on automobiles and we had varying results on different makes and models. Most military vehicles have been hardened against EMP, but those close to the blasts will still likely be taken out. Sensitive electronics in the center of the effective zones will be disabled at 100 percent. Electronics outside of the zones will have various degrees of damage. It was the best we could do with the time frame given, sir."

Anthony Howe nodded his approval. "Just living without electricity will have them in the dark ages and killing each other within a week. Gentlemen, you've all done a spectacular job. I've provided some very fine scotch. Please help yourselves."

Howe poured a glass for Scott Hale from his own decanter. He smiled as he thought to himself, *At least I'll make him gag on the good stuff.*

Most everyone took Howe up on his offer. Many of the Joint Chiefs would be sitting up all night to monitor the progress of the attack. It was now just before midnight. They'd be pretty well snookered by 4:00 AM.

Howe only half listened as the physicist from DOD gave a presentation on the possible nuclear fallout from the high-altitude detonation of the missiles.

Howe patted Alec Renzi on the shoulder and said, "Wake me up around five and let me know how everything went. Tell Jared to have a statement ready for the Federal States tomorrow morning." Howe snorted. "And remind him that he doesn't have to worry about spinning it to win approval in the Coalition. They won't have television in the morning anyway."

Howe retired to his private bedroom and had another drink by himself before he went to sleep.

# CHAPTER 30

"When the tempest rages, when the thunders roar, and the lightnings blaze around us, it is then that the truly brave man stands firm at his post."

-Luther Martin, Delegate
to the Constitutional Convention

Matt woke up early Wednesday morning to the sound of thunder. He opened his eyes to see a dim light. He closed his eyes again. *It feels early. It must be storming outside. The clouds must be blocking the sunrise,* he thought. *What an odd light.* He opened his eyes again to see the strange illumination. It had nearly dissipated.

Karen rolled over. "What was that noise?"

"Thunder," he replied.

"Why are you sitting up?" she asked.

"I thought the sun was coming up. I don't know what happened. It looks like it went back down." Matt looked over at the LED clock radio on the side of the bed. It was off. "Lightning must have knocked out the power. I'm going to check outside."

"What time is it?" Karen asked.

"I don't know. I'll check my phone." Matt walked over to the desk where his phone charged. "My phone is dead. The lighting must have ran through the lines. I'm going to make sure nothing is on fire."

Karen sat up. "Okay. Do you want me to help?"

"I'll be fine," he said.

Matt flicked on his flashlight and hobbled on his injured leg to the kitchen. Justin was already up and checking around.

Doc soon joined them from the foldout couch in the office. "Did you guys hear that?"

"Thunder," Matt said.

Justin commented, "It didn't sound like thunder. It sounded more like an explosion."

"What time is it?" Matt asked.

Doc shined his flashlight on his watch. "4:30."

Matt added, "I thought I saw the sun coming up when I woke up. It couldn't have been."

"Maybe it was lightning," Doc said.

"No," Matt replied. "It lasted way too long to be lightning. Whatever it was, it knocked out the power. It also took out my cell phone."

The three men walked outside and looked around. They looked toward the sky which was filled with stars.

Doc said, "It couldn't have been thunder or lightning; there's not a cloud in the sky."

The thought struck Matt suddenly. "EMP."

Justin said, "Wow, maybe."

Doc asked, "What's that?"

Matt explained, "Electromagnetic pulse. It can be generated by a high-altitude detonation of a nuclear warhead."

Doc inquired, "And it will knock out the electricity?"

Justin said, "At the very least."

Matt said, "We should check the trucks, see if they'll start."

Matt went inside and retrieved the keys.

Doc lectured him, "You get your crutches while you're in there. If you damage that muscle tissue, you won't be able to blame that on an EMP."

"Roger that," Matt replied. He soon reappeared with his crutches and the keys to both trucks and the van left by the men who attempted to rob Matt's home. Justin had been using Wesley's truck. Matt tossed keys to Justin and tried starting his own truck. Doc tried the van. They were all newer model vehicles. None would start.

Matt said, "Well, we better start figuring out what works and what doesn't. We're up now anyway."

Justin said, "Do you think this could be a preemptive strike? Could they be invading right now?"

Matt said, "I don't know, it's possible."

"Maybe I should run over to Adam's," Justin responded.

"That might be a good idea," Matt acknowledged. "Take a rifle, just in case."

Justin agreed and went inside to get dressed.

Matt went inside to tell Karen.

"No!" she exclaimed.

"I've got to start making a plan to implement as soon as the sun comes up," Matt said.

"I'll get some breakfast going," Karen said. "Will the gas stove still work?"

"Yes," he answered, "but be very stingy with it. Once the tank is empty, it may never be refilled again."

Karen said, "We can cook on the wood stove."

"In the winter we can, but without air conditioning, this house won't be bearable with a wood stove going inside during the summer months. We'll start cooking outside when we can to conserve gas," Matt stated.

"What about the solar panels?" Karen asked.

"I'll go check those out right now." Matt headed toward the metal work shed down by the creek.

"Anything I can help with?" Doc followed him down the path to the shed.

"Yeah, maybe," Matt answered.

When they arrived at the shed, Matt looked at the charge controller on his solar setup. "Looks like the charge controller is fried."

Doc asked, "It looks like you had it grounded. Why did it get fried?"

Matt replied, "I don't know. Maybe the cords from the panels acted like an antenna and brought the pulse straight into the controller." He flicked on the inverter. "Inverter and batteries still work. I guess the metal shed protected them. I've got a cheap charge controller that came as part of a kit. I'll see if it works."

Doc said, "Should we go back to the house and have breakfast? The sun will be up by the time we're done and we'll be able to see what we're doing."

"Good call," Matt said.

The two men walked back to the house where Rene and Karen were preparing breakfast.

"The fridge isn't going to stay cold very long," Karen said as the men walked in the door.

Matt replied, "The inverter and battery bank is still working. I'll run a cord up to the house after breakfast. We'll be able to run the fridge off the battery bank for a few days."

Over breakfast the four of them speculated on what the EMP strike would mean for them long term and they wondered if an invasion was coming. As they finished breakfast, they heard an unfamiliar vehicle pull into the drive.

The conversation about a possible invasion was still fresh in Matt's mind. He said, "Karen, go grab some weapons from the bedroom. I can't move fast with my leg, or I'd do it myself."

"Of course." Karen scurried off and returned with a pistol and a rifle. Matt took the pistol so he could still walk to the window with his crutches.

Matt peered out the window. "It's Justin, Adam and Gary. I don't know whose truck that is."

Justin came in the house as the truck pulled away. "None of Adam's vehicles will start."

"Whose truck was that?" Matt inquired.

Justin answered, "It was Michael's. We were keeping it at Gary's. Gary drove it over to Adam's while I was there. Adam is going to drive him home and come back here with the truck."

"Do any of Gary's automobiles start?" Doc asked.

"No," Justin answered. He then gave an abbreviated account of the interrogation of Michael's brother-in-law, Milton. "So Gary has Milton's old Camaro which also works. I think it's a 1972. No computer in there."

Matt shook his head, "There's a lot to be said for having an old beater. What year is the truck?"

Justin said, "Probably a 1978. I'd say most anything from before

1980 should still start."

Justin asked about the solar panels and Matt explained which components had been affected. After breakfast the guys headed to the shed. Matt scratched through some boxes and pulled out several of the small solar panels they scavenged from the top of bus stations during their excursion to Louisville weeks earlier.

"Let's get these hooked up and see what we've got." Matt handed one of the small panels to Doc. "Justin, can you go on the roof and disconnect the cords from the panels?"

"You got it." Justin placed the ladder against the shed and climbed to the roof. He threw each cord down as he disconnected them.

Matt began connecting the small panels from the bus stations to the extra charge controller. "The indicator light says they're charging."

"That's good news," Doc commented.

"Do you want to replace the ones on the roof with these?" Justin inquired.

Matt replied, "The shed gets good sun in the morning, but almost nothing in the afternoon because of the trees. I'm thinking we should get some type of wagon and set the entire system up to be mobile. We can move it around the property to whichever area has the most sun. It'll be a lot less work than clearing an area big enough to not be affected by the shade. We'll break the battery bank into two sets of batteries. We'll use half of them to set up a battery bank near the house for running the fridge and a very few essentials. The other batteries will be on the charging station. We'll have to switch out the batteries from the bank to the charging wagon every day, but we'll have a fridge."

Justin said, "Good plan. How about using your hand cart for a base to construct the solar wagon?"

Matt nodded, "That should work. There's some lumber around back that we can use to build a platform. I guess a two-level table would work best. We can place the panels on top and the batteries and charger below."

Adam pulled up in the old pickup truck and drove down to the work shed. He parked, then walked over to observe the project the men were working on. "What've you guys got goin' on?" he asked.

Matt explained the plan to mobilize the charging station to follow the sun around the property at different times of the day.

"Have you checked out the communications gear in there?" Adam asked.

"Not yet," Matt answered.

"Think it'll still work?" Adam inspected the small, backup charge controller.

Matt replied, "All this stuff works. I don't see why the radio wouldn't."

Adam asked, "So you think anything that was in a metal shed will still work?"

Matt responded, "I have no idea. There's a lightning rod on this shed. I don't know if that had anything to do with it. I read a little on EMPs before, but most of the information out there was fairly speculative. Besides, I think the effects vary greatly on several different factors such as distance from the blast, size of the charge and atmospheric conditions."

Doc asked, "What about radioactive fallout? Can that be an issue?"

Matt said, "I don't know. I think the detonation altitude required for an EMP is above the ozone layer, so I hope that will protect us, but I suspect some amount is bound to make its way through."

Doc asked, "Do you happen to have potassium iodine tablets?"

Matt shook his head. "No. What about water purification tablets? The main ingredient is iodine. Can we use those?"

Doc said, "That's an idea, but I wouldn't know how much to use.

If I could look it up on the Internet, I could figure it out, but that's out of the question. You've got a huge bottle of Betadine. We can paint a large area of skin on everyone's stomach with Betadine. The iodine will be absorbed through the skin and flood the thyroid gland. That should protect us from trace amounts of radiation filtering through the atmosphere."

Matt said, "Okay, you're in charge of that."

Adam said, "I'll take a small amount of Betadine over to the house and take care of my clan. I'll run some by Gary's place, then come back here when I'm finished. I'll bring Lt. Joe with me when I come back and we'll see if he can get the ham radio fired up."

"Sounds like a plan," Matt said.

Adam followed Doc back to the house while Matt and Justin continued working on the solar wagon. They soon had the platforms built out and loaded the equipment on the wagon.

Justin said, "We should get the battery bank set up next, so we can power the fridge."

Matt agreed and Justin carted a couple batteries to the house. Once the battery bank was complete, Matt ran an extension cord to the fridge and flipped the switch to the inverter.

Karen came to inspect the fridge. "It's working!"

Matt said, "Things are going to get tough around here, but having a little bit of power will make a big difference."

Rene followed Karen into the kitchen. "What about the water?"

Matt answered, "When the London water tower runs out, I guess there won't be any pumps running to refill it. We won't have running water much longer."

Justin said, "We can figure out a way to get water from the creek to the house. It's not that far. I can haul it in buckets 'til we get something rigged up."

Matt rested on his crutches, "Thanks, it'll be a week or two before

I can haul water in a bucket. You need another wagon for water."

Justin said, "Who knew wagons would be such a valuable commodity?"

"Yeah, who knew?" Matt laughed. "Where can we salvage wheels?"

Karen said, "You could take the wheels off of the lawn mower."

Matt replied, "That might actually work. We won't have a lawn mower, but water certainly tops a tidy lawn in our list of priorities at the moment."

Doc came in and ordered Justin and Matt to lift their shirts so he could apply a generous amount of Betadine on their abdomen.

Matt raised his shirt, "Any particular reason we're putting this on the stomach?"

Doc answered, "The skin on your belly is fairly tender and you'll get a higher absorption rate. It's also a big enough area to apply an adequate amount of the iodine solution. (Not intentionally, but it's more cosmetic as well. The Betadine leaves a rust colored stain on your skin and the tummy is usually covered.")

"What about Miss Mae?" Karen asked.

Doc answered, "I suppose we can put a little bit on the back of her neck, so she won't lick it off."

Karen answered, "Okay, but you better let me do it. She still hasn't warmed up to you, yet."

Matt said, "Fellas, we better get on that water cart project. Whatever we're going to get done from now on is going to have to be done during daylight hours. We can't afford to run lights."

Doc agreed, "On to the next project, then."

Rene said, "We'll take care of feeding the animals and check on the garden."

"Thanks," Matt headed out the door.

Back at the work shed, the men put their heads together to construct another wagon for hauling water. They soon had a rudimentary cart that would serve the purpose.

Matt inspected the wheels they'd salvaged from the lawn mower. "They won't take a lot of weight. You'll have to take multiple small loads."

Doc added, "I can haul water also. Between the two of us, we can keep the house supplied. Once Matt's leg is better, we'll let him catch up."

Justin laughed at the comment and Matt rolled his eyes. Adam pulled up with Lt. Joe. "You guys ready to check out this radio?"

Matt replied, "We've been running full speed ahead since the blast this morning. Can we break for lunch and then jump on it?"

Adam nodded, "We can do that. I'm just anxious to find out if we're being invaded."

Matt said, "I see your point. Maybe we'll just grab a sandwich and eat while we work on it."

The men walked back to the house, grabbed a few snacks and headed right back to the work shed. They unloaded the components to the ham and carted them back to the house.

"I'm getting a little tight on space," Matt said. "I'm not sure where we should set it up."

Doc replied, "Put it in the office."

Matt said, "But that's your personal space, and it's not that big."

Doc smiled. "I don't mind one bit. If I've got a place to lay my head at night, I'm very grateful."

Matt said, "If you're sure you don't mind."

"I insist," Doc said.

Lt. Joe still had limited use of his injured arm, so he instructed the others as to where and how to set up the radio. Matt ran a power cord into the office to supply electricity from the battery bank to the radio. Lt. Joe asked, "Does your drill still work?"

Matt said, "We've been using it on the other projects. The battery is getting low, but it could go a little while longer. What do you need?"

Joe replied, "If you don't mind, I'd like to drill a hole through the bottom of the window seal to run the antenna cord."

"Whatever you need," Matt replied.

The radio was soon set up and it proved to be in working order. Lt. Joe sat down and started scanning the usual frequency. He pressed the talk key and said, "This is Lima Juliet forty-nine calling CQ CQ CQ." Joe continued to scan. "I'll keep checking the channels generally used by the militia, National Guard, Texas and the Northwest Coalition." Each time he came to the desired frequency, he repeated, "This is Lima Juliet forty-nine calling CQ CQ CQ."

Everyone watched as Lt. Joe scrolled through his usual stops. "Looks like everyone has been hit. This ain't good boys. I'll keep running through to see if anyone else is reaching out. I'll run back through our frequencies and call CQ every thirty minutes or so."

Matt nodded and walked outside to clear his head for a moment. Adam followed him outside.

"What are you thinking?" Adam asked.

Matt peered through the trees to the east. "Do you think they're attacking right now?"

"I don't have a clue," Adam replied. "But I guess we should brace for impact."

"What do you recommend?" Matt inquired.

Adam said, "I think we should consolidate everyone into one house and maintain it as a base. We'll run round-the-clock guard duty and keep everyone at the ready."

Matt said, "That'll get crowded."

Adam said, "If we're getting hit, comfort won't be an issue anyway."

"I see your point," Matt agreed. "Where do you propose to keep everyone?"

Adam said, "The communications hub is here. You've got solar, a good water source; I think we should set up camp at your house and start fortifying a position. The weather's nice, we can set up tents for the guys and the girls can stay in the house. The men can all crowd into the work shed if it rains. I think we should bring Gary and his wife as well. Probably Mr. Miller, too. He's all alone. He wouldn't stand a chance if his house is attacked."

Matt asked, "You think DHS is going to roll all over the hills of Kentucky going house to house, rounding up farmers and killing us?"

Adam replied, "I don't know. My training just tells me to be ready for whatever. They may send small units house to house. If we're ready for them, we can take a small unit."

"Then they'll be back with more troops to squash us," Matt responded.

Adam said, "If we get hit, we'll relocate to my farm. If it gets hit, we'll go to Gary's. We'll map multiple routes out. As soon as we're attacked, the girls will bug out to my house. We'll kill off the invaders, then fall back to my place with the girls before reinforcements arrive."

Matt said, "Let me tell Karen about Fort Bair. I'm sure she'll be excited to know her home is becoming a military base."

Adam laughed, "I'll go round up the rest of my clan. I'll drop them off with their necessities, then go grab Gary and Debbie."

"Okay," Matt said. "Do any of your Baofeng radios work?"

"They're all fried," Adam answered.

"I've got my walkie-talkies in the safe, they should be protected but they're only effective for a mile or two in these hills," Matt said.

Adam asked, "Is your single-side-band, shortwave radio in the safe?"

"Yeah," Matt replied.

Adam said, "I can't respond, but if I take that with me, Lt. Joe could call me on the ham if anything goes wrong. I'd at least be able to race back here if there's trouble."

Matt nodded and went to retrieve the shortwave. He informed Lt. Joe of the plan. Joe then set the radio to the channel he would call if they were assaulted.

Adam jumped in the old truck and said, "I'll bring as much food and provisions as I can."

Matt replied, "You better cache anything you don't want to be stolen. You should stash some food and weapons over there as well, especially if we think we might have to fall back to that location."

"I'll do it," Adam said as he drove away.

Matt wasn't sure how Karen would take the concept of "Fort Bair." He knew Miss Mae would find it disagreeable. Nevertheless, it had to be done.

# CHAPTER 31

"One loves to possess arms, though they hope never to have occasion for them."

-Thomas Jefferson


Paul Randall's security team woke Paul Randall early Wednesday morning to inform him of the attack. They immediately moved him, his wife and Sonny to the underground bunker below his house.

Paul asked the lead officer, "Do we know if there was a physical attack or EMP?"

"I'm not sure, Senator," the man replied. "I saw a bright flash in the sky. I'm guessing EMP. All the radios are shot. We can't get any information right now. You have a backup-comms system in the bunker. I'll get it set up right away."

Kimberly asked, "See if they can get a hold of Ryan. I have to know if he's okay."

Paul explained that it was most likely an EMP attack and that there was probably no life-threatening damage at the moment.

The officer got Paul's backup radio running. He was able to reach Fort Hood's Emergency Services Network and soon had General

Jefferson on the line. He passed the mic to Paul.

"General, can you confirm that we were hit with an EMP?" Paul asked.

"It looks that way. I'm sending a Humvee to pick you up. This may have been a precursor to an invasion. That's what I'd do if I were attacking," Jefferson said.

"The vehicles are running?" Paul asked.

"They were supposed to be hardened against EMP, but that didn't pan out for most of the fleet. All of the vehicles that were inside metal hangars or metal garages seem to be unaffected. Everything on them seems to work." Jefferson said.

Randall voiced his concern. "What if we're hit by a secondary device while we're on the road? Then we'll be totally exposed."

Allen Jefferson said, "That could happen, but I'd say it's unlikely. I've sent men to Red River to pick several old Vietnam-era vehicles that should work. If we're attacked by another EMP, I'll have them pick you up. You'll have an adequate security detail to defend you until they arrive. Besides that, you know how to shoot if you have to."

Sonny asked, "All of our computers are completely dead. Is there any chance the information on the hard drives could be salvaged?"

Jefferson replied, "I don't know, Sonny. Bring them and we'll see what we can do. We have a few Toughbooks in a cage that survived the attack. I'll get one for you to work on. You and Paul will have to share it. We don't have many."

"How long 'til our ride arrives?" Paul asked.

"Hour and a half," Jefferson replied.

"We'll be ready," Paul signed off.

"We have to go to the base?" Kimberly asked.

"I'm afraid so," Paul replied. "We better pack a couple of bags."

Sonny went straight to his quarters and the Randalls went to their room to get ready.

As they were packing, Kimberly said, "I can't believe we're being run out of our home again."

Paul responded, "Jefferson has a nice residence set up for us at Fort Hood. It won't be like hiding out at the Armory."

"It won't be home either," she said.

Paul secured their house and double-checked his pistol. He took two extra magazines and placed them in the bag with his laptop.

His ride arrived right on time and they were on the way to Fort Hood. Kimberly didn't say much on the way to the base. Paul was sure the trip reminded her of the last time they had to leave their home because of a threat from the Federal government. It had resulted in the death of their son, Robert. Paul didn't bring up the subject as he had no desire to relive the ordeal.

When they arrived at the base, General Jefferson met them at the gate. Jefferson jumped into the Humvee. "How was the trip?"

"Uneventful, which was good," Paul said.

Jefferson said, "We'll take you directly to your base residence. I'll give you an hour to get settled in, then we'll have a conference call with the Coalition governors. Larry should be here by then. Kimberly, if you don't mind, Mrs. Jefferson will be stopping by in an hour or so to make sure you have everything at the residence that you could need."

Kimberly perked up a little. "That would be great." She looked out the window and asked, "Are these houses part of the base?"

"Yes," Jefferson replied.

"It looks just like a little suburban neighborhood," she commented.

Jefferson smiled. "We want the soldiers to feel at home here. The place we have for you is a townhome. We don't have auxiliary power for any of the single family residences that were open, but it's a big townhouse. Sonny, you'll be staying in the adjoining townhouse. Larry and Alison Jacobs will be staying three doors down from you. They'll be arriving shortly. Next door is a private security detail that will be making sure you're all safe."

Kimberly brightened up, "It will be nice to see Alison. And Candice too, of course. Maybe we can play cards while we have light."

Jefferson replied, "You'll have electricity, at least for lights, cooking, hot water and other necessities. We have massive auxiliary generators and plenty of fuel stockpiled."

"Thank you general," Kimberly said.

Jefferson responded, "My pleasure."

They pulled into the drive of the townhouse. Jefferson and the security team helped them bring in their bags. Sonny went to his townhouse and the Randalls went to theirs.

Paul asked, "How will we conduct the conference call?"

Jefferson replied, "The Pentagon took several recommendations from the EMP Commission. They installed fiber optic communication lines underground running between several key bases."

"Could the Federal States listen in if they wanted?" Randall asked.

Jefferson explained, "It is a hardline connection between each base. The cables run side by side, but are entirely independent of each other. It is a ridiculously simple system. It operates almost like an old telephone switchboard with each base having their own switchboard. You connect only to the bases you want to communicate with."

Paul inquired, "Could the system be tapped?"

Jefferson shrugged his shoulders. "The system is supposed to alert you if the line is tampered with, but nothing is completely out of the question. It's the best alternative we have, so we'll have to take our chances. We could run encrypted signals, but we would need someone to physically install the software for each node."

Paul asked, "Should I come with you? Do we need to have a conference call right away?"

Jefferson answered, "The governors aren't at the bases yet. Some won't arrive for several hours because of the distance. Several Coalition States don't have a base that's linked to the fiber optic network. We have no secure method to communicate until the governors are at the military bases."

Paul asked, "Have there been any reports of Federal troop movement in the Coalition?"

"None," the general replied. "I've got pretty good information from the major bases and surrounding areas, but we are completely in the dark on the eastern borders of Kentucky and Tennessee. Unfortunately, if the Coalition were being invaded, that would be the most likely place to be hit first. I've got several comms analysts scanning the channels for anyone who may have had a ham radio that was protected from the EMP. Until we find someone, we have no source of information on what's happening in the area."

A voice came over Jefferson's radio. "General Jefferson, this is Governor Jacob's driver. We'll be at the gate in ten minutes."

"Roger," the general called back. "I've gotta go get Larry settled in. I'll be back in an hour."

"See you then," Paul said.

Paul walked into the kitchen where Kimberly was taking a mental inventory of the pots and pans and things she had to work with.

Paul put his hand on her shoulder. "Are you finding everything you need?"

She turned to embrace him. "This is much better than what I had in my mind. I was expecting something like the Armory, when we had mattresses on the floor."

Paul held her tight. "We'll, it ain't home, but we do have electricity."

"Plus, I'll have Alison and Candice. We can make each other laugh in any circumstance. This won't be so bad." Kimberly kissed Paul and turned to take her things upstairs to the bedroom. Paul grabbed his bags and followed her.

Paul was still putting his things away when he heard a knock at the door. He walked down the stairs and opened the door.

Jefferson was there. "Do you need a little more time?"

"No, I'm ready." Paul replied. He called to his wife, "Kimberly, I'll be back later."

Larry was waiting in the vehicle when Paul got in. Paul joked, "Did the lights go out at your house, too?"

Not to be outdone, Larry replied, "Yep, I think Alison blew a fuse with the Cuisinart."

Sonny entered the Humvee and they drove away. The men arrived at a low-level administrative building. Larry joked, "Did you get kicked out of your office, General?"

"Don't judge a book by its cover," Jefferson replied.

The men followed the general to a small conference room. The general slid a keycard into what appeared to be an air-conditioning thermostat. This triggered a panel that receded back and exposed a false wall. Inside was an elevator door. The men went in the elevator and took it to a subterranean level.

"You never told me about this!" Paul exclaimed.

Jefferson winked, "You never asked."

The door opened and revealed a massive cave-like area.

Jacobs said, "Wow, this reminds me of Cheyenne Mountain. You've done a good job of keeping this place secret."

Jefferson replied, "We've tried. There are a couple of places like this."

Larry asked, "Is one of them at the Denver Airport?"

Jefferson laughed. "No, that was a red herring. The conspiracy theorist who put out that story worked for the Pentagon. All of the signs and clues that there's a mega-bunker under Denver were put there on purpose. We actually have storage space under Denver International. It's mostly bottled water, MREs and outdated computer hard drives. All the reports from contractors that say they worked on an underground facility in Denver are true. It was all part of an elaborate cover-up to keep people looking at the right hand when we were working with our left."

The men walked several yards down a dimly lit corridor to a conference room. Jefferson flipped several switches on a panel and engaged the speaker phone. The men selected chairs around a pristine table and the general called, "Malmstrom, this is Fort Hood. Are you online?"

A voice called back, "This is Governor Shea. Go ahead, Fort Hood."

Jefferson asked, "Have Governor Goldwater and Governor Schmidt arrived, yet?"

Mark Shea replied, "We sent two twin engine planes to pick them up. Goldwater is in Boise which is over 500 miles away. Schmidt is in Cheyenne, nearly 700 miles away, so it may be a while before they arrive."

The situation was the same for Minot Air Force Base. North Dakota Governor Abrams was there, but South Dakota Governor Donald Barlow would be arriving much later.

The governors of Kentucky and Tennessee were in a smaller subterranean bunker located at Fort Knox. Both governors of the Carolinas had arrived at the underground command post in Fort Bragg.

Paul began right away, "Gentlemen, I'd love to wait for

Governors Barlow and Schmidt, but we've got to get started. This is certainly the worst crisis we've had to face, yet. Sonny will be taking notes and he'll brief the others when they arrive.

"Let's start with Tennessee and Kentucky. Have either of you heard any reports of invading forces other than the ones we know of?"

Harvey Simmons of Kentucky replied, "We've not received any news either way. I dispatched eight recon teams consisting of four men each to check out the eastern borders. They're instructed not to break radio silence unless they observe enemy troops that we were not previously aware of."

Paul replied, "So you do have radios that are still operational?"

"Very few," Simmons replied. "We had a few mobile command posts that were hardened against EMP and a few hand-held radios that were either in storage cages or metal hangars that survived the attack. The mobile command units are going to be acting as relays for the hand-helds which the recon teams are carrying. We'll let you know if we hear anything at all."

The North Carolina Governor stated, "We had a fair amount of redundant communications systems, backup power and vehicles in underground storage here at Fort Bragg. I'll be sending out troops with comms equipment to set up a network throughout North Carolina and South Carolina first thing in the morning. They are staging that operation as we speak. By tomorrow night, we'll be able to send and receive information to communication outposts in all of our cities and larger towns. As of right now, we have no information coming in."

Paul complimented, "That's a great plan, Governor."

Mark Shea spoke next. "We have a network of ham operators that are in the AmRRON network that have been practicing for this sort of thing for several years. They're spread out all over Montana, Idaho, Wyoming and the eastern halves of Washington and Oregon. I expect many of them have redundant systems to set up after an EMP. It may be a while before they get online with their backup radios, but when they do, it should be an effective way to get information and send out updates."

Paul Randall said, "That's fantastic. I wish we had more citizens who thought like that."

General Jefferson said, "Paul, I recommend that we begin to discuss a response to this attack. I think we all know that the purpose of the EMP was to disable our ability to effectively defend the Coalition. I don't think it would be prudent to sit around and wait for the next shoe to drop. We need to take action immediately."

"What would you recommend?" Paul asked.

"A nuclear strike," Jefferson proclaimed.

"No!" Paul came back definitively. "No way. That is not an option."

Mark Shea jumped in. "I agree with Paul. We can't justify a nuclear strike and it may incite a direct nuclear retaliation. I would be willing to support a like-kind response. What would you say to an EMP attack against the Federal States, general?"

Paul interrupted, "I think we all need a little cooling-off period before we start talking about retaliatory strikes. We should at least wait until the other governors are present. This is not the type of thing any of us have the authority to do without approval from our other elected representatives."

Jefferson said, "An invasion may have already been launched. I pray we have enough time for your diplomatic process, Senator. We don't need to take a vote on whether or not the people of the Coalition want us to do our duty and defend them against Federal troops."

Randall said, "General, you will not be making that decision unilaterally."

Deafening silence fell over the boardroom.

Tennessee Governor Richards was the first to speak. "Why don't we all take a breather? We'll take an hour break. When we come back we can discuss the possibility of an EMP strike against the Federal States. That would serve to level the playing field. During the break, let's all try to remember that we're on the same side."

Paul collected his notes and left the room without speaking. He knew Jefferson had never intended to make a nuclear strike. The whole thing was a military-political tactic. He had overpriced the attack by suggesting the nuclear option. Then he could bargain for an EMP strike and appear to be settling for less. The EMP assault was the plan all along. He respected the general, but he did not like the fact that he was playing politics and manipulating the rest of the governors.

Larry Jacobs followed close behind Paul Randall. He left him a little space then gradually caught up with him. "You're right about the nuclear strike, Paul," Jacobs said. "But Jefferson is right about not waiting for the other shoe to drop."

Paul didn't look at Larry, "It sounds like he's already won his consensus."

# CHAPTER 32

"But let all who take refuge in you be glad; let them ever sing for joy. Spread your protection over them, that those who love your name may rejoice in you. For surely, O LORD, you bless the righteous; you surround them with your favor as with a shield."

-Psalm 5:11-12

Matt and Karen were still trying to work out the arrangements when Adam arrived with provisions and his family packed tightly into the bed of the truck.

"Thanks for being so patient about all of this," Matt said to his wife.

"We have to make the best of it," Karen replied. "No one asked for a civil war."

"Let's go try to make everyone feel welcomed," Matt said.

Karen nodded, "We all know each other pretty well and get along with one another. If you're going to be stuck in close quarters with a bunch of people, this is the bunch you'd want."

Shelly and Janice helped Adam bring some supplies up to the

porch. Mandy and Carissa ran in the house to find the cat.

Adam asked, "I guess it's going to be pretty tight. Where should I put the dry goods?"

Matt said, "Let's drive them on down to the work shed. I've got plenty of room down there."

Matt jumped in the truck and the two men drove down to the work shed. Justin walked down behind them and helped them unload.

Adam gave them a lift back to the house. "I'm going to pick up Eli and run by Gary's. He won't be able to fit much stuff in the Camaro, so I'll throw his big items in the truck."

Shelly waved them down before Adam drove away. "Hey, I had an idea. When I was in college, some of the girls built lofts in their dorm rooms. It was basically a few studs that elevated a plywood platform four feet high. One girl would have her bed on the bottom, and the other girl would have her bed on the top. It was sort of like bunk beds, but half the room had the platform. It provided more storage and personal space when sharing those little-bitty dorm rooms. You still have all of that thick plywood from your roofing business, Adam. We could build the platforms in the two bedrooms. It would make more space since we are all going to be crammed in there like sardines."

Matt nodded. "What do you think, Adam?"

Adam shrugged, "I can build them, but it's your house. Whatever you say."

"Let's do it," Matt said. "We can put mattresses on top and bottom. It'll stretch the space and essentially make four bedrooms instead of two."

Adam drove away and Matt, Justin and Shelly went in the house with the others. Matt explained the concept that Shelly had come up with. It was decided that Karen and Janice would share the top level of the master bedroom and Carissa and Mandy took the lower level. Shelly and Rene would share the lower level of the second bedroom and Debbie, Gary's wife, would take the top level.

They began by clearing the areas so the platforms could be built. Additionally, Matt, Doc and Justin stowed the bed frames in the work shed. With only four feet of overhead clearance on each level, the mattresses would have to go directly on the floor.

On the way back from the work shed, Matt said, "We need to start dedicating someone to a lookout position right away. If we're being invaded, we could get hit at any time. The most likely direction an attack is going to come from would be the road. I think we should start taking shifts up by the road. I've got two walkies, we'll keep one at the house and the lookout will have the other one. Everyone should carry at least a pistol at all times."

Justin said, "I agree. The girls can take shifts on lookout as well. That will allow us to work shorter shifts. Everyone will be fresher and more alert."

Matt said, "Let's put up a lean-to shelter over by the road. We'll camouflage it so it won't be visible to anyone driving up to the property."

Doc said, "Why don't you take first shift on lookout. Justin and I will bring some materials to construct a blind. That'll give you a chance to get off that leg. You've been overdoing it today. If we're going to fight any more battles, you'll need that leg."

Matt argued, "I've been keeping my weight on the crutches…mostly."

"Mostly," Doc said sarcastically.

Matt retrieved the walkies. He took one and handed the other to Justin. He slung his rifle over his back and headed to the tree line near the road. As he sat down his leg began to throb. Doc was right. He had overdone it. This was a bad time to have an injury.

Justin called over the walkie, "What about a tent for a lookout shelter?"

Matt replied, "We'll probably need those for the men to sleep in. Let's stick with a lean-to. We can build them out of forest debris and they'll be naturally camouflaged."

Justin called back, "Roger."

Matt added, "Bring some zip ties and paracord. We'll use that to attach the basic structure. Bring a tarp also. We'll use it for a roof to keep the rain off."

Matt sat still and waited. It wasn't even noon yet, but he was already tired. Justin called back over the walkie. "Lt. Joe found someone on the ham. It's some guy from Idaho. He says he is part of a network of ham operators called AmRRON. He said he'll be gathering and relaying information as he gets it."

Matt sat up. "Did they get hit by an EMP?"

Justin called back, "Yes, they're completely in the dark also. He says other people in his network will be online by tonight."

Matt asked, "How do we know he's legit?"

Justin said, "Joe's heard of them before. He even remembers the guy's call sign, Foxtrot five one niner."

Matt said, "Then I guess we have to trust him."

Matt signed off and waited for Justin and Doc to arrive with the supplies. When they made it to the observation post, Justin filled Matt in on the rest of the details about the radio communication. "The guy says he'll relay all the information he receives every hour on the hour. He spoke with someone from Texas and they're dark also. There are no reports of an invasion yet, but everyone seems to expect one."

Matt spotted Adam coming up the road from a good distance away. Doc stepped out into the open to wave Adam down as he drove by.

"Hey," Adam yelled out the window as he stopped the truck near the observation post.

"Where is Eli?" Matt yelled back from the edge of the tree line.

Adam shook his head. "He said if he leaves his property that the Feds will have already won. He won't leave his animals. He told me that he's old and ready to die if it comes down to it, but he ain't leavin' his animals. I told him we'd bring him back every day to feed them and check on them, but he's digging in. He gave us some beeswax to make candles."

Matt yelled, "That was nice."

"Yep," Adam replied. "I'm going to get Gary and Debbie settled in. I'll come up when we're done."

Matt waved as Adam drove on to the house. Gary and Debbie followed Adam in the old Camaro.

Justin and Doc continued piecing together a shelter for the observation post while Matt kept watch. It was hard for him to sit back while the other two men worked, but Doc wouldn't have it any other way.

Shelly and Rene walked up to the outpost. Rene said, "Adam wants you guys to see something. We'll keep an eye out for a while."

Matt thanked them and explained how to work the walkie. Shelly assured him that she was familiar with the operation of a walkie-talkie.

Matt grabbed his rifle and crutches and hobbled down to the house. Doc and Justin followed. When they arrived, they saw a big wall tent already set up.

"How do you like that?" Adam asked.

"It's great!" Matt said.

"Gary used to be a Civil War reenactor. This was his tent." Adam explained.

Gary said, "I guess we're all Civil War reenactors now."

Justin joked, "As long as it wasn't no Yankee tent. I ain't sleepin' in no Yankee tent."

Gary said, "I ought to whip you for even thinking I'd play a Yankee."

Matt laughed and said, "That should easily fit four cots."

Adam added, "And someone will always be on watch, so there will never be more than four men sleeping at one time anyway. On Navy subs, they call it 'hot racking.' Space is limited on submarines, so sleeping space has to be shared. With the pull-out couch in the office, we should have enough space for everyone to sleep."

The men continued to get the accommodations set up then moved on to erecting the platforms for the girls in both bedrooms.

# CHAPTER 33

"May God give us wisdom, fortitude, and perseverance, and every other virtue necessary for us to maintain that independence which we have asserted!"

-Samuel Adams

Ryan Randall arrived early Friday morning at Fort Hood to meet with the other pilots who volunteered for the counterstrike against the Federal States. As he was getting settled into his temporary barracks, General Jefferson walked in. All the pilots stood at attention.

"As you were, gentlemen," the general said.

Jefferson walked over to Ryan's bunk. "I thought you'd be staying with your parents."

Ryan replied, "I'm still not on speaking terms with Dad."

Jefferson said, "That's no reason to punish your mom."

Ryan replied, "If I tell her that I'm here, she'll want to know why. If she finds out I'm flying in the assault, she'll worry from the time I tell her until I get back. Ignorance is bliss."

Jefferson said, "I can't keep the fact that you'll be flying from your father. You're your own man. He can't stop you, but he deserves to know. That's part of being a man, Ryan. I think you should tell him."

Ryan agreed. "I'll tell him. I want to wait 'til just before takeoff. I'm in no mood for a long argument about it. He can decide if he wants to tell Mom."

The general said, "I can respect that. I'll be going over the attack plan with everyone in the briefing later this afternoon. However, I want to discuss it with you in private. I may have a special role for you if you accept the task. Can we have lunch together after you get settled?"

"I'd be honored," Ryan said.

"Good. Head on over to my residence at twelve o'clock," Jefferson said.

Ryan replied, "Twelve o'clock, sir."

The general left and Ryan continued to put his things away. He got several looks from the other pilots, but no one said anything. It was common knowledge that Ryan had been fast-tracked through training by the general. He had proven himself as a good pilot, but he could still sense the contention from the other men.

Ryan put on a ball cap and sunglasses before walking over to meet the general. He kept a lookout for his father. He was in no hurry to explain why he was on the base. He arrived and was escorted to the dining room by an MP. Ryan took a seat and was soon joined by the general.

"I hope you like roast beef," Jefferson said.

"We don't get anything like that at Kelly Field. Things are pretty tight on base," Ryan commented.

Lunch was served and Ryan had to make a conscious effort not to be a pig.

Jefferson said, "I'll show you some maps after we eat, but the assault is going to be a combined attack utilizing ICBMs launched from Malmstrom and missiles launched from fixed wing aircraft. The ICBMs will be used to strike the larger geographic areas such as the Southwest, West Coast, and Midwest, but you'll be part of the attack that will launch smaller missiles against the Northeast. We want that to be more surgical so we minimize the effect on Canada. We need to do what we can to keep the few friends we have."

"Has Canada been supportive of the Coalition?" Ryan asked.

Jefferson took a sip of his iced tea. "No, but they haven't been supportive of the Federal States, either. Hopefully, we can rebuild a relationship with them after the dust settles."

Ryan inquired, "What about China? How will they react to their forces on the west coast being hit by an EMP?"

Jefferson said, "I'm not sure, but they are an invading force. They've aligned themselves with the Federal States. They should expect retaliation for the action taken against the Coalition."

Ryan quizzed, "You mentioned that you wanted to discuss a special role for me in the assault?"

Jefferson wiped his mouth. "Yes. I hope I can depend on you to keep this between us. I know how angry you are at D.C. for the murder of your brother."

Ryan answered, "I'll never get over that. And yes, you can count on me to keep a secret."

Jefferson said, "You have no obligation to accept the mission, but I'd like to propose an opportunity for you to collect your pound of flesh from Howe. There is no political will for anything other than an EMP against the Federal States, but we need to take the head off the snake. You'll be launching a small nuclear warhead over D.C. If the guidance system on the delivery missile were to malfunction, the warhead might detonate at a lower altitude. Rather than generating an EMP, it would eliminate all of the corruption inside the beltway. There would be collateral damage. You have to decide if you can live with that. Your father has no stomach for it. I wish it were not something that had to be done, but I see no other option if we want America to survive."

Ryan asked, "So you're talking about nuking Washington? Wouldn't I have to launch from a different altitude? That could cause speculation. It might make people think that I was part of a conspiracy or at the very least, blame it on pilot error."

Jefferson said, "You'll launch the missile from miles away, at the same altitude as all the other pilots. It could have been done without any pilot ever knowing. If you're uncomfortable with it, I'll assign you to launching the EMP over New York or some other place."

Ryan said, "No, I'll accept the mission. I want to be the one who blows that cesspool to the devil. I don't care if we're exposed. I'll do it and I'll never have any regret."

Jefferson said, "We won't be exposed. The only trace evidence will be in the guidance system which will be destroyed on detonation."

Ryan countered, "But it'll look awful fishy that it was the missile over D.C. that malfunctioned."

Jefferson lifted his ice tea for a toast. "We'll blame it on the EMP strike from the Federal States. I'm sure people will believe that it could have affected the guidance system in the missile."

Ryan toasted the general. "There will be no way to prove otherwise, so they'll have to accept it."

# CHAPTER 34

"I have hidden your word in my heart that I might not sin against you."

-Psalms 119:11

Early Monday morning, Matt woke to a firm nudge on the arm. Doc said softly, "It's five o'clock. Time to get up." Matt took a second to remember where he was. For a second, he thought he was back in the work camp prison. Why else would Doc be waking him? As soon as he saw his pillow, the blanket over him and the fold-out cot beneath him, he knew he wasn't in the work camp. There had been no such comforts there.

"Okay, thanks. I'm up," Matt replied with a smile. Doc returned to the office or what was now being referred to as the radio room. Matt's six-hour guard shift began in one hour. He would be stationed at the observation post near the road and Karen would be watching the backside of the property from a second position that had been erected atop the metal work shed. This secondary position allowed them to keep watch for assault teams approaching from the forest. Between the two observation points, all possible angles of approach were covered. Matt stoked the fire outside of the men's tent and started a pot of coffee on the metal grate over the fire. He used Gary's blue enamel coffee pot for his morning fix. There was still plenty of natural gas in the tank, but making coffee outside when the weather permitted was one way to stretch the depleting resource.

Matt went inside and quietly opened the door to the master bedroom. He climbed the short ladder to the upper level of the sleeping platform and gently stroked his wife's leg until she awakened. "Time to get up," he whispered.

Karen nodded that she heard him but continued to rest her head on the pillow. Miss Mae, however, needed no coaxing. She came out from under the lower level sleeping area where Mandy and Carissa slept. She met Matt at the bottom of the ladder with a soft "meow." She was ready for breakfast.

Matt went to the kitchen and took a few pieces of leftover chicken from the fridge to give Miss Mae. Her supplies of cat food were dwindling, but she didn't seem to mind. In fact she much preferred the leftovers on most occasions.

Matt made a small batch of pancake batter and took it outside to cook over the fire. The coffee was ready when he arrived so he poured himself a cup.

Karen joined him just as the pancakes were ready. "It's been five days now since the EMP. Does this remind you of Florida after Hurricane Wilma?"

"Sort of," he replied. "At least we knew power would eventually be back on. And we still had radio stations. This feels a little more permanent."

Karen asked, "If we haven't been attacked yet, do you think we're safe?"

Matt shrugged. "I don't know. They may be waiting for things to descend into chaos. It's possible that they figure we'll use up all of our resources and get weaker. The opposite is probably true. Most folks who live in rural areas are probably adapting and becoming more resilient, like we are. Lt. Joe has been able to reach others who had some type of communication equipment that survived the attack. He thinks there are even more who may have had shortwave radios that survived. They would be able to receive information being passed around, even if they have no way of letting us know.

"The Northwest Coalition has several of their AmRRON participants operating a communications net. They're able to pass information or call their militias and military if any region comes under attack. The Carolinas have established a fantastic emergency communications network utilizing military radios that were stored in EMP resistant locations. It's only a matter of time before Kentucky and Tennessee get a network set up like theirs. The time to have hit us was right after the EMP attack. Now we're getting stronger day by day."

While the two were eating their pancakes at an outside picnic table near the men's sleeping tent, Mandy came outside to join them. "Matt, I want to be on lookout with you. I can watch, and I'm a good shot if I have to shoot somebody."

Matt said, "I don't mind if you come along, but you have to ask your mom."

Mandy rebutted, "Can't I ask my dad? I know mom won't let me. She thinks she can protect us, but if anything bad ever happens, I might have to shoot somebody. It would be better if she let us learn more about fighting."

Matt said, "Climb up to the observation post on top of the work shed and have Shelly call your dad on the walkie-talkie."

"I can tell him that it's okay with you?" she asked for clarification.

"It's fine with me," Matt smiled.

Mandy ran off and Karen said, "She just turned thirteen. Do you think this is a good idea to have her out on the front line?"

Matt said, "She makes a good point, if we do get hit, she may have to fight."

Karen countered, "The plan is if our house gets hit, the girls are supposed to fall back to Adam's house."

Matt said, "That's the plan, but what if you get cut off, or what if they run you down in the woods on the way? We could get boxed in from multiple directions. War is unpredictable. We try not to dwell on all the horrific things that can happen, but the reality is that it can get ugly. If Mandy is brave enough to embrace the thought of having to fight, we should encourage that bravery and try to get it to grow. It will serve her much better than fear."

"Whatever you say," Karen didn't sound convinced when she conceded.

Mandy was soon back with a smile that stretched from ear to ear. "Dad said I can come with you!"

Matt chuckled, "Then you better eat a good breakfast."

Matt made her a small plate of pancakes and poured himself another cup of coffee.

Mandy began eating. Between bites she said, "Dad said it was alright for me to bring my .22 rifle."

"You might need it." Matt looked over to see Karen's reaction. She didn't say anything, she just rolled her eyes.

After breakfast, Karen headed to her post above the work shed to relieve Shelly. Matt grabbed his rifle, some water and his Bible. Then he and Mandy went to the post near the road to relieve Adam.

When they arrived, Adam gave Mandy a quick rundown of what was expected of a sentry. "Sweet pea, you have to be very still and very quiet. You have to stay low and do what Matt tells you. Is that understood?"

"Yes, sir," she answered.

Adam smiled and placed his camouflaged boonie hat on her head as he kissed her. The hat swallowed half of her small head but Mandy beamed with delight from her father's approval.

Adam left the post while Matt and Mandy settled in for their shift. Matt pulled out his Bible and began to jot down some scripture on a three-by-five-inch index card.

Mandy whispered, "What are you doing, Matt."

"I'm writing Psalm one on an index card so I can memorize it," he replied. "I recite the part I remember in my head, then when I get to a section that I can't remember, I can pull out the card and memorize the next section."

Mandy was curious. "You're going to memorize the whole Psalm?"

Matt nodded. "The first psalm is only a few verses. I should be able to do it this week. Did you know Jewish children used to have to memorize the entire Torah? Some still do."

"What's the Torah?" Mandy whispered.

Matt replied, "It's the first five books of the Old Testament."

"Wow!" Mandy exclaimed. "But why are you memorizing a whole psalm?"

Matt spoke softly. "When I was captured and held in the work camp, I didn't have a Bible. The only Bible I had was what I had memorized. When I had no hope at all, those few verses I could remember were a great source of hope for me. I wished I had known more verses to meditate on when I was sitting inside my cell."

Mandy sat with her eyes wide open. "That must have been horrible. I can't imagine being in a cage like that. Can I read your card?"

"Sure." Matt handed her the index card.

Mandy recited the words from the card. "Blessed is the man who does not walk in the counsel of the wicked or stand in the way of sinners or sit in the seat of mockers. But his delight is in the law of the LORD, and on his law he meditates day and night. He is like a tree planted by streams of water, which yields its fruit in season and whose leaf does not wither. Whatever he does prospers. Not so the wicked! They are like chaff that the wind blows away. Therefore the wicked will not stand in the judgment, nor sinners in the assembly of the righteous. For the LORD watches over the way of the righteous, but the way of the wicked will perish."

She sat quietly for a moment as if she were digesting what she had read. "Why is the guy who meditates on God's law like a tree by a stream of water?"

Matt smiled. "A tree planted by a stream gets its water from underground, sort of an unseen source. (Other trees are dependent on the weather. They have to have rain or they'll wither away.) The man who gets his peace from God's word isn't dependent on outside circumstances. For that tree, it doesn't matter if it rains or not. Do you understand?"

Mandy nodded. "So if you're planted by the stream, it doesn't matter if DHS throws you in a cell, your peace comes from inside."

Matt smiled and patted Mandy on the head to let her know that she got it.

Mandy asked, "Do you have another index card?"

Matt handed her the one he had written on. "I'll get another one back at the house."

Mandy and Matt sat diligently watching the road and the surrounding area all morning. At noon, Gary arrived to relieve them. "Did Matt sleep all morning and make you stand watch?"

Mandy laughed. "No!"

Gary snickered, "Well then, you're lucky. That's what he used to do to me when we were guarding the border."

"Really?" Mandy was unconvinced.

"It was the other way around, the way I remember it." Matt grabbed his things and headed back toward the house, with the young sentinel trailing close behind.

When they returned to the house, Janice was preparing a huge meal to feed everyone at the homestead that was now being called

Fort Bair. "Everyone can't eat at once anyway, so just grab a plate and eat when you're ready."

Mandy asked, "Is Dad awake, yet?"

Janice said, "He's still asleep. He needs at least another two hours. You can wake him up later."

Karen had been relieved from her post by Debbie. She went to the bucket to wash up then came to eat next to Matt and Mandy.

Janice asked, "Matt, do you think it would be too much of a drain on the batteries to run the dehydrator?"

"What do you want to dehydrate?" he asked.

Janice replied, "Adam is planning to kill another cow. They are exposed over at our place, anyway. He thinks it's best to cull the herd as low as possible. He goes over there every other day to check on them, but it's inevitable that they'll be stolen if no one is around to watch them."

Matt said, "The dehydrator sucks a lot of juice. We could dehydrate on top of the metal roof of the work shed. We can use the racks out of the ovens to place thin strips of beef on."

Janice thought. "What about bugs? Won't they get on the meat?"

Matt said. "There is always someone up there on guard duty. They can shoo the bugs away."

Karen said, "It's my shift in the mornings. That's the only time there would be enough sun to dehydrate. Maybe I can enlist your helper to give me a hand at my post; and shooing bugs."

Mandy nodded, "I'll help you, Karen."

Everyone greeted Doc as he came out of the house and sat down to eat at the big picnic table. "How is everyone today?" Everyone exchanged pleasantries, then Doc said, "Lt. Joe picked up some concerning news this morning. Foxtrot five one niner sent a coded message. Lt. Joe deciphered it using the book cipher they're using. It seems Texas has intercepted some very credible intel that D.C. is planning a secondary EMP attack."

Matt sat up very attentively. "When is this supposed to happen?"

"Wednesday," Doc said.

Matt began processing the ramifications of another attack. "I guess they are targeting the backup power and communication systems. I'm going to go wake Adam up. We need to start rolling everything up right away."

Doc said, "But we have two days before the attack."

Matt replied, "Unless D.C. figures out that the plans have been intercepted. In that case, they may launch early to catch people off guard."

Doc said, "You could be right. Just let me know what to do."

Matt said, "Why don't you and Lt. Joe start taking down the radio. I'll get Justin and Adam to help me with the solar array."

Doc said, "Okay, but you take it easy on that leg. It needs a few more days before you start playing football again."

Matt chuckled at the comment and went to wake Adam. Once Adam was awake, Matt relayed the information to him.

Adam said, "It sounds fishy. I'm wondering if it could be a ploy by D.C. to get us to take down our communications."

Matt said, "It's coming from the AmRRON network hub. They are pretty good about vetting the information. But you're right. How would we know if it is misinformation from D.C.?"

Adam said, "On the other hand, it could be misinformation from the Coalition. They could be planning a counterstrike against the Federal States. They may be releasing the information this way so we'll roll up our comms and power systems but not risk tipping their hand to D.C. Whatever the case may be, we should roll everything up."

Matt agreed. "I'd say we should build a Faraday cage inside the work shed to keep everything in. We can build it out of the extra chicken wire I bought for the coop."

Adam said, "The work shed kept everything safe last time. Don't you think it will protect everything?"

Matt replied, "It's impossible to know. It depends on the magnitude and proximity of the blast that generates the EMP. I think we should take every precaution we can."

Adam put his boots on. "Then let's get started."

# CHAPTER 35

"Is it not High Time for the People of this Country explicitly to declare, whether they will be Freemen or Slaves? It is an important Question which ought to be decided. It concerns us more than any Thing in this Life. The Salvation of our Souls is interested in the Event: For wherever Tyranny is establish'd, Immorality of every Kind comes in like a Torrent. It is in the interest of Tyrants to reduce the people to Ignorance and Vice. For they cannot live in any Country where Virtue and Knowledge prevail. The Religion and public liberty of a People are intimately connected; their Interests are interwoven, they cannot subsist separately; and therefore they rise and fall together. For this Reason, it is always observable, that those who are combined to destroy the People's Liberties practice every Art to poison their Morals. How greatly then does it concern us, at all Events, to put a Stop to the Progress of Tyranny."

-Samuel Adams

Ryan Randall entered the hangar Tuesday evening for his pre-flight inspection. The missiles were being loaded into the cargo bays of the planes. He had never seen the new Gen 6 JSM 19-C. It was a lighter, more compact competitor to the AMG 158 from Norway's Kongsberg designed to fit in the weapons bay of the F-35. The larger

AMG 158s were recently integrated to be carried externally on the F-35, but it increased the overall radar signature. The downside to the new Gen 6 JSM 19-C was that it had less range than the extended range version of the AMG 158. Maximum range for the new stealth cruise missile was one-hundred-fifty miles. This meant the pilot had to get much closer to the target to launch the attack. The upside was that once the missile was launched, it was completely invisible to the most sophisticated radar systems in existence.

Ryan looked around the hangar. There were other F-35s as well as some aircraft being outfitted with larger missiles, mostly F-15s. All military aircraft had been hardened against EMP, but the proximity to the blasts had still crippled many of the bombers and fighters in the Coalition fleet. No doubt, Howe had specifically targeted military installations to receive larger pulses.

Ryan noticed General Jefferson, who had come to personally see how the preparations were coming along. Ryan walked over to the general. "Hello, General."

"Hey, Ryan. Are you all set to go?"

"Yes, General," Ryan said.

Jefferson said, "We'll be living in a different world tomorrow."

Ryan said, "I know everything is on a need to know basis, so forgive me if I'm being too nosy, but did I see B-83 gravity bombs being loaded into those Raptors?"

Jefferson said, "I suppose you've earned a position in my inner circle. We'll be making physical strikes against several military installations around the Federal States. After D.C. falls, our analysts predict that many of the states will fall into the hands of regional warlords. It's best that we just eliminate the threats immediately."

Ryan asked, "Do the Coalition governors know there will be physical nuclear strikes?"

Jefferson half answered his question. "They understand that we will be physically attacking military installations. Everyone wants an end to this conflict. After the EMP attack on the Coalition, we're struggling to stay alive as a country. We need a decisive victory. We can't sustain a multi-year conflict against D.C."

Ryan agreed with the general, but he knew that Jefferson was taking a lot of liberties by making these unilateral decisions. He wasn't about to rock the boat. Ryan wanted to be the one who took out Washington. He wanted to put an end to the criminals who murdered his brother.

Jefferson said, "You should try to get some sleep. You'll be in the air in a few hours."

Ryan laughed. "I don't think I'll be sleeping tonight, General."

Jefferson bid the young pilot farewell and Ryan began walking to his parents' residence, which was a couple of miles away from the hangar. The walk would give him an opportunity to compose his thoughts and think about what he would say. Ryan arrived on the street where his parents were staying. He walked up to Sonny's front door and knocked.

Sonny opened the door. "Ryan, what are you doing here?"

"I'm participating in the attack tomorrow. Can I come in?" Ryan asked.

Sonny opened the door wider. "Of course, come right in. Did your father not answer the door?"

"I came here first," Ryan stated. "I'm flying tomorrow. I don't want to tell my mom. I wanted to see if you'd have my dad come over so I can tell him without her knowing."

Sonny replied, "I'll call him over here, but your mom deserves to know also."

Ryan shook his head, "She'll worry until I get back. I don't want her to fret the whole time I'm gone."

Sonny said, "She's a big girl. I've never been in combat, but I'm sure regret weighs a ton. I think you'll be more focused if you go into it with a clear head. I don't think you'd be at peace knowing that your mom has no idea what you're getting into."

Ryan considered the wisdom of Sonny's counsel. "Okay, you're right. I should give her a big hug and tell her I love her."

Sonny smiled as Ryan left to knock on his parents' door.

Kimberly opened the door. "Ryan! How good to see you. Paul, Ryan is here!"

Paul came down the stairs. "Hey, son."

Ryan told them the news. Kimberly was upset and Paul held her close.

Paul said, "You could be reassigned to fly a drone in the attack. You'd still have a role in the assault, but you'd be safe."

"I need to do this, Dad," Ryan said.

Kimberly insisted that they all pray together for a while. Afterwards, she scurried around the kitchen to fix Ryan something to eat. As the family sat down to have a small meal together, Paul and Ryan avoided any subjects that might instigate an argument. Tonight was not the time to be fighting. After dinner, Ryan hugged his parents, wished them good-bye and headed back to the barracks.

Ryan sat quietly on his bunk and focused on his breathing. He was anxious about the mission, but determined to get it done. The hour finally came for him to depart. He suited up and headed to the hangar. Ryan boarded his plane and taxied to the runway. Ryan watched the hypnotic glow of the afterburners of the jets taking off before him. Soon, he was on deck and airborne shortly after.

The handling of the F-35 was incredible. Ryan's speed was calibrated so the detonations of all the weapons systems would be only minutes apart. Ryan could see nothing below him as he flew over Tennessee and North Carolina. The EMP attack made the area below him an ocean of darkness. The first glow of the sun began peaking over the horizon as he turned north toward Virginia. Just before he arrived over Petersburg, Ryan opened the weapons bay and launched the missile. Ryan smiled as he thought, *The twenty-kiloton warhead on the missile will radically change the tourist industry in D.C. for years to come.*

In less than an hour, there would be no more White House, no more Capitol Building, no more Lincoln Memorial, no more US Treasury building and no more Federal Reserve. The slate was being wiped clean as the sun rose over the pristine Atlantic Ocean.

Ryan made a turn to the east and proceeded toward his rendezvous point. He was to use the F-35's vertical landing capability to set down at a remote location on the outer banks near Elizabeth City, North Carolina. The plan was to have as few aircraft in the air as possible when the weapons detonated.

# CHAPTER 36

"And this shall be the plague with which the Lord will strike all the people who fought against Jerusalem: Their flesh shall dissolve while they stand on their feet, their eyes shall dissolve in their sockets, and their tongues shall dissolve in their mouths."

-Zechariah 14:12 NKJV

Anthony Howe awoke to the sound of pounding on his door. He drank quite a lot the night before and did not wake up quickly. "Mr. President, Mr. President, we have to get you to the bunker!" the Secret Service agent yelled as he unlocked the door and opened it.

Howe looked up, confused, as he forced himself to sit up in the bed. "What's happening?"

The agent said, "We have to get you below ground. I'll explain on the way."

"You'll explain now!" Howe snapped.

The agent stated, "NORAD has reported that ICBMs have been launched from Malmstrom."

"They're headed here?" Howe's voice was filled with panic.

"No sir," the agent explained. "They are headed west. That doesn't mean there aren't other attacks targeting the White House."

"Get Scott Hale on the phone," Howe barked. "I want to launch a nuclear strike against all Coalition states."

"Sir!" the Secret Service agent demanded, "we have to get you to the bunker now! I promise, Secretary Hale will be my second priority."

Howe conceded, "Okay! Let me get some pants on and we'll go."

Howe turned to his closet, and grabbed a pair of comfortable slacks. The light of the sun flooding into his closet was burning his eyes. It quickly became so bright that it washed out the colors of everything in the closet. Everything was white. Howe closed his eyes, but the light flooded right through his eyelids. His final thought was that he had somehow been transported into the center of the sun and was looking right at it with no ability to close his eyes or look away.

# CHAPTER 37

"The Constitution shall never be construed...to prevent the people of the United States who are peaceable citizens from keeping their own arms."

-Samuel Adams

Matt approached the observation post near the road at 6:00 AM Thursday morning. He would be relieving Adam from his twelve-to-six shift.

"Any action last night?" Matt inquired.

"Nothing." Adam removed the whistle from around his neck and handed it to Matt. Since the walkie-talkies had been stowed away to protect them from the EMP threat, the post nearest the road had been using the whistle in case an alarm had to be sounded or backup requested.

Matt said, "Maybe we should pull out the shortwave and see if we can pick up any news. If we don't get confirmation that there's been a strike, we'll put it back. We could keep checking for a few days before we set everything back up. Once we hook up the comms and backup power, it's at risk."

Adam agreed. "I'll pull the radio out of the shed and come back

242

up here with Lt. Joe."

Adam left to retrieve Joe and the shortwave receiver. He returned in less than fifteen minutes.

Lt. Joe switched the shortwave radio to single-side-band mode and began searching the ham channels. He started off with the known frequencies. He found nothing while scanning the other ham networks in the Eastern Kentucky area. They were likely in the dark, just as Fort Bair was. Finally, Lt. Joe found a signal being transmitted from Fort Bragg. It was a recorded message that was being transmitted on a constant loop. The entire message gave a short brief of what had happened the day before.

"On Wednesday morning, Coalition forces launched a counterstrike against the Federal States. The strike was carried out by a variety of methods and weapons systems. Intercontinental ballistic missiles were fired and detonated at high altitudes to generate an electromagnetic pulse over many of the Federal States. In smaller geographic areas, strategic strikes were launched by manned and unmanned aircraft to generate EMP attacks. The Coalition also dropped munitions on key military bases which crippled the Federal States' ability to respond to the strike.

"The strike was considered successful by Coalition leadership except for one nuclear delivery system which malfunctioned. The error occurred in a JSM 19-C stealth cruise missile which was programed to detonate a high-altitude nuclear strike over Washington D.C. The warhead detonated at a much lower altitude and resulted in a direct nuclear strike against the capital of the Federal States. The failure is being accredited to either a lack of fuel which caused the missile to lose altitude or faulty components within the guidance system. Some speculation has been made that the guidance system could have been damaged by the EMP attack launched against the Coalition. The direct strike eliminated all structures for nearly a one mile radius. The deaths of those inside the city were instantaneous. Those who live in the immediate area will likely die of burns and radiation poisoning over the coming days and months. Those who live east of the Appalachian Mountain chain should take precautions against fallout. The prevailing winds have been in a northeasterly pattern. Those living north and east of D.C. should take particular caution. No further threats are anticipated at this time, and those with communications capabilities inside the Coalition States are encouraged to re-engage their networks."

Matt spoke first. "Wow! I guess that leveled the playing field. What does that mean for us? Do you think the war is over?"

Adam shrugged. "I don't know. I suppose it will depend on the other Federal States. Without D.C., I doubt they'll be able to get organized. Without their key military bases, I don't think they'll be able to sustain a war going forward even if they do get organized."

Lt. Joe asked, "Do either of you fellas buy that bit about the strike on D.C. being a malfunction?"

Matt said, "It was a very lucky malfunction if it was."

Adam replied, "It was deliberate. Someone is trying to save face."

Joe said, "I can't say I'm upset about it."

Adam replied, "Yeah, I won't lose any sleep over it."

Matt commented, "But we should pray for the folks who'll be affected by the fallout. That's a terrible way to die."

Lt. Joe said, "I'm going to grab Doc and get the ham set up. We need to find out what else is going on around here as quick as possible."

Adam said, "I'll grab Justin and Gary and start setting up the solar wagon. All the batteries are just about dead. We'll be losing everything in the fridge if we don't get some juice running today."

Matt asked, "Adam can you send someone up here with a walkie-talkie? This whistle isn't the best option for comms."

Adam nodded, "See you in a bit. Stay sharp, DHS in Pikeville will be doing everything they can to try and hang on to what they've got."

Matt said, "I suppose evicting them from the state will be our next big task."

As he walked away, Adam said, "They've got no means of resupply now. We'll have them out of here soon."

# CHAPTER 38

"Experience hath shewn, that even under the best forms of government those entrusted with power have, in time, and by slow operations, perverted it into tyranny."

-Thomas Jefferson

Friday afternoon, Paul Randall was still managing the political fallout from the attacks against the Federal States. He spoke with Montana Governor Mark Shea over the military radio.

Paul said, "Governor Shea, I understand your concerns, but I hope you'll consider the broader picture here. China is moving troops and infrastructure into California. I'm sure you're aware that Eastern Oregon and Eastern Washington will soon follow. We need to stick together."

Shea replied, "Paul, you know this isn't just up to me. All of the representatives from the Northwestern Coalition have voted on this issue. We will be formalizing the language to create an agreement between our states based on the Articles of Confederation. We'll be happy to extend that agreement to individual states in the Coalition or to a broader federal agreement between Texas and the Southern Coalition, but we've decided against obligating ourselves to a federal government."

Randall replied, "I think you should at least wait for evidence concerning the missile's guidance system. You're basing your decision on rumor and hearsay."

Shea shot back, "Senator, we have a myriad of proof that federal military installations were hit with strategic nuclear devices. Whether the strike on D.C. was intentional or a mishap, we were left out of the loop on what manner of strike would be taken against those installations. If it was the only option, we should have been told in the planning phase of the operation. I think this presents an excellent case for absolute state sovereignty. The disagreements between states and federal governments are bound to come. A confederation is the most any Northwestern Coalition state is willing to offer. Please relay our sentiments to the other states. I've got to let you go now, Senator."

Paul sounded defeated. "I'll talk to you soon, Mark. Thanks."

Paul left the communications room and returned to his office. Sonny came. "There is a ship flying a United Nations flag seeking to dock in Corpus Christi. They've stated that their intentions are to send an envoy to speak with you about humanitarian aid to the Northeast."

Paul buried his head in his hands. "Humanitarian aid means UN Peacekeepers. I won't sign off on it, but what am I going to do? We're in no position to start a war with the UN."

Sonny didn't offer his advice. He simply asked, "Shall I tell them that you'll receive the envoy?"

"Okay, I'll talk to them, but they won't like what I have to say," Paul said. "Do we have to provide transport?"

Sonny answered, "It's my understanding that they have a helicopter on the ship."

"Clear them to land at Fort Hood then," Paul stated.

"Very well, sir." Sonny closed the door behind him.

Allen Jefferson walked in shortly after Sonny left. "You wanted to speak with me, Paul."

"Yes, have a seat Allen." Paul's tone was somber. "The governors have elected me to inform you that your service to the American Coalition Forces will no longer be required. I'll be happy to accept a resignation if you'd like to tender it, but the subject isn't open for discussion."

Jefferson rebutted, "I hardly think that is an appropriate way for the Coalition to express gratitude for my role in putting this conflict to an end."

Randall stood up as he shouted, "The conflict, General, is just beginning! China is moving troops and equipment into California, an envoy from the UN is on his way here to inform me that New England is being occupied by UN peacekeepers and the Northwest Coalition has decided against a formal government with Texas and the Southern Coalition. I think not having you locked up and sent up on charges of treason pending an investigation on the 'malfunction' in D.C. is more than generous. I hope I don't find out that was a planned event. That was my son's plane that delivered the missile. You should take your freedom and be happy with it. In fact take it and get out of my sight before I change my mind."

Jefferson didn't look at Randall as he left the room.

Paul Randall had just over an hour to cool off before the UN envoy arrived. Sonny introduced him.

"Senator Randall, this is Wei Long Qian, representing the UN Security Council."

Qian bowed, but Randall merely offered his hand as was customary in Texas.

Qian shook Randall's hand but seemed a bit put off by Randall's unwillingness to bow. "I offer greetings from UN Secretary General Gavrikov."

Randall said, "Mr. Qian, pardon me for saying so, but I find it curious that you're here representing the Security Council. It was my understanding that this meeting was to talk about humanitarian aid."

Qian asked, "May I sit down?"

Randall said, "State your business, Mr. Qian. I'm very busy as I'm sure you must be also. After all, I'm sure the Security Council needs to speak with China about putting military assets on the sovereign soil of another nation. That is certainly a more pressing issue for the UN than a meeting over humanitarian aid."

Wei Long Qian remarked, "I understand that you must be under tremendous stress, Senator, but this is hardly the manner I would expect to be treated by a member nation."

Randall laughed, "Mr. Qian, the American Coalition is not a member of the United Nations. We do not seek to be a member of the United Nation nor will your troops, assets or personnel be welcomed in any Coalition state. If you're here to ask permission to have UN peacekeepers in former states that have not yet joined the Coalition, I have no authority to grant you that permission nor would I if the authority were mine. If you so choose to occupy those states, for military, humanitarian or any other purpose, pay very close attention to the borders. If UN troops are spotted on Coalition soil, they will be regarded as a hostile force and shot. There will be no warning shots nor courtesy calls. Do I make myself clear?"

Qian replied, "I'm very insulted, Senator. I'm sorry for your country that they have such a rude man to represent them to the rest of the world."

Randall said, "Sonny, make sure Mr. Qian makes it safely back to the helicopter. And inform General Jameson that Mr. Qian needs to vacate Coalition sea and air space in no more than two hours."

Qian gathered his things and stormed out the door.

Minutes later, Sonny entered the room again. "Paul, Captain Steven Shaw of the Oklahoma Militia is requesting to speak with you on the radio."

Randall asked, "Do you know what it's about?"

Sonny replied, "I think they've taken the capital. It may be about an agreement between Oklahoma and the Coalition."

Randall said, "Okay, I'll be right there."

Randall soon arrived in the communications room and the radio operator called the frequency for Captain Shaw.

Paul said, "This is Paul Randall of the American Coalition, what can I do for you, Captain Shaw?"

Steven Shaw came back over the radio. "Senator Randall, I wanted to express my gratitude for the counterstrike. When the EMP detonated over Oklahoma, it took out the communications and surveillance capabilities of the Federal troops occupying our state. It leveled the playing field and we were able to regain control of Oklahoma. We are in the process of reinstating the state government. Once that process is finished, we would like to know the procedure for joining the American Coalition."

Randall said, "I'm very happy that you've been able to retake your state. I must say though, we wouldn't be able to form an agreement without a motion from your governor or state legislature."

Shaw said, "I understand, Senator. I can assure you, the people are very much in favor of joining the Coalition. Our governor was slow to act in joining before the DHS invasion. If he doesn't show some initiative now, he will be turned out of office by the people."

Randall said, "Once your house is in order, have the governor or a delegate from your state senate contact me and we'll arrange a meeting. I wish you the best in this endeavor, Captain Shaw."

Shaw signed off and Randall headed over to the pilots' barracks. He wanted to catch Ryan before he went back to Kelly Field. When he arrived, Ryan was packing his things.

Randall said, "Leaving without saying good-bye?"

Ryan didn't look up. "Rumor has it that General Jefferson will be asked to resign."

"Bad news travels fast," Paul Randall replied.

"You planning to have me busted down to potato peeler?" Ryan asked.

Paul said, "Ryan, Jefferson concealed plans to use nuclear devices against Federal military targets. No one can prove what happened in D.C., but the whole world knows it was no mishap. Whatever you knew or didn't know, keep it to yourself. You were following orders and no one faults you."

"Including you?" Ryan asked.

"Including me," Paul replied. "I've lost one son. You're all I have. I love you more than you can imagine. Your mother misses you also. Why don't you take a couple weeks to cool off, then come stay for a week with your mother and me? We should be back at the ranch by then, as long as the borders can be secured and we're not attacked by any outside forces."

Ryan looked up. "I'll do that. If I can get my R&R approved. I'm not in with the Commanding General anymore. Who will be taking command of the Coalition forces?"

Paul said, "Jameson out of Fort Bragg. I'm sure you'll be approved. I think everyone who flew in the raid will be getting a week off."

Ryan said, "There is some chatter about Kentucky and West Virginia requesting help from the Coalition to take out the remaining DHS troops and private contractors. Will you be approving that?"

"Kentucky is part of the Coalition. We'll give them whatever support we can to get rid of any remaining Federal forces. As far as West Virginia goes, we have to make sure everything is put back together in the Coalition States first, but I'll consider it," Paul said.

"I'd like to volunteer to fly support for those missions, if and when, that is," Ryan said.

Paul nodded, "If and when we decide to designate aerial assets to the region, I'll put in a good word."

Ryan said, "Thanks. I'll respect your decision. I'm sorry I've been so stubborn. If I may add though, the private contractors in the region will become warlords if they aren't dealt with soon. Even the former DHS troops have no leadership now. They'll look to the contractors for employment opportunities. I know we can't force freedom down anyone's throat, but if we have states like West Virginia who just need a nudge to gain their freedom and perhaps join the Coalition, it's in our own best interest."

Paul agreed, "We'll work with any state that agrees with our core philosophy. Those that don't sign off on the new laws to safeguard the Constitution and Bill of Rights will be on their own. Our country has learned the hard way that oil and water just won't mix."

# CHAPTER 39

"You will keep in perfect peace him whose mind is steadfast, because he trusts in you. Trust in the LORD forever, for the LORD, the LORD, is the Rock eternal."

-Isaiah 26:3-4

Matt and Karen took a walk around their property after lunch Saturday afternoon. Matt held his wife's hand firmly with one hand, and the other rested on the sling of his rifle. As they walked, Karen inquired, "Do you think we'll be decommissioning Fort Bair soon? The threat of a DHS invasion is over."

Matt adjusted his boonie hat to sit lower on his head. "We're not out of the woods, yet. There is still speculation about people fleeing the radiation zones through the mountains. Those that do will be desperate for food, shelter, whatever they can get."

"And how long will we have to keep watch for that?" Karen asked.

Matt said, "Until we can secure the borders. Everyone is tired of the tight quarters. We have to be patient a little longer. Once we retake Pikeville, we can focus on securing the borders."

Karen said, "You mean once 'they' retake Pikeville. You can't fight with your leg."

"I'm going to do whatever I can," Matt replied.

Karen's voice got a little louder. "It hasn't even been two weeks since you were injured. Besides that, it hasn't been two weeks since I was wondering if you were alive or dead. You just got off your crutches. You won't be able to run if you have to. There is no way you are participating in the raid on Pikeville. I'll tell Adam not to let you go. It's too much to ask. It's too much to ask of me, Matt. I'm sure it was tough on you being in the work camp, and I haven't complained about what it was like for me, but it was tough. I cannot go through that again. Everyone else knew if their husband was alive or dead. Even Shelly knew Wes was dead. She at least had closure. I'm not saying I'd rather be in her shoes, but that was the roughest thing I've ever been through."

Matt said, "I won't be on the front line. I'll probably have some type of support role. You're right, I can't run. But there are several other things I can do like communications support, help Doc with the injured, whatever. You know I can't sit around the farm while everyone else is in the battle."

Karen dropped her head. "I know."

Matt pulled her close. "But I'll be safe."

When they returned to the house, Adam was awake. Since his shift was from 12:00 AM to 6:00 AM, he typically slept until after one o'clock.

"Ready to roll out?" Adam asked.

Matt asked, "Where are we going?"

"Over to the house to check on the cows and dig up some coffee from the cache to bring back over here," Adam replied.

Matt saw Justin and Doc loading into the truck. He knew it was more than Adam was saying.

Matt kissed Karen, "We'll be right back."

"Where are you going?" her voice was frantic.

Matt said, "No one is geared up to fight. Adam probably wants to talk about Pikeville. He may be meeting some other guys over at his place. I'll fill you in when we get back."

Karen's face softened. "Okay, be safe."

Matt got into the old Camaro with Gary. Shelly opened the door and said, "Move the seat up so I can get in the back."

"You're going?" Matt asked.

"I'm in charge of the cows," she said with a note of sarcasm.

They arrived at Adam's in a few short minutes. Matt looked around. Everything seemed to be in its place. When he looked at Smokey, he noticed she was much thinner than the last time he'd seen her. Matt jumped out to go check on the horse.

Adam called out, "Looks like we've got a new addition."

Matt looked over to where Adam was pointing. He saw that Smokey had finally given birth. Her young foal was nearby, pouncing around on the other side of the barn.

Matt said, "Mandy will be excited to see this."

Adam said, "She will. You better remind her that the foal will be yours."

Matt said, "I'll make sure she knows she is welcome to see it any time. Maybe I'll let her name it."

Adam said, "That would be really nice."

Matt asked, "So are we planning the attack on Pikeville?"

Adam said, "Yeah, a few guys are driving up from Manchester to discuss the raid. But we did need to check on the cows and dig up some coffee from one of the underground caches."

Sam Hart, Jeff Hillier and Jeremy Pence drove up in an old,

rusted-out truck.

Everyone went inside and Sam began explaining the plans. "We're going to clear Pikeville at dawn on Monday. The Kentucky National Guard is going to push in from the south on Route 23. The town is still full of citizens who are effectively imprisoned. We don't want to box DHS and the private contractors in. We want them to have a back door. We'll leave 23 northbound wide open so they can retreat. We're sure they'll run toward West Virginia either by Route 23 to 119 or out the side door on Bypass Road and up Town Mountain Road to 119."

Justin spoke up, "So we're going to let them run to West Virginia and hole up? Doc and I are from West Virginia. We'd like to go home someday. There are a lot of West Virginia Militia that have been fighting and helping to hold borders in Kentucky. I don't think that's fair at all. We're letting them go now, only to fight them later."

Sam said, "Hold your horses, young man. Let me finish. We don't want to engage them in Pikeville because of the citizens. The National Guard will come with a superior show of force from the south and push them out of town. The entire Eastern Kentucky Liberty Militia will be laying in ambush all along the road to West Virginia. As soon as the first vehicle of Federal forces reaches the border, we'll commence firing from the sides of all the roads between West Virginia and Pikeville. The Coalition has promised four F-16s to provide close air support. They know to focus their fire on armored vehicles. I'm sure I don't have to tell you to make sure your position is a good distance from the road. The F-16s will be moving fast when they strike.

If any Federal troops are still in town at that time, the National Guard will engage them. There are about fifty men with the Lexington Militia that will be waiting for them at the border making sure no one gets across. Our boys from McKee Company will take the stretch of road from 194 to 119. The men from Mount Vernon will cover 194. DHS has to take 194, the bridge is still out in that section of 119 from the last time you were there, Adam. We'll all take the front section of 119 and the guys from Somerset Company will take Bypass Road and Town Mountain Road."

Adam studied the map. "Monday is the twenty-first. That's exactly one month since I lost my brother on that same road in a failed ambush."

Sam said, "Then this is your chance to make it right. We'll get 'em this time."

Adam looked at Matt. "My cousin was captured there also. I'm sure he harbors bad memories of the location as well. I don't want to sound superstitious, but can you see if the men from Somerset will switch with us? It's not that I think it'd be bad juju or anything, I just think the memories will cloud our ability to be as effective as we need to be."

Sam nodded. "I can respect that. I'm sure Somerset Company will understand the reasoning and won't mind a bit."

Adam said, "Thank you."

Sam continued explaining the plan. "We'll have six-man fire teams spread out about every half mile or so. If you start taking concentrated fire, bug out, head into the woods. There's plenty of cover all along the way. The enemy will be totally exposed."

Adam asked, "Any idea how many armored vehicles they have that are still operational."

Sam said, "McKee Company sent a recon team there last night. I should know a little more by this evening. We got hold of a few AT-4s from the National Guard."

Adam said, "Wow, those would have come in handy. They were being stingy with them before."

Shelly asked, "What's an AT-4?"

Adam explained, "They're shoulder-fired anti-tank weapons."

Sam continued, "We should have enough for each fire team to have two AT-4s. The Guard sees this as their mission. Maybe that's why they're handing them out. It may also be that they didn't know how long the conflict was going to go on."

Adam said, "At any rate, I'm glad we've got some real munitions for this fight."

Sam said, "And we'll hang on to any that we don't use. We'll just say they were left in the woods or whatever. We've been doing the Guard's job for a few months. It's the least they could do for us. Let's all meet up here tomorrow night just after dark. We'll do a pre-combat inspection and roll out to our positions.

"It's going to be a mess out there. We'll have good guys and bad guys all mixed up. We don't know if they'll be in uniform or what. Some of our militia in other companies have a wide variety of uniforms. We've come up with a code system for movement to identify ourselves. The challenge question is 'trick,' the response is 'two' for National Guard and 'three' for militia. Get that wrong, and you'll be detained. So if someone approaches my position and I'm not sure he is who he claims to be, I'll say 'trick.' If he's militia he'll say 'three.' If he's wearing National Guard insignia and says 'three,' we've got a problem. Does everyone understand?"

Shelly clarified, "Because National Guard should answer 'two.' He may have stolen a uniform and overheard a pass code if he says 'three.'"

"Bingo." Sam answered. "Anyone have any other questions?"

No one did.

"Alright," Sam said, "get lots of rest and eat a couple good meals between now and then. We'll see y'all tomorrow night."

When Matt arrived home, Karen quickly pulled him to the side to get the skinny on what was happening. Evidently, there was a lot of speculation between her, Rene, Debbie and Janice.

"So what's happening?" Karen asked.

Matt said, "The National Guard are actually the ones that will be invading Pikeville. We'll just be sitting outside of town to pick off anyone who decides to run."

Karen said, "Oh, I guess that's not so bad."

Matt nodded. He could tell she wanted details, but he knew more details would give her more to worry about. While he hadn't lied, he'd left out a few pieces of information that would give her more cause for concern if she had them.

"So the horse gave birth since the last time Adam was there," Matt stated. Nothing like baby animals to help shift the direction of the conversation.

"Did you see it?" Karen asked.

Matt smiled. "Yes, it's so cute. You won't believe it. The foal is walking around just like a full-grown horse. A little clumsy, but not bad for the first day on its feet."

Karen reminded him, "You better not say anything to Mandy; none of us will get any sleep."

"I'll take her over there after my post tomorrow. It'll be a surprise," Matt said.

# CHAPTER 40

"I have sworn on the altar of God eternal hostility against every form of tyranny over the mind of man."

-Thomas Jefferson

The next day, there was an air of apprehension about the raid. Wesley's death, as well as the death of so many other members of London Company was still fresh on everyone's mind. Matt felt the heaviness on the hearts of all those at Fort Bair.

After lunch, Matt called to Mandy, "Do you want to walk over to your house and help me feed the cows?"

"Sure." Mandy was a little somber as well. The new horse would lift her spirits.

Carissa shouted, "I want to go, too!"

Matt said, "Okay, ask your mom."

They cut through the woods and Matt soon arrived at the fence with the two girls.

Mandy put her hands over her mouth and gasped when she saw the foal.

Carissa pointed. "A baby horse!"

Mandy said, "It's beautiful! It's going to be your horse, Matt. What will you name it?"

Matt said, "That's true, it will be my horse, but you're so good with horses, I was hoping I could count on you to help me raise her. After all, you'll only be a couple miles away."

"Of course I'll help," Mandy said. "I'll do whatever you need me to do!"

Matt said, "For starters, why don't you name it?"

Mandy was filled with joy. "Spirit!"

Matt said, "Okay, Spirit it is. Any particular reason?"

Mandy said, "Because the horse reminds me of a new American spirit. The war is almost over, and we'll have the opportunity to make a better future."

Matt wasn't expecting that for an answer. "Wow, that's fantastic."

Matt had taken the girls to give them something to be excited about and shift their focus from the battle lying ahead. But he had been blessed even more. Matt saw the true spirit of America in Mandy's dreams for the country. Suddenly, the small horse was an icon of hope for Matt. He had been closely watching the country in a death spiral for decades. It had been year after year of things deteriorating and getting worse and worse. Finally, it seemed that there was a glimmer of hope. For the first time since he could remember, things might actually be getting better.

Once they arrived back at Fort Bair, it was time to start gearing up. Matt packed his assault pack, oiled his rifle, checked his gear and stocked up on food and water. The others who would be participating in the raid did the same.

The team began loading up into the truck shortly after sundown. Janice said, "We want to say a prayer for you all before you roll out."

Adam said, "That'd be great."

Everyone formed a circle and held hands as Janice asked God to watch over and protect those that would be participating in the raid. Karen added a plea to God to bring them home safely.

Lt. Joe would be staying to operate the radio while they were gone. He joked, "Y'all better hurry up. I don't like bein' left here with all these women. They might get tempted."

Shelly winked at Lt. Joe as she racked a round into her rifle. "Then you better run, Joe. If I find out you were cheatin' on me, we'll need a new comms operator."

Everyone had a chuckle and the team pulled away. They rendezvoused with Manchester Company and headed toward Pikeville. The men from McKee Company stated that the former DHS troops were manning checkpoints on the south and north sides of Pikeville, roughly half a mile outside of town. Since the militia couldn't approach from the south on 23, they would have to take a detour which would take them roughly twenty miles out of the way. They would pass Pikeville heading north on State Road 80, then follow 194, a winding country road, through the mountains and south back down to their ambush positions.

They soon arrived at their position. Adam dropped them off on the side of the road and took the truck back a few hundred yards to a side road. He had informed them that he would drop the truck, stash the keys and walked back to the ambush position.

The moon offered a fair amount of light between the clouds for them to select defendable positions. Matt did not have the confidence he had at the ambush one month earlier. He was still a little gun-shy and continued to recite a Bible verse in his mind to keep him at peace.

Their position on Town Mountain Road was just over a mile away from the DHS checkpoint. They had to be very alert for patrols and be ready to peel back into the woods if a patrol drove by. Everyone was positioned on the west side of the road and split into two teams. Adam, Gary and Justin were in the forward position, closest to the road. They held the two AT-4s and would be initiating the assault. Matt, Doc and Shelly would be doing clean up with sniper shots from a more fortified position. Adam didn't hide his reasoning for splitting the team up in this manner. Shelly was in the rear position because she was one of the best long-range shooters. Doc was in the rear in case they needed him to address an injury. Matt had been assigned to the rear position because he couldn't run if they had to make a hasty retreat to the truck.

Adam explained to Matt, "If we have to run, everyone is going to slow down to cover you. It will put us all in jeopardy. Your rear support position is critical. When the front team falls back, we'll be counting on you to cover us."

Despite wanting to be part of the front team, Matt knew Adam was right. Matt took his position and settled in for the night. He shared some cookies Karen had made with Doc and Shelly. They whispered softly about what morning would bring. The three of them took shifts resting, but no one could relax enough to actually go to sleep.

Morning finally came. The break of dawn was met with the sound of gunfire ringing through the hills from the distant south. Matt said to Doc and Shelly, "Sounds like we're on."

Within minutes, a convoy of vehicles was streaming along Town Mountain Road toward US 119. Matt and his team sat silently as vehicle after vehicle passed them by. There were several armored vehicles that survived the EMP or had been retrofitted to function without the damaged components. The convoy also contained many old trucks that had most likely been stolen from the people of Pikeville.

Matt waited anxiously for the Lexington Militia to break radio silence and signal for the ambush to commence. Suddenly, the radio squawked, "Brace for air assault." Seconds later, F-16s were low overhead.

Matt covered his head as the Maverick air-to-ground missiles fell from the last plane. The eruptions shook the ground beneath him. The vehicles destroyed by the missiles left burning piles of rubble strewn across the narrow mountain road. There were three vehicles in Matt's vicinity that were trapped behind the flames. The first was a late 70's Jeep which tried to plow through the rubble. As it passed through the flames, it hooked a piece of burning material in the axle. The Jeep could still move, but the flames were quickly heating up the vehicle. The driver stopped and five troops bailed out. Matt saw Adam engage the troops. Matt followed suit along with Shelly. Three hostiles were down before the remaining two had a chance to return fire. The second vehicle was a Humvee. Justin fired one of the two AT-4s at it. It was a direct hit. The vehicle flipped over and everyone inside was killed. The last vehicle was a white, 1976 passenger van. It quickly turned around to head back toward Pikeville. Adam fired the second AT-4 at the moving vehicle. The projectile hit the road and exploded on the right front side of the fleeing van. The explosion caused the van to go off the east side of the road and careen down the hill until it was suddenly stopped by an old oak. The passengers poured out and Matt's team engaged them. Eight men rushed out of the van to find cover. Adam called over the walkie, "Gary, Justin, follow the two men from the Jeep to the north. Once you take them out, stay on the east side of the road and flank the guys from the van. I'm coming to you Matt."

Adam soon arrived near Matt's position to fire on the enemy. The men from the van were shooting and retreating into the woods. They were moving in two teams of four. Four would lay down cover fire while the other team would peel back into the woods. The two teams used a leapfrog method to take turns moving away from Adam and the others. Shelly hit one of the men during his retreat and Adam shot one from the same fire team as he was taking cover. Matt shot one from the next fire team when he got up to move back. They were soon out of range.

Shelly yelled, "Should we pursue them?"

Adam thought for a moment. "Matt, you and Doc stay here and cover us, we'll move to the other side of the road to see if we can catch a couple more of them."

"Roger that," Matt said.

Adam and Shelly made a quick run across the road. Almost immediately, the enemy revealed their position when they began firing.

Matt saw one who exposed himself a little too much from the tree that he was using for cover. Matt took the shot and hit him in the chest. Shelly caught a bullet in her shoulder which spun her around before she reached the other side of the road. She got back up and finished crossing. Before she did, another bullet hit her in the calf. She fell to the edge of the road. She still did not have proper cover. Adam called to Matt, "Lay down heavy cover. I'm going to crawl to Shelly and drag her back to my cover position. Doc, see if you can scoot over here. She needs medical attention fast."

Matt changed the magazine of his M4 and moved the selector to full auto. Matt took a general aim toward the enemy and laid down bursts of five or six rounds while Doc ducked and ran to meet Adam near Shelly. Matt emptied his magazine, hit the release, inserted a new magazine, slapped the bolt catch with his palm and resumed firing. Adam had made them repeat this series of movements in training until they were sick of it. He had made them perform the function in the dark, blindfolded, while he threw stuff at them and under every other imaginable condition. Matt had really not enjoyed that part of the training, but it just paid off. The rapid magazine change allowed him to continue firing, which kept the enemies' heads down long enough for Doc and Adam to move Shelly to a safe position.

Once they were safe, Matt changed his magazine again and moved his selector back to semi-auto. He and Adam continued to take shots at the enemy from cover while Doc went to work on Shelly. Doc began by using his EMT shears to cut the lower portion of Shelly's pant leg off and then her sleeve to expose the wound on her shoulder.

Adam took out one more hostile before they were out of sight and out of range. He called Justin and Gary, "You guys alright?"

Gary called back, "We got one of them, and the other is way back there. Should we pursue?"

Adam replied, "Negative. Shelly's been hit. We're pulling out. You guys come on back. Take turns covering and moving. We've still got three hostiles out here in the woods."

"Roger," Gary replied.

Gary and Justin soon met up with the rest of the team. Doc continued to address Shelly's wounds. He gently probed each wound. "It looks like they were full metal jacket rounds. I don't see any fragmentation. It looks like they're both through and through. She has a lot of tissue damage and has lost a lot of blood. She needs to get to the medical tent where a surgeon can work on her and get her some blood. I need another med kit so we can get her ready to move." Matt offered his kit to Doc. He put a Quickclot sponge on each side of each wound and wrapped each wound with an Israeli Battle Dressing.

While Doc dressed Shelly's wounds, Matt found two saplings and began fashioning a stretcher with the saplings and the duct tape he kept in his bag.

Justin commented, "There's not much you can't do with duct tape."

"Don't leave home without it." Matt put the finishing touches on the stretcher.

Justin and Doc carried the stretcher while Adam took point to lead them back to the truck. Matt and Gary walked backwards behind them to cover the rear. They kept a particularly tight watch over the areas the Federal troops had fled to.

They soon reached the truck, loaded Shelly into the back and headed out. Adam drove and handed the radio to Doc. "Let them know we have wounded, what type of truck we're in and where we're at."

Doc followed the instructions. "We need to get her to the medical tent in the south National Guard staging area," he called over the radio.

National Guard Operations Command called back, "The south staging area is overwhelmed. If your wounded are stable, you need to get them to Combs Field. It is a small airport just north of Prestonsburg. National Guard has a complete field hospital set up there. We're using it as our forward operating base. The staging area to the south is just to stabilize patients, then move them to Combs."

"How far?" Doc asked.

Command called back, "Thirty-five miles from Pikeville. What's your location?"

Doc told the communications operator, "Town Mountain headed to 119."

The operator said, "Then you have to go north. There's still heavy fighting on US 23 between you and the southern staging area."

"Roger that, thank you, command," Doc said.

When they reached US 119, it was littered with burning trucks and military vehicles. Adam had to drive on the side of the road in some places to avoid the flaming debris. Minutes later, they were on US 23 headed north. Almost immediately, they hit a National Guard checkpoint. The guards held their weapons pointed at Adam's team. The lead guard approached the vehicle. "Trick!"

Adam kept his hands raised with his foot on the brake. "Three!"

The guard motioned for the other guards to lower their weapons. "ID."

Adam pulled his driver's license out of his pocket. It was his proof that he was a Kentucky resident. There was no formal ID for the militia.

The guard inspected it, "Where you headed?"

"Combs Field, we've got wounded," Adam replied.

The guard motioned the driver of the Cougar blocking the road. The driver backed up revealing a gauntlet of armored vehicles stretching for about one-hundred yards.

Adam proceeded slowly through the mobile barricade which created angles to navigate around for anyone forcing their way through. Once he passed through the gauntlet, he was able to speed toward Combs Field on the open road.

Twenty minutes later, they were in Combs Field. The guard at the checkpoint directed Adam to the field hospital. Medics rushed to get Shelly into surgery. Doc found the lead medic and offered his services. He was promptly assigned to a station and went to work.

The others were directed to the chow tent where they could get something to drink and eat. Matt was just very thirsty. He got some water and found a place to sit down. Adam joined him while Gary and Justin got a plate of food and came to sit next to Matt and Adam.

Matt asked Adam, "Do you think they'd let us use the radio to call Lt. Joe so he can tell the girls that we're okay?"

Adam replied, "They're probably swamped right now, but we could try walking back down to the camp checkpoint. That Cougar had a long-range radio. As long as it wasn't damaged by any of the EMPs, maybe they'll let us use it."

Matt nodded. "We'll be right back."

Gary said, "We'll be right here."

Adam approached the vehicle and asked the driver to use the radio. The driver pointed to the guard that was calling the shots and Adam repeated his question.

The guard recognized that Adam was prior military. "Where'd you serve?"

"Fallujah and Helmand Province," Adam answered.

"Marines?" the guard inquired.

Adam nodded.

The guard instructed the driver to give Adam and Matt access to the radio.

Matt was soon talking to Karen, "We're fine. We should be home tonight. Shelly got hit, but she's stable. She is in surgery. We may have to leave her here overnight."

Karen was alarmed. "How did she get hit? I thought you were just watching the roads outside of town."

Matt said, "Yeah, we were, but some of the Federal troops made a run for it and we had to engage them. We're on the National Guard's radio. We just wanted to tell you all that we're fine. I love you, see you tonight."

Karen's voice came back over the radio. "I love you, too. Be safe and hurry home."

Adam took one minute to say hello to his two daughters then signed off.

They returned to the chow tent where a colonel was debriefing Gary and Justin. Adam filled in a few more details when he arrived. He told the colonel about the four men that got away.

"They won't last long out there. The National Guard will keep guards around the city until Pikeville can reform their militia and police department. You fellas did a great job. Y'all stay as long as you like. When you get ready to leave, stop by the fuel truck. Give the man this gas voucher and he'll fill up your tank.

An hour later, Doc found the men in the chow tent. He got a plate of food and sat down with them. "Shelly is out of surgery and resting. She'll have to stay for a couple days. I'm going to stay here and help out. I'll keep an eye on Shelly as well. You guys head on back and I'll call Lt. Joe and keep everyone updated on when we'll be coming back."

Adam nodded, "Do you need anything from us?"

Doc said, "They're short on medics. They've assigned me a tent, given me clothes. They're making me feel right at home."

Matt said, "Don't get too comfortable. We need you back at Fort Bair eventually."

Doc said, "Thank you very much. And thank you for the hospitality, but this is my calling. If they have a place for me, I may stick around a while. You know I'll come visit though."

Matt felt a pang of sadness for a moment. He had been through a lot with Doc. They had kept each other sane in the work camp.

"Okay, but if it doesn't work out, you'll always have a place to lay your head."

The men said their farewells and headed out.

# CHAPTER 41

"We owe our unceasing gratitude to the Supreme Ruler of the Universe, who safely carried us through our arduous struggle for freedom."

-Samuel Adams


The next morning Shelly lay on her bed after Doc finished changing her bandages. She noticed a young pilot walking through the recovery room and talking with some of the injured. He walked past her bed and glanced. He turned back around and walked over to her. She couldn't help but notice that he was an attractive young man.

"We'd never let anyone as pretty as you get shot in Texas," he said.

Shelly rolled her eyes and tried to fight back the smile. It didn't work. Soon her face was glowing red. "I didn't get shot. It was shrapnel from an F-16's missile that hit me."

The pilot's facial expression changed rapidly. A look of horror overtook the light-hearted smile. "No! Really?"

Shelly laughed. "I'm kidding."

"I'd hate to see what you're like when you're not injured. My name is Ryan," the pilot said.

Shelly felt a sliver of guilt as she replied, "I'm Shelly."

What could it hurt? The pilot was just being friendly. She wasn't doing anything wrong. Wesley had only been dead for a month, though. It was too soon to even look at a boy the way she was looking at Ryan. But this guy looked familiar.

"Wait, what's your last name?" she quizzed.

"Randall," the pilot answered.

"No way!" she said. "Big fan of your dad's. My whole family is a big fan. Well, the people I call my family anyway."

"Thanks," Ryan said. "What do you mean by 'the people you call your family?'"

Shelly had the perfect out. She explained everything. She told Ryan about Wesley and how she had no other family besides Wesley's now.

Ryan said, "I'm sure Wesley was very brave. All of your family sound like real patriots. And, you know, that's what family is. It's not necessarily who you're born to, but it's the people you share your life with. I'd love to meet them some time. I'll be back in Kentucky in a couple of months. Would it be possible to stop in and meet them?"

Shelly couldn't see the harm in that. After all, Adam and Matt were such fans of Paul Randall, who was she to deny them the opportunity to meet Ryan? "I suppose that would be okay." She gave him the address.

Ryan put his hand on Shelly's and her heart jumped. "Get well soon. It was very nice meeting you, Shelly."

"Likewise." Shelly didn't feel so bad. After all, she couldn't help it if it felt nice to be noticed. Ryan seemed to get the message as well. She wasn't trying to say "No." She was just trying to say, "Not now."

Back at Fort Bair, Rene relieved Matt and Mandy from their post at noon. After the raid on Pikeville, the post near the road was the only post being manned. The observation post on top of the work shed was decommissioned for now. The men were rotating the late-night and early-morning shifts, and the women were taking the day shifts.

Matt returned to camp with the newest member of the security team. Karen was preparing lunch for everyone who was hungry.

Karen said to Matt, "I hope you'll be able to manage your post alone next week, Mandy will be starting school with me."

Mandy spoke up, "We're having school? Where?"

"Right here," Karen said. "At least for now. Once things settle down, we'll try to move it to the church."

"Who's coming?" Mandy asked.

Karen replied, "A few other kids from church. I'm sure it'll grow in time."

Mandy asked, "Are Alison and Tammy going to be coming?"

Karen replied, "I spoke with Alison's mom on the radio. She'll be attending. I'll probably see Tammy's mom at church this weekend. I'm sure she'll want to come."

Mandy said, "That's great. Since the collapse, I hardly ever see my friends."

Matt said, "Things will start getting back to normal. It will be a slow process, and things will never be the way they were before, but things will be getting better. In fact, I think it will be much better."

Lt. Joe wandered out to the picnic table for lunch. "Matt, you've got a fella on the radio who wants to talk to you. Says he's in Florida."

Matt asked, "Frank?"

Joe replied, "Yeah, Frank. You better hurry up though. I might eat my lunch and yours, too."

Mandy and Carissa both chuckled at Joe's comment. His sense of humor did a lot to keep things light around the camp.

Matt shook his head. "I'll run you out of Kentucky if you eat my food."

"I'd like to see you try," the lieutenant joked.

Matt proceeded to the office which was now set up as the communications room. He picked up the mic. "Frank?"

"Hey man," Frank said.

Matt said, "Wow, it's good to hear your voice. So you made it. Are the blockades coming down? Have you heard anything?"

Frank said, "I'm sure things have been rough all over, but you wouldn't believe what it was like down here when they cordoned off Florida. Yes, the barricades came down. After D.C. fell, most of the troops abandoned their posts. The gangs in Jacksonville broke through the barricades into Georgia. They've pretty much cleaned out Florida, so they needed new territory.

"By the grace of God, my family is fine. Most others around here have lost someone. Disease, starvation and attacks from the gangs have thinned out the population around here. I'm sure it's much worse in the population centers. You did the right thing by getting out of here when you could. Your buddy, Jack, didn't make it. Our community was hit by a gang out of Jacksonville. He was shot and killed in the firefight. He took two in the chest. He didn't suffer."

Matt was stunned. "What about Tina?"

Frank said, "She's in bad shape. She never really snapped out of it after their ordeal of trying to make it up here from South Florida. After Jack died, she really took a turn for the worse. She doesn't talk, hardly eats. I doubt she'll make it much longer. We give her food, shelter and everything she needs, but she has no hope."

Matt inquired, "Don't you have church services in your community?"

Frank shot back, "Bro, who are you talking to? I lead a Bible study at my house every Wednesday night. We have a worship service every Sunday morning here. I've tried to talk to her, but she's hung up on the opinion that if there was a God, he wouldn't let all of this happen. I've explained how Deuteronomy 28 actually says all of this stuff will happen when a nation turns its back on God. I told her the fact that all of this happened is proof that the Bible is true and that there is a God. But at the end of the day, people choose what they want to believe. We're all free moral agents.

"Enough about me. How is your family?"

Matt proceeded to tell Frank about his capture and rescue, Wesley's death and all the other trials they had faced. Then he asked, "Would you consider moving up here?"

Frank replied, "Once the militia can reorganize, we'll get these gangs under control and Florida won't be a bad place to be. The current population is a fraction of what it was before. We've got fresh water, lots of good farm land and you know how nice it is down here in the winter."

Matt inquired, "Do you think Florida will join the Coalition?"

Frank said, "Most folks around here felt abandoned. We understand that Randall's plate was full without having to lend us a hand, but I think we'll be trying to do things on our own for a while. I'm sure we'll want a good relationship with the Coalition. We'll be happy to establish free trade and that sort of thing, but we made it on our own this far."

Matt agreed, "That's understandable."

The two men finished their conversation and bid each other

farewell.

Matt returned to lunch where everyone else was finishing up.

Lt. Joe said, "Karen made sure I left you something to eat."

Matt shook his head and made himself a plate. "As soon as the borders are secured, I'm going to make rebuilding your cabin a priority. You're too mean to keep around here, Joe."

Justin finished his meal but was still sitting at the table next to Matt. "Rene and I are heading out next week. We're going up to Louisa. All of the former West Virginia Militia are meeting up there. They're petitioning the Coalition for support to retake Huntington. Once we take Huntington, we'll have momentum to clear out the rest of the state."

Matt inquired, "You're taking Rene? She would be more than welcome to stay here."

Justin smiled. "I know. I told her that, but she's determined."

Matt slapped him on the shoulder. "I'd go, too, but Doc says my fighting days are over. I'm a little past my prime."

Justin said, "You've done your share. And I'll never forget what you've done for Rene and me. You gave us a home and kept us well-fed."

"It's been our pleasure to help out," Matt said.

Justin added, "I think Adam is coming. He said he's depending on you and Gary to keep an eye on things around here. The crops are already starting to come in. Hopefully we'll have West Virginia settled in time to come back and give you a hand with harvesting and canning. You know I'll always be available to help out with anything."

Matt said, "Thanks."

Matt finished his meal. He looked around at his home that had been transformed into a military base. It had seemed like such a hardship at the time, but now everyone would be leaving. Once the borders were established, Gary and Debbie would be returning to their home. Adam's family would be going back to their farm. Lt. Joe would have a new cabin up on his property by Wood Creek Lake and Doc seemed to have found his calling as a military physician.

He and Karen had come to see Justin and Rene as family. The house would seem empty without them. Soon it would be just Karen and himself. And Miss Mae, of course.

# CHAPTER 42

"If my people, who are called by my name, will humble themselves and pray and seek my face and turn from their wicked ways, then will I hear from heaven and will forgive their sin and will heal their land."

-2 Chronicles 7:14

Six months after the attack on Washington, D.C. the political landscape of the former United States transformed immensely. Paul Randall was elected as the President of the American Coalition. While the states within the Coalition still held their sovereignty, they pledged mutual defense to one another. They adopted the original Constitution with an enhanced Bill of Rights. The enhanced amendments would attempt to safeguard against the injustices that had grown out of the oversized Federal government. Attempts to pass laws which violated the Bill of Rights in word or principle were deemed to be treason and punishable by death. This measure would cause every lawmaker to carefully consider the peril of their very lives before proposing a law that could be construed as unconstitutional. After the final count, the Coalition States would come to consist of Kansas, Oklahoma, Texas, Missouri, Kentucky, Tennessee, West Virginia, the Carolinas and Georgia.

The northwestern states solidified a confederation that was based on the original US Articles of Confederation. Those states included Eastern Washington, Eastern Oregon, Idaho, Montana, Wyoming, the Dakotas and Northern Colorado. Utah later petitioned to join the confederation as did Nebraska.

New Mexico and Southern Colorado formed the Southwestern Union. The majority of residents in several counties of Arizona pushed to join the Southwestern Union, but others vehemently objected. The schism resulted in a mini-civil war within Arizona. Borders were regularly redrawn with the sovereign state of Arizona losing more and more ground to the Southwestern Union. The Southwestern Union formed strong trade and mutual defense treaties with Mexico which helped to squeeze the remaining holdouts in Arizona.

Arkansas, Louisiana, Mississippi, and Alabama retained all the laws of the former United States as they had stood before the collapse. The strong Federal government of those states came to be known as the Southern United States of America.

The cities of the northeast were completely unrecognizable. The United Nations sent in massive humanitarian aid as well as UN peacekeepers. They established a foothold in the Northeast and began to push toward the West. They eventually held all of the Northeast except for New Hampshire. They took control of Michigan, Wisconsin, Minnesota and Illinois. The UN claimed authority over New Hampshire, Pennsylvania, Ohio and Indiana, but insurgents regularly attacked UN installations killing UN peacekeepers and looting supplies. The insurgents were decentralized fighters made up of freedom fighters, independent militias and large street gangs that migrated out of the population centers. Each geographic region had its own group dynamic. There were also freedom fighters in upstate New York, but most were eventually pushed out by the UN and forced to migrate to the Coalition or join other factions to continue the battle against the United Nations.

The UN took control of the states they deemed to be war-torn disaster areas and stated that they were there to foster democracy and help the states return to prosperity. Technocrats from the UN Security Council were appointed over those states as governors.

Democratic elections were promised to those states, but never came to pass.

Virginia was a battlefield for many months. The eastern portion of the state, like Delaware and Maryland, was decimated by the nuclear fallout from the attack on Washington D.C. The western portion of the state was hotly contested ground in a fight between local militia and a consortium of private military contractors that sought to rule the land. The private military group that came to be known as Dark Horse eventually took possession of the state. It was ruled by a council of three men who came from the three largest defense contractor firms that made up Dark Horse. They represented Black Water, KBR and DynCorp. The UN recognized Virginia as a corporate state and regularly employed Dark Horse in fighting insurgent cells within UN-held territories.

Florida and Alaska both remained independent nations. Both maintained very good trade relations with the Northwest Confederation, the American Coalition and the Southern United States.

China established military bases all along the west coast, Nevada and Hawaii. The official narrative was that it was a humanitarian effort, but the fact that the Chinese flag flew all along those regions told a different story. The Chinese established hard military borders that extended from the southeastern border of California, up the eastern border of Nevada and down the middle of Oregon and Washington. They now held complete control of the west coast of the former United States. The region was soon recognized by the UN as a territory of China known as the People's Republic of Western America.

This fragmented arrangement of the former United States created new tensions along the borders of the new nations and territories. The ideologies that were so close geographically were worlds apart philosophically. Still, these borders were respected and the policy of live and let live was observed by all; at least for the time being.

Matt sat on the porch next to his wife and breathed in the cool November evening air. He contemplated the dramatic events that had made so many changes in the population and borders of what he had always known as America. Karen took Matt's hand and placed it on her slightly rounded stomach. Matt took comfort in knowing that what was left of his country would be a free land to raise his child.

His child would grow up free to worship God, free to speak, free to carry a gun, free from warrantless searches and invasions of personal effects. His child would be born a free citizen of Kentucky who would never see the effects of inflation from a central bank which steals the wealth of its people through criminal devaluation of the currency. His child would use silver and gold as money and currency. His child would keep the fruits of his labor, free from state and Federal income tax. His child would own the land passed by Matt and Karen without threat of seizure by property or death taxes. Matt and Karen's child would live under a Federal government constrained to the necessary evils it could commit on the limited budget of what it collected through tariffs. The revenues extracted by taxing imports would have to be enough for the Federal government to perform the minimal tasks of protecting borders, enforcing contracts and very little else. Kentucky would be constrained to the revenues collected through a state sales tax. This would fund the state militia, roads and a handful of government salaries.

In Kentucky, at least, schools would be funded by parents who formed cooperatives through their churches or communities on a voluntary basis. Welfare would be the business of the church or other community organizations.

Voting in the Coalition was a privilege. Those who wanted to be involved in selecting leaders had to take a test and prove they had a rudimentary understanding of history, economics and government. Men and women had been forced to take a test to prove they were competent enough to drive a car for over a century, but something as sacred as selecting the nation's leaders had been open to the most ignorant of men. In the end, it was the low-information voter that destroyed America.

Matt would be careful to teach his child the importance of being faithful to God and defending liberty. He would be sure to teach his child the dangers of an obese central government. Matt's child would learn the words of George Washington, "Government is not reason;

it is not eloquence; it is force. Like fire, it is a dangerous servant and a fearful master."

Thank you for reading
*American Reset,*
*Book Three of The Economic Collapse Chronicles.*

Amazon reviews are the most important method of getting The Economic Collapse Chronicles noticed. If you enjoyed the book, please take a moment to leave a 5 star review on Amazon.com. If you don't feel the book quite measured up to 5 stars, drop me an e-mail at prepperrecon@gmail.com and let me know how I can make future books better.

**Keep watch for**
*The Days of Noah,*
*A Novel of America in the End Times*

Stay tuned to PrepperRecon.com for the latest news about new books and preparedness related subjects. While on the website, you can link to our Facebook page and YouTube channel to stay up-to-date with the most recent posts.

Listen to the Prepper Recon Podcast to get great interviews from preppers around the world. It will help you to be better prepared for everything from a hurricane to the end of the world as we know it. You can download or listen to the podcasts at PrepperRecon.com, or subscribe to the show on Stitcher, iTunes or YouTube.

Made in the USA
Lexington, KY
15 August 2015